Words We Didn't Say

AUBREY WHITTEN

Copyright © Aubrey Whitten, 2025.

This novel is entirely a work of fiction. The story, all names, characters, and incidents portrayed in it are the work of the author's imagination or are used fictitiously. Any resemblance to actual persons, living or dead, events, or locales is entirely coincidental.

All rights reserved.

No part of this publication may be reproduced, distributed, decompiled, reverse engineered, stored, or transmitted in any form or by any means, including photocopying, recording, or other electronic or mechanical methods, now known or hereinafter invented, without the prior express written permission from the author.

Aubrey Whitten asserts the moral right to be identified as the author of this work.

Cover beautifully designed by The Bookshelf Studio.
www.thebookshelfstudio.com

Chapter illustration by Larek.

eBook ISBN – 978-1-7636050-2-2

Paperback ISBN – 978-1-7636050-3-9

*To the man who waited for me outside the firm past midnight,
and the readers who stumbled on this story years after I'd left,*

Thank you.

I wouldn't have made it this far without you.

Prologue

Eden

Six months ago, when the first word was "Hey."

"My dead grandma can run faster than you!" Andie shouted over her shoulder.

Maybe that was Andie.

I squinted into the morning sun. Tourists shuffled along the boarded path, gawping at the blue sky, the patchwork of cotton ball clouds, the cliffs, the beach, too busy taking photos to get out of my way. I dodged one tourist. Another. I could barely keep track of the blur of red tank top and loose grey sweats disappearing ahead of me.

No way had I fallen *that* far behind. The smudge on the horizon wasn't my best friend. That could've been anyone.

"Come on, Ed!" she called back. "Move your arse!"

Or not.

Gasping, I staggered another four steps before admitting defeat. My hand flailed for the railing, and when my fingertips brushed the edge, you can bet your booty I latched on for dear life. That bit of metal was the only thing stopping my exhausted body from tumbling off the trail and plunging into the ocean below.

"I just—" I hunched over, gulping in breaths, my palm pressed over a heart thumping overtime. "I just need—"

What I *needed* was to travel back in time and leave my adorable pink high-tops tucked safely away in my wardrobe where they belonged.

I should've ignored the fun run poster on the noticeboard outside the coffee shop. I never should've listened to my personal trainer. All the times that overstuffed beefcake had told me I was "killin' it, babe"—lies! And so what if the fun run was for a good cause? I didn't have to be one of Sydney's biggest fundraisers fighting youth homelessness. I *was*. But I didn't *have* to be.

I slumped against the railing.

Now, I was just lying to myself. I had to be the best. Exceptional. My childhood scarred every twist of my DNA. If years of therapy and skimming the occasional self-help book had taught me anything, it was that I was in a never-ending race to win the approval of a father who'd never wanted me. Not when he'd yanked my tiny hand off my mother's cold, wooden casket. Not when I'd threatened to run away at fifteen or when I'd made good on my promise the following year. Not even now, when I was *someone*.

My grip tightened around the railing.

Should I let that man's failings tear down the confidence I'd clawed together despite him?

No. *Hell* no.

I took a deep breath and pushed away from the edge. I managed one step…and then…another. That was enough. Sometimes, that was how life happened—wobbly baby steps, walking, running, and finally, *soaring*.

Who stopped Eden Phillips? No one.

Andie loomed around the bend. She was a storm cloud blotting the picture-perfect view. She rarely smiled—including when she saw me hobbling closer—but her tomboy aesthetic suited grim. The full sleeve of intricate black floral tattoos on her arm was the closest she got to 'cute.'

"Thank you for gracing me with your presence, your majesty," she said.

My reply was a glare.

"I thought you'd been training for this fun run?" She cocked her head, one eyebrow up. "What exactly do you do at the gym? Clearly, you're not logging many hours on the treadmill."

"My time at the gym is better spent looking adorable and scouting the weights room for eligible bachelors to corrupt. We don't all need to waste our mornings bench pressing a bus like you do, you know."

Andie smirked.

"That wasn't a compliment," I said.

"Sure sounded like one. So? You've farted around long enough to get your breath back. Ready to go?"

"No." I flopped against the railing beside her. "I'd prefer to sit my little cutie booty at a café and order a fresh macchiato and a bacon roll." I pouted. "Why didn't you talk me out of this stupid scheme?"

Andie's eyebrow was up again. "When have I ever managed to talk you out of anything?"

"What about those curtain bangs and, um, my goth phase or the, um…" I huffed out a breath. Alright, Andie had a point. No one could stop me once I'd set my mind to something. "I've learned my lesson this time, okay? No more scheming. I'm done." When Andie's frown deepened, I doubled down. "I swear."

But even as the promise tumbled out of my mouth, my mind shifted into gear, speeding full throttle towards a brilliant new plan.

Supporting the fun run didn't have to end with me scrubbing sweat off my face or sniffing my armpits to make sure I'd rolled on enough mineral deodorant. Where did I excel? Talking. People. Instead of charging ahead, I could slip to the back, motivate the stragglers, and cheer everyone on. I'd let others shine—for once.

I twittered a wicked laugh.

"That's gotta be an all-time record," Andie said.

I shot her an innocent look. "I've got no idea what you're talking about."

"Uh-huh. Sure thing, troublemaker." She nudged her shoulder into mine. "Dig deep, finish the run, and we'll get you a bacon roll. The end is just around the corner, up those stairs—"

I groaned. *"More stairs?"*

"There's like...two..."

My posture perked up from slumped over to standing tall. "Just two?"

"Or, you know..." Andie lifted a shoulder. "Twenty."

My eyes narrowed. "Twenty."

"Maybe forty. Hardly any." She waved away my impending heart attack like it was nothing. "Come on."

"I want two bacon rolls out of this," I grumbled.

Andie started jogging down the boarded trail.

And I lagged behind.

Again.

"Come on, loser!" she called.

And I was struggling along just fine—slow but steady—dodging the barbs Andie tossed back at me on the sea breeze until a man pushing an empty stroller passed me, a toddler wailing on his hip.

My footsteps slowed.

It was just some dude. Some *dad*. But the sight of that man's strong arms around his child was a crowbar that wedged in the crack in my chest, prying it open, the morning sun threatening to wake up the secret sleeping deep inside me.

The dream of a family.

The impossible.

I'd skated past the dreaded 3-0 without a breakdown. Some people stressed about missing milestones—a husband, kids, settling down—and I was living my best life, wasn't I? As thirty-two hurtled closer, everyone still believed the only thing I craved was collecting more designer shoes to stuff in my closet. They had no idea. I ached for a family of my own more than anything in the world.

I pressed a hand to my chest to stop the feeling from spreading. Too late. The thread of loneliness around my heart twisted until it knotted tight. My chest heaved, but no air got in my lungs.

I...can't...

Defeated, I flopped on the bottom step, my head falling between my knees. The dribble down my cheeks wasn't tears. The salty sting was sweat. I never cried.

"Hey." A man. Footsteps padded closer. "Um, are you...okay?"

Just peachy.

Would the humiliation ever end? I quickly dashed my palm over my eyes and craned my neck, ready to shoo my good Samaritan on his way so I could crumble in peace.

I blinked.

Oh no.

The man crouched in front of me.

Yeah, not just any man.

The man.

His mouth flattened to the same serious line he always wore at the coffee shop, and his dark brows furrowed like he was examining—judging—every tiny detail about me from behind his black-rimmed glasses. I squeezed my eyes shut.

Not him. Anyone *but him.*

Maybe I was delirious. Maybe on death's doorstep, you hallucinated the suit you'd been seducing with flirty smiles for the last month. I cracked one eye open. No suit today. His workout gear seemed strangely casual after only seeing him in fine tailoring, and his dark hair flopped adorably over his forehead instead of being slicked back, but—

I gulped.

It was him.

The God of Nerds.

This isn't happening.

Our first official meeting wasn't supposed to happen when I sat defeated at the bottom of some stairs in Clovelly, drowning in sweat and the bitter memories of childhood. I'd schemed up a plan to be coy for another week or two before sinking my claws in him for one night we'd never forget. You had to be patient with a man like him. He was shy. Every time I'd ducked my head in a calculated, demure smile, his cheeks had burned the sweetest shade of pink. Only sometimes had he been brave enough to smile back.

"I can find help," he said, his eyes travelling up the stairs. "Or maybe I could wait with you until your friend comes—*oh.*"

Sneakers pounded down the steps two at a time. Frantic, I shooed Andie away. She rolled her eyes and mimed a phone with her hand.

"Call me," she mouthed before disappearing.

This wasn't her first rodeo.

I turned my attention back to my good Samaritan. Oblivious to the commotion, he was back on his feet, his eyes on their new home examining his running shoes.

"I appreciate you stopping to help." I waited for him to lift his gaze before flashing my cutest smile. "Thanks, um—" I gestured to him to share his name.

He stared at me blankly. A beat of silence. His eyes grew wide. "I'm, um..." He braced his hands on his hips and gulped down a breath. "Yeah, you know, I'm...Zach."

This man was adorable—*awkward,* but adorable. "You sure?" I grinned.

He nodded, a cautious smile spreading across his face.

"Well, thank you, Zach. I'm—"

"Eden." My name whooshed out of him like he couldn't believe he was saying it out loud. "Long macchiato with an extra dollop." His brows shot over the top of his glasses. "I—I'm not a weirdo o-or anything. I've seen you at Brew HaHa a few times."

A few, huh? Smooth. "And you noticed me all the way out here?"

"Yeah, I noticed your—" Zach's guilty eyes darted in the direction of my backside and then everywhere—any-where—else. "Um—" He coughed into his fist.

"Sir!" I faked a scandalised gasp. "Have you been peeking at my booty?"

His cheeks flushed a brighter pink than my high-tops. "Well..."

Oh, he'd been peeking, alright, and I loved it. "Sir!"

"In my defence"—he bit back a shy smile—"you have a very *nice* booty." He chuckled. My strait-laced companion had probably never said that word before in his life. "Can I help you up?"

Out shot his big hand. His palm swallowed mine when I curled my fingers around his, and he tugged me up, pulling a little too hard, my chin bumping against his shoulder.

"S-Sorry," he whispered.

I fought the urge to burrow my nose into his neck. How did he smell so clean? Cologne and just...luxe. "That's okay." Why did I whisper back?

"So, um..." Zach puffed out a nervous breath. "Now we've officially met... If you're not busy later this week, there's this restaurant... Montecito."

Spanish food. He was talking my love language. "Sir, are you asking me out on a date?"

"Attempting to. You'll be shocked to discover I don't usually approach unsuspecting women for dinner dates."

"What about peeking at their booties?"

"Also exclusively a you thing." He grinned. "So... Dinner?"

"Sounds fun."

"How about tonight?"

"Tonight?"

Zach rubbed the dark stubble on his jaw. "You're right. We shouldn't wait that long." His grin was back. "I hear Montecito also does a great lunch special."

I laughed and bumped my shoulder against his. I'd misjudged this shy Casanova. I should've pounced sooner. "Sir, I accept. There's just one thing I need to do first."

I waved for him to keep walking.

Cautious, Zach's brows furrowed, but off he went.

I nibbled my lip, enjoying the view of his powerful stride from two steps behind. He was a fine example of a man. Slimmer than some. Definitely no beefcake. But he had the perfect triangle of broad shoulders cutting to narrow hips, and damn, what a sexy li'l butt.

He'd been worth the wait.

A confused look turned over Zach's shoulder when I didn't follow. "E-Eden?"

I grinned. "Now, we're even."

1

She didn't say, "It hurts to be forgotten."

Eden

If a woman's thirty-second birthday kicked off with not one but two orgasms, she'd be forgiven for thinking it was going to be the best day ever, right?

Rookie error.

The writing had been on the sterile white walls of Zach's apartment the moment he'd crawled out of bed. He'd showered, dressed in his suit, and knotted his tie *just so*, all without a word. Birthday wishes? Gifts? None. His lips had lingered a little longer on my forehead on his way out the door, but still...nothing.

"Promise you won't forget?" I'd said.

Dark brows had popped over the top of his glasses. "I'd never forget," he'd said.

Except now, the sunset was melting into Sydney Harbour, and city lights dotted the skyline. The party—*my* party—had already started.

And Zach wasn't there.

A watch didn't match the vibe of the tassels and sequins of my vintage cocktail dress, but Andie was tracking the time for both of us. She'd been sliding a look to the doors for a while, always as she readjusted her bowtie or checked her cufflinks, but yeah, she'd been looking.

"Even Cinderella wasn't this late to the party," she muttered.

"He'll be here," I said.

My delivery was as unconvincing as the last time I'd said it. The certainty in my voice had started wavering about ten songs ago when I'd shifted from hopeful to defensive.

I had every reason to be worried.

This wasn't the first time Zach had let me down.

Yvette's attention flicked to the doors, too. An eternal optimist, complete with a halo of bleached blonde curls, she preferred to see the champagne glass half full even when only a sip was left. But blue eyes narrowed. Full lips thinned. Even she had her doubts.

"You reminded him, right?" Yvette asked.

A note stuck on the fridge. The text message of heart eyes and cake emojis I'd sent him when I'd gulped down a smoothie so the rest of my staff could take a proper lunch break. Wasn't that enough? I'd talked about my party for weeks. At least three influencers had featured it as *the* place to be. That was more rope than I'd tossed off the cliff for any other man to rescue himself.

Andie frowned even more than usual. "Why does Ed have to remind him? It's her damn birthday."

"We all know Zach's a little, well, *you know,*" Yvette said.

Socially awkward? Distracted? A workaholic? The ugly voice in the back of my mind whispered the word 'selfish.' But when Zach's attention was on me, his arms snug around my middle and his nose nuzzled in my hair, the only word I heard was 'perfect.' The problem was that his attention was rarely on me anymore.

"What a fucking cop-out," Andie snapped. "The three of us work our arses off for twelve hours a day at Voom, and we still found time to plan a classy do for a hundred people. Zach had two jobs tonight. One"—Andie held up her index finger—"bring the cake. Two"—her middle finger went up next—"get here on time."

The flutter of Yvette's false lashes was a declaration of war. "Sweetie, I hope you're planning to stick those fingers somewhere useful."

Andie stammered out a few curse words, tugging on the cuffs of her jacket, her cheeks red hot. She had no real comeback. Yvette grinned. She'd won this round.

I sighed. This wasn't how I imagined my birthday. My two best friends bickering. No man on my arm. Where *was* Zach? I'd blow out the candles flickering on top of my birthday cake and wish this disastrous night was over…if there were candles…or…a cake. I couldn't keep standing around, hoping he'd make time to prioritise me. I looked like a fool.

"I'm going to call him," I said.

"Don't." Andie's eyes pleaded with me to change my mind.

"I won't go easy on him," I reassured her. "A girl's allowed to make a scene on her birthday."

"I approve," Yvette said. "You give that man hell."

I planned to—if he ever picked up his phone or answered my messages. History told me neither was a certainty.

Chin held high, I squared my shoulders, and my taffeta gown swished with the confident swing of my hips as I weaved through the crowd. A dazzling smile masked my disappointment. Air kisses on my guests' cheeks and my sincere thanks for coming concealed any vulnerability. I laughed away awkward conversations asking me about the mystery man who'd finally convinced me to settle down.

"You'll meet him soon," I always said, as if it were part of the plan to keep them on the edge of their seats.

But when the corridor narrowed into shadows, old memories creeping up the walls, I escaped into the bathroom where no one could see my facade unravel. I slumped against white tiles. My gloved palm clutched over my mouth to block a scream—or even more humiliating, a sob.

Zach forgot.

He forgot my birthday.

He forgot...me.

Again.

My shoulders trembled as a breath squeezed into my lungs. I'd forgiven Zach for all the date nights he'd missed. I'd even shrugged off him missing my salon's picnic. Three years in our new location, number one in all the reviews, and another nomination—but still no win—for me as Hairstylist of the Year were things to be celebrated. And they had been—by everyone except him. But I'd already set the bar too low. An uninspired apology was all it had taken to earn back my smile and a mumbled agreement he deserved another chance. I'd broken all my rules for Zach.

Where had we gone so wrong?

Our relationship had shot off like a crazy, sexy rollercoaster. That man had swept me off my feet and spoiled me with fun dates, staying up all night talking, and eventually, weekends rolling around in bed. He'd made me wait and wait.

He wasn't a one-night stand kind of guy. He wanted a commitment. Someone special. Or so he'd said.

Six months later, the roller coaster sat parked and rusty at the station. Worley and Stone owned Zach's soul. He was *always* at the office.

I was the first to sing from the rooftops about how much I loved his drive and determination. He wouldn't be one of Sydney's top lawyers if he didn't have that edge. But he'd captured me, convinced me to move into his apartment on a whim when my lease had been up, and now, he was never there.

I slipped away from the wall, pinned my reflection in the mirror, and examined my face with critical eyes.

I could see her. The confident woman who'd escaped a childhood better forgotten to claw her way to the top was still inside me. The courage and the same steely determination shone through, but a heavy truth weighed behind my eyes.

My impossible dream was slipping through my fingers.

Huddled under my covers late at night, I'd squeeze my eyes shut and fantasise about a future that wasn't just me against the world. The empty shell of the bedroom warmed up, and my imaginary husband snuggled closer, laughing about how we needed to buy a bigger bed because our kids kept sneaking in and we needed more room. It was the opposite of how I grew up, and the craving had only gnawed deeper once Zach became part of my life.

But I couldn't lose myself. I had to stay strong. Courageous. Sometimes, it was still me against the world.

My black satin gloves balled by my side, and I challenged my reflection head-on.

It was time for the pep talk.

Who are you?

"Eden Phillips," I told the mirror.

Who made you the woman you are?

"I made my damn self."

Who needs a man?

I scoffed. More than one hook-up had complained I had *daddy issues*, but I wasn't a card-carrying member of the 'I Hate Men' club. Men were easy on the eye, and I'd stumbled on plenty who didn't need an hour-long seminar and a personalised map to find my clit. Sex was a joy and one I'd always indulged in with abandon, but outside the bedroom, most men were walking disappointments.

My head bowed.

Until Zach.

I prowled through the world like a tiger, seeking opportunities, staking my claim as the queen of the urban jungle, but with Zach, I purred like a kitten. His whispered promise to take care of me was a drug. Addictive. When I'd only ever relied on myself, words like his tingled on my skin, braided around my heart, and twisted too tight.

I hadn't whispered the three magic words: *I love you*. Neither had Zach. We'd jumbled up the steps to a relationship. Maybe because we lived together, he didn't think he needed to tell me. Maybe everything about this relationship was a mistake. How would I know? I'd never been in a relationship before.

Sighing, I turned my back on my reflection and headed for the door. I'd never find my true strength hiding in the bathroom.

"Happy Birthday!"

I fluttered through the crowd. More air kisses. More superficial conversations. More of my sincere thanks to my guests for choosing to spend their Friday night celebrating with me.

A yelp turned my head.

The crowd split. Two waiters spun, trays swooping out of the way, barely avoiding a collision. Guests on the dance floor scrambled. An enormous white box pirouetted through the chaos. It wobbled. Spun. Expensive black dress shoes with laces tied *just so* stumbled left, then right, before the awkward dance ended with a sigh and a mumbled, "That was close."

Wait.

My eyebrows pinched together. I'd recognise the velvety rumble of that voice anywhere. "Zach?"

His head popped out from the side of the box. "Hey." A sheepish grin followed.

I waved at the chaos. "What the heck is all this?"

"Your cake."

He didn't forget. Warm tingles filled my chest. "You sure there's just one cake in there?"

"Oh, uh." His head tipped back with a nervous laugh. "I guess we did go a little overboard."

"We?"

"Me and Mum. Actually, one hundred percent my mum. I'm just the delivery boy." His gaze roamed for a safe place to deposit the cake. "Where should I, um...?" Another helpless look turned around the room.

I pointed to the empty stand. Zach flashed me a relieved smile and headed for the table. He slipped the box from his arms, and with trembling fingers, he stripped off the sticky tape, lifted the lid, and folded down the sides.

He stood back and stuck out his hand. *"Voila!"* A proud smile lit up his face.

My hand fluttered to my mouth, a tear threatening to spill down my cheek. Oh, that cake, it was the stuff of dreams—three tiers of white frosting decorated with elegant black and gold Art Deco trim, feathers, pearls, and a beaded edge identical to my dress.

"It's a *Great Gatsby* cake to match your theme!" he said. "It's all edible, even the feathers. Crazy, huh?"

My chin wobbled.

Zach's face fell. "You don't like it?"

I clutched his arm and pulled him close, hiding my tears in the safety of his chest. "I love it. But I—" I swallowed the shame blocking my throat. "I didn't invite your parents."

Forget a party invitation; I hadn't even *met* Zach's parents yet. They'd asked us over plenty of times since I'd moved in with him, but I'd always found an excuse to weasel out of more rejection.

"Next birthday." He booped me on the tip of my nose.

"Yeah." The smile on my face was shaky. "Next birthday."

I buried my emotions by tidying Zach up. He smiled, head lolling to the side, as I straightened his bowtie and his collar and then ran a fingertip along the sharp lapel of his tuxedo jacket. My touch on his cheek finished the routine. He shaved every morning, but when evening rolled around, delicious dark stubble contoured his jaw.

"We're the perfect couple," I said, beaming. "You looking handsome in your tux. Me in my gown. Can you believe I got my little paws on this vintage piece? It's one of a kind. Handmade in Milan." I twirled so the beads fanned out. "I thought for sure someone would've already rented it for the weekend."

Zach's lips flattened into a grim line. He was weighing up whether to say something difficult. Something I wouldn't like.

I bit my lip.

He probably thought I should've chosen something less fancy. But an event like this called for a special dress, and this one hadn't cost much. I spent my money on shoes and timeless accessories that could be mixed and matched for every occasion. One-off dresses for a party? Rented only. Frugally chic.

I kissed Zach's cheek. "I'm going to snap some piccies of my cake."

Light bouncing from the chandeliers made the cake sparkle in every direction. I scrolled through the photos, selected my favourite, and whipped up a quick post for my social media. Nibbling my lip, I read over it three times.

> Thank you to the most talented mama in the world for my beautiful birthday cake. Maree, you're the best!

My stomach knotted.

A stupid post wasn't enough to say thanks—even if I did have half a million followers. I smacked a few heart emojis after the message. Still not enough. I'd have to make Zach's mother one of my famous gift baskets. Maybe I should buy her a car. Anything was easier than disappointing that woman in the flesh.

Zach stole a kiss on my cheek. "You're quiet tonight."

Lips pressed together, I avoided his eyes. My palms beaded with sweat in my gloves.

"Denny Dee?" he gently urged. "What is it?"

"I just—" I cleared my throat, forcing a smile. "I thought you'd forgotten." I stopped myself from adding 'again.'

His smile was confused. "I wouldn't forget your birthday. Why would you—" He glanced at his watch, and his eyes widened. "*Shit!* I didn't—the time—I just—" His failed excuses ended with a frustrated breath.

"I wish you'd called," I whispered.

"I'm so sorry. I meant to leave work early, but Mac and I got stuck finishing a settlement, and then the traffic across town was a complete mess. I was too paranoid to speed in case I ruined your cake. Mum said three hunks of wood are holding it together, but I didn't want to take any chances."

I nodded, barely listening. Zach had so many excuses, always beginning—and usually ending—with his job.

"I'm sorry." Zach wrapped me in a hug and kissed my forehead. "I'll get better at this. I promise I'll try harder."

"It's okay." It wasn't. "You're here now." And that fact made my toes tingle.

"I wouldn't be anywhere else."

Except work.

Zach's face brightened. "Hey, I almost forgot. I've got something for you." He patted his pocket. "Right here."

Clapping my hands, I bounced on the spot.

I *loved* this game.

I could buy myself anything I wanted, but I still adored gifts. The trinkets Zach surprised me with proved he thought about me while he did whatever lawyers do all day. Sometimes, he hid a packet of sweets in his pocket. One time, it was tickets to the movie I'd desperately wanted to see. Not-so-secretly, some of the appeal of digging around in his pocket was sneaking a cheeky touch *down there*. I'd always say, "Oopsie," and smirk suggestively, but not tonight. My classy birthday party was a hard-on-free zone.

So, even though the smile I tipped up at him was pure sin, when I slipped my hand in Zach's pocket, the search was entirely chaste. My fingertips skimmed the sharp edges of a box. I pulled it out.

Oh.

My heart exploded at the sight of Tiffany blue, all wrapped up with a white bow.

Yvette squealed in the background.

I snuck a peek over my shoulder. Her hands were slapped on her cheeks. Andie stood beside her, scowling. We were all thinking the same thing.

Zach was proposing.

Finally.

His face turned fuzzy from my unshed tears, but...

This proposal was all wrong. I'd imagined Zach would be the type of man to do things the old-fashioned way. He couldn't ask my father's permission, but I thought he'd still drop to one knee, make a heartfelt speech, and present me a ring he'd designed himself. Maybe he'd even whisper, "I love you," to catch up on the step we'd missed.

Zach grazed his nose along my cheek. "I wanted to get you something special to celebrate your special night." His smoky voice curled around my heart and tingled over my skin. "Open it, Denny Dee."

I tugged off the bow.

It's really happening.

I edged the lid off the box.

I'm going to have a family. A good man truly wants me. Loves—

I choked on my disappointment. Maybe to Zach, it sounded like delighted surprise. I hoped it did.

I blinked down at the delicate diamond earrings in the box. "Zach, they're..." Beautiful. Absolutely stunning. The teardrops dangling from platinum gold would've cost him an absolute bomb, but they weren't the engagement ring I'd been hoping for. "I adore them." I did. I *did*. "Help me pop them on."

And I flaunted those damn earrings to anyone who'd look at them. I delighted in twisting my head to show off how they sparkled, and I told everyone the handsome man on my arm had given me my precious gift.

And it *was* precious.

But if there had been candles flickering on top of my cake, I wouldn't have blown them out to wish for those earrings.

2

He didn't say, "I love you."

Zach

Say the word 'lawyer,' and most folks imagine the guys in the movies. You know the kind I mean. Confident. Big dick energy. That lawyer swaggered into a courtroom in a slick suit, swept back a full head of hair, and smirked at the jury because he had a trick in his back pocket to win the unwinnable case.

But a *real* lawyer? Someone like me?

I wore an expensive suit. A few wayward strands of silver had made an unwanted debut around my temples, but I still had the same mop of dark hair I'd been failing to tame all my life. I'll be honest, though. I'd never swaggered...anywhere. And a courtroom? Me in front of a jury? Once. I'd puked. That's right. All over the floor.

My client had taken one horrified look at the vomit splattered on his sneakers, leant over, and whispered, "You sure you're a lawyer?"

Top of my graduating class.

But if my boss had taught me anything—and, truthfully, Chris Stone had taught me everything about being a lawyer—it was that my success didn't begin and end in that courtroom.

Brains and hard work counted at Worley and Stone. Grinding in solitude behind a desk was valuable. I had a future. For a kid who'd grown up in the western suburbs of Sydney, poorer than dirt, the promise of never living pay cheque to pay cheque was worth never seeing the sun…

Most of the time.

Yawning, I adjusted my glasses and squinted at the computer. Another night, another contract. The long list of clauses blurred into smudged black lines, and my fingers were sluggish over the keyboard with each tap, tap, tap.

I refused to even acknowledge the shaky stack of files parked in the corner of my desk. I hadn't touched a single folder on that pile, and it was already—I glanced at the computer—ten o'clock.

My phone buzzed.

Eden
> Miss you, handsome man xoxo

Eden's message tugged a smile out of me. The curve of my lips was rusty. Strange, even. It was the first time I'd smiled all day. I quickly responded.

Zach
> Miss you more. xx

Eden
> Is tonight a wait-up night?

When would I head home? My gaze cut to the pile of work still untouched on the desk. I grunted. At this rate, I'd never leave. I couldn't fail. Not now.

Not…again.

Promotions—a chance at partnership—loomed closer. The arrogant prick with the receding hairline three offices down was just itching for me to implode. He wasn't the only one. Worley and Stone may have been my home, but running the gauntlet of the office was survival of the fittest. Worse. It was the Ministry of Love—if you'd snuck under the school steps to read *1984* as many times as I had.

And now, I had Eden to think about, too. I needed to build stability for the two of us, and I couldn't dump all the worries about mortgages and how much life costs on her shoulders. She was a hairdresser. How much could she possibly earn? Minimum wage? She avoided every awkward conversation about family and money, but she shouldn't have to rent a fancy frock to wear to her birthday party.

My groan echoed in the empty office.

The birthday party.

The cake had been a big win, but I'd been late, and she'd frowned when she saw the earrings. When we'd tumbled through the door at 2:00 a.m., she'd unbuckled my pants without any ceremony, pushed me on the sofa, climbed on top, and edged me almost to insanity, all while wearing a defiant glare. Hot. I'd wanted it. But sex was a barometer with Eden. When the pressure ratcheted up to cool, detached, and her in control, she was pissed off. That night, she'd been furious. She probably still was. It was just another awkward conversation she preferred avoiding.

Screw it.

I flipped my laptop shut. Impossible deadlines disappeared. I slipped on my jacket, straightened my collar, and adjusted my tie. Armour on.

Zach

> It's a wait-up night.

The shuffle of my feet picked up speed down the empty corridors as the elevators appeared. When I reached for the down arrow, a polished pink fingernail hit the button first.

"This is an early finish for you," Michaela said, dropping her bag on the floor with zero care as she shrugged on her coat. "You're slacking off, Rawles."

Her smirk confused me. Were we on speaking terms again?

Michaela fooled most people, talking about her need for authenticity and finding joy in the small things, but she was all show. Gloss, no grit. The bag was the perfect example. She'd huffed when I hadn't noticed it on the boardroom table. Designer, apparently. A paralegal had squealed and jingled the gold charms, but when Michaela had searched across the table for my approval, my disinterested nod had earned me a glare and a reminder of exactly where I'd come from.

"We can hardly expect the son of a grease monkey to understand the craftsmanship in a piece like this," Michaela had laughed.

A low blow, and she knew it. My father was a good man. He was proud of being a mechanic, and yeah, maybe scholarships had paid my way through university, but I was senior to Michaela now in every way. I'd be one of her bosses soon. At the minimum, I was her equal, but not in her eyes—or many others who walked the same corridors.

I ignored her teasing with a tight smile. "Maybe keep my early departure to yourself." I'd prefer not to be the subject of her pillow talk with Chris.

"You didn't hear the news?"

I grunted. When would I hear any gossip? I never left my office and even more rarely took breaks. Lunch? What the hell was that? Two times a week, I dragged my backside to the gym under the misguided advice of a therapist from years ago who'd suggested boxing classes for my mental health. Every other day,

I scoffed whatever sandwich my executive assistant dumped on my desk on her way back from Pilates.

"Chris proposed," Michaela said.

"To...*you?*"

"To the timid doctor with the glasses."

"Lola? I thought they broke up."

Michaela's lips curved, but she wasn't smiling. "So did I."

The elevator chimed. Silver doors stretched open, and I gestured for her to head in first. "So, what does that mean for you?"

"I doubt I'll get an invite to the wedding, but Chris promised to pencil me in every second Tuesday if I'm interested."

"Mac..." *Shit.* "I..."

What else could I possibly say? Don't? Value yourself? Leave me out of it?

I slumped against the wall of the elevator. That was the last thing I needed to know about Chris, and I sure as hell didn't want Michaela dragging me into any drama. He wouldn't.

Personal lives stay personal—his motto, ruthlessly enforced.

Nothing—nobody—was bigger than the firm. Elijah Johnson learned that the hard way. Who was he? Nobody. He'd become *persona non grata* and hauled out by security the day after he'd prioritised his daughter's ballet concert over a client meeting. I wasn't about to stick my nose where it didn't belong and become the next Elijah Johnson.

The pointy toe of Michaela's stiletto tapped against my shoe. "Where are you headed?"

I shrugged. "Home."

"I've heard good things about a new bar on the harbour. Want to grab a drink?"

No. "Ah..." *Absolutely not.*

Michaela's hand slid along the handrail. "There's live music until midnight." Her floral perfume was so strong I could almost taste it. She'd gotten too close. "A quiet crowd."

Clearing my throat, I edged away until I bumped into the corner. "You know crowds don't help the sales pitch with me."

She smiled. "I do know a lot about you." The gaze she dipped to my belt made me uncomfortable enough to clumsily button up my jacket. "You and me. We had a good thing once."

"We had...a...thing."

But it wasn't good. She'd called it casual. An *arrangement*. I called it four times too many.

"So," she pressed, "can I tempt you?"

"Mac, I..." The word 'no' was simple, yet I couldn't spit it out. She was confrontational and still too close to Chris to risk any more frayed feelings.

I shook my head.

The elevator doors opened, and I waited for Michaela to head out first.

"Always the gentleman," she said, the cut of her voice making the words anything but a compliment. Her heels echoed through the empty foyer. When she glanced back at me, she smiled. "You sure I can't change your mind?"

"See you tomorrow."

I didn't wave goodbye.

·♥·♥·♥·♥·♥·

THE FRONT DOOR BUMPED to a stop. Sighing, I wedged myself through the gap, careful to sidestep the cardboard boxes stacked against the wall.

Day thirty-two.

Why hadn't Eden unpacked yet? She'd moved in over a month ago, and I wanted her to crowd my space. I wanted to see her in every inch of the apartment. The cup on the bathroom vanity looked less lonely with two toothbrushes stuck in it instead of one.

But it was almost like Eden had one foot out the door, never quite all in. My chest tightened. Was she waiting for someone *better?* I ticked most of the boxes of being the better kind of man, didn't I? I hadn't fully outgrown my blue-collar roots to become as successful as someone like Chris, sure, but *almost*.

I took off my shoes and butted my socked toe into the box until it slid flush against the wall. I dropped my briefcase on top.

Lights burned in every room. I flicked off the switches as I wandered through the apartment—hallway, living room, kitchen—and, shaking my head with a smile, I switched off the bedroom light, too. I liked Eden's quirks. The apartment was never dark when she was home. The scattered vegetable scraps on the kitchen counter after one of her late-night cooking frenzies was an adjustment, but it wasn't a dealbreaker. Some people were just messy cooks.

Light splintered through the gap of the door to the ensuite. I peeked inside. Eden stood at the vanity. She had drawers stuffed full of cute pyjamas, but she'd thrown on one of my T-shirts, the hem barely skimming the tops of her thighs. Her dark hair hung loose over her shoulders.

She didn't notice when I leant against the doorframe. All her concentration was on squeezing cream into her palm and dabbing it on her face. I smiled. I'd binge-watch Eden in front of the mirror before any TV show. She was all my favourite things—the bone-deep sigh of the first sip of coffee in the morning, the contract with no red lines through the terms.

She sniffled and rubbed at her nose, the red tip matching the blotches on her cheeks.

Shit, what did I forget this time?

I shuffled behind her. Wrapped my arms around her waist. Breathed in a whiff of her powder-scented face cream. She was the little patch of heaven in all my gloom.

I kissed the crook of her shoulder and murmured, "Why the tears, Denny Dee?" *Please don't say me.*

"Tears—wha—oh! No!" Flustered, Eden flapped her hands and capped the bottle of face cream. *"Allergies.* One of my clients dropped by with flowers this afternoon to say thank you. Roses." She wrinkled her nose. "It was thoughtful of her, but those weeds are havoc for my sinuses."

"Need something from the pharmacy?"

"Nah, now that you're finally here, I'm not letting you out of my sight." Grinning, she twisted around and threaded her arms around my neck. "You know, this is the first time we've seen each other today."

"Mmm?"

"You'd already left for the office when I woke up. It's time to pay up and say hello." Her smile turned sly. "Properly."

"Properly, huh?" I pecked a kiss on the corner of her mouth.

She huffed—that wasn't the *proper* kiss she wanted—but I laughed away her frustration, my grip tightening on the curve of her hip, fingers embedding my old T-shirt possessively into her skin. I needed her closer.

The kiss was slow to start, my lips soft on hers, soft again, and then, grinning, I pinned her minty little mouth with mine. I devoured her, slipping in my tongue, meeting hers, her throaty moan encouraging me to keep going…and going…until one final peck sealed the end of her *proper* kiss.

"Hello." I bumped the tip of her nose with mine.

Eden dissolved into a breathless giggle. "Hi." She popped a kiss on my chin before turning around to fiddle with the potions on the vanity. "So, how was your day, handsome man?"

I lifted a shoulder. Same old, same old. Emails. Phone calls. Constant fires to put out—with none of the fluffy kittens stuck in trees or grizzled firefighters rescuing them to make the stories even remotely interesting.

Eden's eyes caught mine in the mirror. She frowned. "That good, huh?"

"Work's work. Mac and I settled a big contract that's been hanging around for a while. How was your day?"

"Amazing!"

Her excited chatter bounced off the white tiles, but her stories about clients and colours wove into worries I thought I'd left at the office.

Did I remember to reply to the email from the developer?

"—and then you won't *believe* what Yvette said—"

When's the settlement for Pitt Street? Monday? Shit. I need to check if Mac talked to the bank.

"—and Andie totally lost her shit!"

Eden twittered a laugh that I matched with a shaky smile. Guilt made it hard to swallow the lump in my throat. It wasn't the first time I'd missed listening to her stories.

I stepped closer, pulling Eden's back against my front, looping my arms around her waist, and letting my chin nuzzle into her hair. Her gaze locked on mine in the mirror. Her tube of cream dropped to the vanity. Long, slender fingers curled over mine, and she bit her lip as she slid my hand down, down...

I brushed my lips on the shell of her ear. "You want me to make you feel good?"

As her head bobbed up and down, my hand was already wandering past the elastic waistband of her knickers. She whimpered when I ghosted a touch along the warm, delicious skin of her pussy, gently spreading her open, searching for the delicate wet patch to slick my fingers.

"Denny Dee." I groaned into the hollow of her neck. "What got you feeling like this?"

"Us." Her eyes shut tight. "Our first time." She rocked her hips against my hand, deepening the pressure of my fingers swirling over her clit, just the way she liked it. "You kept me waiting so long."

I had. "I needed to be sure." Eden would've broken my heart if I hadn't. Discarded me. I knew she would've. I teased her with a slow and steady rhythm as I pressed languid kisses up her neck. "I don't fuck just anyone. I'm selective."

"You"—her pretty pink tongue darted over her bottom lip—"chose me?"

I hummed a yes in her ear.

She whimpered. A red flush crept higher up her neck, and her hips rocked faster and faster against my hand. She was racing for her prize.

"That's it," I whispered. "Almost there. Show me I made the right choice."

Her throaty sigh shot straight to my cock, but there was no relief for me except to let out a groan. This was about her. But what was it about this game she liked so much? Why did she get so turned on pretending she didn't hold all the cards? She could've chosen any man she wanted. I'd only shifted the odds because I wasn't the type of guy who enjoyed being used for one night.

"Z-Zach." Her dark eyes fluttered open and locked with mine in the mirror.

Say the words.

Her hand squeezed mine, and breathless gasps escaped her lips in time with the fingers I swirled over her smooth, wet skin. My pulse pounded. I pressed myself even closer into her spine, tugged her hair, and exposed her neck, grazing my teeth, enjoying her sweet taste on my tongue, reminding her who was making her feel so good.

Eden was perfect. Not just like this. Everywhere. Always.

I'd wanted to confess how I felt about her since the day she'd moved in. Fascinated, I'd stared at her toothbrush stuck in the cup beside mine. I'd wanted to say it then...and so many times since.

I love you.

"I'm going to take such good care of you," I whispered instead.

More of her favourite words, and enough to tip her over the edge with a filthy string of curses whispered so prettily.

I love you so much.

I kissed Eden's shoulder, blinked watery eyes into her hair, and let the sweet tremors against my hand distract me until I could swallow all the emotion somewhere safe.

We weren't ready for those words yet.

Soon.

When I'd made it.

When she had a reason to say them back.

3

She didn't say, "Please choose me."

Eden

Hit play on the evil genius theme song.

This was my best scheme yet.

My sneakers squeaked on the marble floor as I exited the elevator. Those shoes were the shit, glittery gold designer kicks perfect for scurrying around the offices of Worley and Stone after dark.

But no beady little lawyer eyes would spy my shoes—or me. Every office, every desk was empty, probably abandoned hours ago for Friday night drinks and weekend plans.

I seesawed to a stop.

Or *abandoned* like a creepy warehouse in those horror movies where the killer was waiting…just around the corner…ready to pounce.

My heart bumped faster.

Was this really my best scheme ever?

I glanced at the brown paper bag clutched in my fist and smiled.

Yeah. *Hell* yeah.

Delivering Zach his favourite takeout, sharing half an hour, sure, some people might take something so simple for granted. It was a small gesture, but another way of showing Zach I supported him chasing his dreams. We were doing it together…even if some nights I'd never felt more alone. A moment like this was worth pushing past silly phobias. The dark was no match for me.

I squared my shoulders and focused on the city lights.

Proud but adorably humble, Zach had mentioned he'd scored prime real estate in the firm and could look over the whole city from his desk. Those same lights flickered in the sleeping offices at the end of the corridor.

The *never-ending* corridor.

My eyes darted everywhere. Why was this floor *so dark?* Who turned out all the lights? A prickle of sweat dribbled down my back. Why was it *so hot?* My fingers trembled to open another button on the cotton blouse clawing at my skin.

I was never making it out of the building alive.

I plastered myself against a glass wall and sank to the floor.

Takeout, safe. Handbag, open. Phone, already calling for backup via video chat.

Yvette's grinning face bounced onto the screen. "Deenie!" She slurped a sip of her cocktail, swaying to the music thumping in the background.

I scrunched my eyebrows. "Where are you?"

"El Diablo Cantina. And may I just say tonight's patronage is above average." She cackled but suddenly stopped and leant closer to the screen, squinting. "Where the hell are you?"

"Losing my shit at Zach's work."

Yvette plonked down her cocktail. "Okay. *Okay.* I'm the chosen one for once. I can do this." She shook out her hands and arms before settling into a prayer position. She screwed her eyes shut and hummed. "Follow me. Big breaths." One eye slitted open. "I don't hear any big breaths."

I laughed. "Sorry, but this is too weird."

"Isn't this what you do with the grouch?"

"No way. Andie usually says something like, 'Get over yourself, loser.'" I shrugged. "It works."

"Tough love, huh? Well, on that note, please tell me your office booty call is the only reason you're wearing that outfit. Wait! Is that—" Her hand flew over her mouth. She inched it down again only to ask in horror, "Are you wearing a purple cardigan?"

"It's, um, corporate chic." I winced. It was ugly. *Really* ugly.

Yvette's nose wrinkled. "If you say so."

"Look, this was the best outfit I could scrounge together at the last minute, okay? I don't exactly have a row of dull lawyer wear hanging in my closet."

"And the universe thanks you for having better taste." Yvette lifted the glass to her lips and muttered, "Usually."

"It got me in the building and up the elevator."

Truthfully, the security guard's dopey smile after I'd sobbed a made-up story about lost paperwork and popped enough buttons to *accidentally* flash him my bra got me in the elevator. No one needed to hear that version of the story, though. I grinned.

"A smile!" Yvette squealed. "Feeling better now?"

I bobbed my head in a quick nod. "I'm good."

"I expect a bridesmaid's dress as payment for my efforts."

"Deal." I waved.

Yvette flapped a wave back. "Oh, and Deenie?"

"Yeah?"

"Get over yourself, loser!"

Yvette's cackle ended the call, and that reminder of my friend picked me up off the floor. I slung my bag over my shoulder and grabbed the takeout. The corridor wasn't endless anymore.

Confident steps powered me past the offices to where only one light still burned.

Hey, stranger.

Zach was scowling at his computer, nibbling on the end of his fancy fountain pen. His jacket was off, the cufflinks I'd bought him on display, and his tie hung loose enough to flick open the top few buttons of his shirt. My heart squeezed. He was *so* handsome. He had no idea. He walked around oblivious to the eyelashes fluttering in his direction, always too busy inspecting his shoes, never paying much attention to anyone—except me. I smiled.

My footsteps fell in sync with a new echo from the other end of the corridor. Heels. I paused, plastering myself back against the glass, my breaths silent.

Closer...and closer...

A woman sauntered out of the shadows. Her hair was more caramel than blonde, a balayage that desperately needed smoother blending, and she was wearing the typical bland black suit my business clients seemed to prefer. Her shoes had a little more personality, though—designer stilettos with red soles that tapped along the marble floors to Zach's office.

The woman drummed her knuckles on the glass door. When Zach didn't look up from whatever he was reading, she nudged the door open.

"Rawles." She held up a black coffee mug. "Thought you might need this."

"Oh, uh..." He barely lifted his eyes off the computer. "Thanks, Mac."

Mac.

This was Mac? I'd imagined some guy in his mid-forties with thinning hair wearing a suit jacket that didn't quite button up around his middle—not her!

Apprehension dripped down my spine.

This wasn't right.

Mac slid the coffee mug along the desk, and the grateful smile Zach rewarded her with splintered my heart. I glared down at the takeout bag clutched so tight in my fist I could feel my nails biting into my skin. Spoiling Zach was *my* job. I deserved that smile instead of the scraps of attention he tossed my way.

Zach turned back to his computer.

I took a step. Only one.

Mac made quite a production of taking off her suit jacket and tossing it over a chair. Her back arched, boobs straining the buttons of her silk blouse, as she stretched with an exaggerated yawn. Zach's eyes didn't leave the computer.

I slapped a hand over my mouth to muffle a giggle. This woman was ridiculous.

Mac frowned. Recalculating her game plan, she skimmed her fingers along the wood before perching on the edge of the desk. Nothing. She crossed her legs. When he still didn't look up, she reached over and flipped his laptop shut.

"Hey!" Zach snapped. "What the f—"

"Forget about work tonight," she said.

"I can't—"

"If this is about the other night—"

"Don't."

"—I promise no crowds this time."

This time?

My heart pounded louder. The corridor narrowed. The dark hung heavier. My next step faltered.

When were the other times?

Zach sagged in his chair. He watched the woman in his office with a cautious expression, his mouth opening like he was about to say something. He shook his head.

"It'd just be you and me," she added. "My place. Like before."

I struggled to force air into my lungs. What did these words mean? Old ghosts clawed too tight, too real, around my throat. I wanted to run, but my feet hovered on air, the world ripped out from under them. Was I watching the end of my relationship in real time? No, I had to be making too much of this. Zach wouldn't cheat. He *wouldn't*.

Teeth buried in my lip, I darted my eyes between the scene in front of me and my phone. I tapped out a message to Zach and hit send.

> Eden
> **Is it a wait-up night?**

His phone pinged on the desk.

Please. My eyes begged Zach through the shadows. *Please.*

He didn't pick it up.

I swayed, my knees forgetting how to keep me upright. It was a mistake. Yeah. Sometimes, it took a message or two to get his attention. He was busy. My eyes narrowed on the woman crowding his desk. Not busy with her. With work.

The next message was harder. My phone shook, fingers trembling as I fumbled over the screen.

> Eden
> **I want to spoil you xoxo**

I hit send.

Another ping.

All eyes in the office snapped to his phone. This time, Zach grabbed it. I didn't imagine the smile tugging at the corner of his lips. Mac saw it, too. Jealousy twisted her features, and she uncoiled her legs like the viper she was and slithered off the desk.

"Got a secret admirer?" She sauntered beside him, trying to peer over his shoulder.

Zach's chair slid away. "Ignore that." He shoved his phone across the desk. "It's no one."

I sucked in a breath.

No one.

I was swaying again, toppling around on the spot like I was on the ocean, trying—no, failing—to stop my knees buckling.

No one.

I hit the floor.

"Messages at this time of night are usually important," Mac said.

"It's literally no one important." Zach opened his laptop. "No big deal, okay? Don't even think about it." He started typing again.

No one.

It was just like the nights all those years ago that I'd spent cowering in a ball on the laundry room tiles. I'd crept through the dark and peeked under the gap of the door, searching for the crack of light, screaming my tiny lungs out.

"Who's that?" the women's voices had always whispered.

"No one," my father had always barked back. "Ignore her. She'll learn her lesson."

Sometimes, my father had kicked the door or promised me a damn good hiding if I didn't quit making so much noise. He'd taught me a long time ago to stop screaming in the dark.

I thought Zach saw me, though. I didn't think I needed to scream, or send messages, or be hidden away. I was *someone* now. I blinked at the light shining down the corridor. He didn't see me. Had he ever?

"Want me to help you relax?" Mac asked.

He only saw her, and she was slithering closer…and closer…

"Zach?"

"Oh, um… Yeah—"

The broken whimper torn from my throat blotted out the rest of Zach's words. I couldn't sit there and let my heart get ripped out, too. I jolted to my feet, lurching in the other direction so I didn't have to see what happened after Mac dug her claws into his shoulders. I scampered down the corridor like a drunk mouse, knocking into the walls, my handbag thumping against my hip until light burst through the suffocating darkness.

The elevators.

I jabbed at the down button over and over. No waiting, just *ding,* and the doors opened.

I stumbled inside on shaky legs and pounded the lobby button with my fist. Agitated, I paced in the small space, anxious to escape the tiny elevator, the building, the memory of that woman touching the man I thought I'd spend the rest of my life loving with all my heart. A lifetime passed. The scene in Zach's office replayed too many times.

When the elevator stopped, I exploded out, my sneakers squeaking on the shiny floor as I ran through the foyer, my phone out of my bag and pressed to my ear as I fled the building.

"Pick up." I dodged people walking on the street, the rings bleeping on and on. "Pick up."

Andie yawned. "Eden?"

My eyes lifted to the sky to whisper a silent *thank you.* "Andie. Shit—he—I c-can't—"

"What's going on?" Andie suddenly sounded wide awake. "Is everything okay?"

"No, it's not—I—"

I jerked to a stop and hunched over. My chest ached, and my breath stuck in my lungs no matter how many times I tried to wheeze in more air. People passing glanced at me with big eyes before skating closer to the edge of the road to keep their distance.

"Eden, you're scaring me." Andie was on high alert, her voice edged with worry. "Tell me where the fuck you are. I'm coming."

"M-Meet—" The stammer in my voice wasn't me. I needed to pull up my big girl pants. I was strong as shit. A survivor. No man had broken me before, and I sure as hell wasn't about to set a new record. "Meet me at the apartment."

And like the best friend she was, Andie replied without even hesitating, "I'm already out the fucking door."

4

She didn't say, "I'm not as strong as I pretend to be."

Eden

I STABBED THE KEY at the lock and missed—again.

"Stupid piece of—" The kick I landed on the front door didn't make me feel any better.

Why were keys impossible to use when you were in a rush?

I rolled my shoulders and forced a breath in, then out. Now wasn't the time for emotions. If I could claw my way out of a broken home and build a million-dollar business, I wasn't letting a damn *door* beat me.

It took three attempts, but I stuck the key in the lock, turned it, and pushed my way inside. I didn't get far. The door jammed to a stop about halfway.

"Fu—*oof!*"

My feet tangled around the stack of cardboard boxes Zach had been nagging me to unpack for weeks. I lurched forward, landing a hand on the wall to steady myself before my face kissed the hallway floor in a dramatic hello. Fitting. The perfect end to my day...or perhaps...the perfect start to my new life?

I smiled.

The boxes were a sign. Not the sign my therapist had told me—dysfunctional fear of commitment. *Please.* Future Eden was a genius leaving the mismatched Tupperware and last season's clothes untouched in boxes by the front door. Leaving was so much easier this way.

I stormed through the apartment, only pausing for a quick stop in the kitchen. Green numbers blinked on the microwave. 10:05 p.m. Zach wouldn't stumble through the door until well after midnight...if he stumbled in at all.

Would the stench of that woman's perfume linger on his shirt? Would he sneak into the shower and scrub the memories of her from his skin before tugging back the bedsheets to snuggle beside me as if nothing had happened?

I wasn't about to find out.

I hauled every bag, every box, off the shelves in the walk-in closet and tossed them on the bed. Clothes hangers disappeared from the railing. I was sweeping my jewellery into an empty shoebox when footsteps padded to a stop behind me. Armed with a sheepskin boot, the box of trinkets, and my chin hiked up, I was ready for battle.

But it wasn't Zach.

Andie smirked. "I come in peace." Her shoulder fell against the doorframe, cool and casual. Chaos? Nah. Business as usual.

I lowered the sheepskin boot.

"You left the front door wide open, you know," she said.

I dumped the box of jewellery on the bed. "I'm in a rush."

To prove my point, I charged into the closet, ripped open a drawer, and grabbed a handful of my lacy knickers. A neat pile of boxer briefs was stacked beside them. I glared at all the sensible cotton, my jaw clenched tight.

Had Zach's other woman seen him wear anything in the pile? Had she shoved any down his thighs, impatient to get her greedy hands on what should've only been mine?

An ugly laugh bubbled out of me. I ignored the knickers. Instead, I scooped up the folded briefs until they spilt from my arms, and I stormed to the balcony. With a casual toss of my hand, cotton danced on the night air, and—I raced to look over the railing—fluttered to the balcony below.

"Oopsie."

Oh well, Zach could enjoy the awkward conversation with the old dame in Apartment 14C explaining why his undies were now draped all over her potted lavender.

Andie watched my act of revenge with one eyebrow up. "Wanna explain what's going on?"

"I'm leaving."

"I can see that."

My hands propped on my hips, I paused in the middle of the room, planning my next move. "Did you get here on the Triumph?" The ancient motorcycle Andie was restoring wouldn't cut it for this trip.

"Nah, I had a feeling I might need the Pajero."

"Please tell me you're joking."

"Little Miss Choosy, who prefers not to own a car, can call a taxi if she likes."

Unamused, I glared at her through slitted eyes.

Andie raised her palms. "The rusty old beast might not look like much—"

"It has the fuel consumption of a small country!"

"It'll haul all your shit to my place, though, no problemo."

"Fine," I huffed, "but I'm planting a tree to apologise to the environment when this is over."

Snagging an empty duffel off the bed, I headed back to the closet. Andie shuffled close behind me.

"So..." she said.

"So?"

"What did the suit do? Weren't you going to surprise him with dinner from the Spanish place all the hipsters drool over?"

How long had Yvette waited before blabbing my stupid plan to Andie? Two minutes? "I went." I crammed a fistful of bras into the duffel.

"And...?"

I sighed. "I schemed my little booty off to get inside the building and talked myself off a cliff to sneak to his office. Too bad I was beaten to him by some blonde with a balayage so bad it should be criminal."

Andie's mouth dropped open. "He's screwing around?" She bit out the words in complete disbelief. She wasn't at the top of Zach's fangirl list, but she hadn't pinned him as a cheater. "That fucking bastard is *dead*. After everything you've done to support him! All the times he blew you off and didn't put you first. No fucking way."

"All the fucking ways."

"What did he say when you confronted him? Tell me you chopped his dick off."

Shaking my head, I sagged against the wall. "I just—I kinda—freaked out." I sighed. "I bolted like a pathetic coward."

"No way, Ed. He's the coward."

I stood there, a blank stare settling on the floor. I fought to smother the memories, but it was as helpful as throwing a cup of water on a forest fire. *If this is about the other night.* The words echoed in a dark whisper at the back of my mind. *That's no one.* I folded over, braced my hands on my knees, and forced down a slow breath.

Andie cursed under her breath. "Do you need a—?" Her arms opened wide like she was ready to comfort me with all the hugs I needed.

I raised my hand to stop her. "No hugs. Hit me with all your tough love, but I'll be a basket case if you get your arms around me. I refuse to collapse in a heap in this apartment. I won't give him the satisfaction."

Andie's chin dropped in a quick nod. "Tell me what you need me to do."

"I need to get the hell out of here."

"Then I'm right behind you."

We shared a sad but familiar smile. The simple exchange mirrored the one we'd had sixteen years ago when we'd stood shell-shocked in Andie's bedroom. Her mother had wailed while her father had torn apart the living room, hitting walls, demanding to know from his God why he was being punished with a daughter *like that*. Andie had to stop me from flying out there to plough my fist into his fat jaw, but I would've done anything to erase the evil words she'd heard that afternoon. Andie wasn't broken. She was perfect. And when she'd decided to stuff a backpack full of clothes and run from their disapproval, she hadn't done it alone. We'd done it together.

Now, it was my turn to run.

The two of us were like a team of well-trained professionals, removing every scrap of evidence I'd ever lived in Zach's apartment. The photos on the fridge—reminders of brief moments of happiness between his broken promises—were ripped up and tossed in the rubbish bin.

The rest of my belongings were stuffed into whatever bags I could find. There was a mix of suitcases, duffels, and reusable shopping bags for Andie to lug down to the rust bucket parked illegally out front. When we ran out of space in the back, Andie secured the leftover boxes to the roof racks, and I pretended to be useful by tugging on the straps when she barked instructions down to me.

It's really over.

My steps were silent as I drifted around the apartment, casting one last look over the life I was leaving behind. White, sterile walls. Modern and cold. A house, not a home. I'd convinced myself the colour and warmth would flood in if I just loved Zach enough. We'd be happy. We'd get married, maybe even start a family. We'd grow old together. A sharp jab dug under my ribs. Yeah, that dream was the hardest to let go.

I was successful. I'd *made it* despite the odds stacked against me. But every achievement was a smokescreen to protect the tiny girl who'd lost a mother she barely remembered and the teenager who'd run away at sixteen, got a job, and a grown-up life way before her time. The celebrity scene had been fun, but Zach had shown me the possibility of a life I'd never dared to hope for. I'd been right to keep my heart locked up tight. Those dreams weren't for women like me.

Andie cleared her throat.

I appreciated her warning. It gave me enough time to take a deep breath and brush the tears off my lashes. All traces of weakness were hidden under a fake smile when I turned around.

"Wanna torch the place before we go?" Andie scanned the living room. "Too much? We should break something. What does the suit love more than anything?"

Not me. "Work."

Andie snorted her acknowledgement. "Want to add to the collection of shit you've thrown off the balcony?" She nodded to the flatscreen on the back wall. "We could convert that bad boy to a few hundred Lego bricks."

"I doubt he'd even notice." Zach was never at home. He probably didn't even remember he owned a TV. He'd missed every movie night I'd planned with some sorry excuse about losing track of the time.

Andie swallowed. "You're going to be okay, Ed." She reserved the softness in her voice only for moments like this. "You're too good for some jerk who can't see past his own dick to understand your worth."

"I know."

Buried feelings of never being enough had erupted through the clumsily patched cracks in my heart, but I meant my words. Zach was out of the picture. My first proper relationship had ended in disaster. So what? I still had my friends and my business. I'd lived a fantastic life before him, and I'd make damn sure I lived an even better life now that I was kicking his sorry booty to the kerb.

I locked in the promise to myself with a nod.

I dropped my fluffy cat keychain on the kitchen counter, and I didn't look back before slamming the door shut behind me.

5

He didn't say, "I'm in over my head."

Zach

My head throbbed, a tight band squeezing around my skull. Words on the computer screen blurred. Two aspirins hadn't helped. I was never shaking this headache...or my damn desk.

How had Chris talked me into taking on another contract? I'd stood up for myself—my team—and yet, somehow, I was sitting in front of a mountain of new work, about ready to gnaw my own arm off because I was that hungry, and the finish line was further away than ever.

Hunching over the laptop, I massaged the pain spearing through my temple and scrolled to the next page of the contract.

A tap against my shoe dragged my attention from where it needed to be. Frowning, I glanced down. The tip of a black stiletto. Rapid blinks made my office flicker back into focus.

Michaela's hip was propped against my desk, her head tilted. *She's* still *here?*

I flexed my hand, stretching stiff fingers that had been clawed over the computer too long, careful to school my frustration under a blank expression. The coffee was a nice gesture, I suppose. It'd been a long day of too much work and too many meetings—and far too much Michaela.

She'd been hovering around me all day. She'd been put on notice that she'd been relegated to one of the many women Chris had on the side instead of being his main event—if the quips I'd heard in the men's room were true.

I'd been shocked that other people in the office knew about their fling. I hadn't even been able to process that a man I deeply respected was apparently acting in such a shameful way behind closed doors. But I wasn't Michaela's babysitter or the security blanket she could pull out when she needed a dopamine hit. Been there, done that, didn't want the T-shirt.

Was she ever going to piss off and let me finish my work?

"Zach?"

"Oh, um… Yeah." I waved my pen, shooing her away. "Sure. Whatever."

Squinting through the pain, I focused my attention on the screen. Where was I? Right. Page twenty-six. Elevator maintenance. I scanned the contractor's pricing and scoffed out loud.

Not bloody likely.

I clicked into my notes and started typing a reminder to renegotiate those bullshit terms, but—

A gasp jerked into my lungs before I stopped breathing altogether. My spine stiffened. The smell of earthy coffee was doused by the burn of too much floral perfume. A sharp breath heated my neck. And then…icy fingers gouged my shoulders. Massaging.

No.

Michaela had her hooks in me.

Absolutely not.

I jerked out of her grip. "What the hell are you doing?" I scrambled to my feet so fast the chair spun.

Her eyebrows squished together. Her hands froze in midair. "Helping you relax." She said it like she was surprised I was questioning the insanity of what was happening in my office.

I barked a laugh. "I don't think so." Three quick steps, and I was at the door. "Out." I pointed to the corridor.

Almost smirking, Michaela cocked her head. "You can't be serious."

"Deadly."

She didn't move. I stared at her, eyes widening every beat she challenged my gaze. *What the...?* Scowling, trying to ignore the vice tightening behind my eyes, I glanced around the office. Her jacket was slung over the spare chair in front of my desk. When the hell had she taken that off? Obviously, I'd missed the memo that she planned to stay.

I leant over, snatched the black wool off the back of the chair, and held it out to her. "Out."

Open-mouthed, Michaela stared at me before shaking off her surprise with a laugh. "Oh, come on, Zach. Even you can make time for a little fun—"

"Out!"

Michaela stomped over and snatched the jacket from my hand. Her unspoken "Fuck you" was punctuated by her slamming the door so hard the frames on the wall rattled out of place.

I nudged each of the certificates back into a neat line and collapsed into my chair. The mug stared back at me. Frowning, I shoved the coffee away, propped my elbows on the desk, and buried my face in my hands.

I *knew* her bringing me a coffee was bullshit. She hadn't done a nice thing for me in months...other than moving on to Chris. How long was I going to keep paying for my lapse of judgement? Forever, at this rate.

I was too distracted to focus on the contract I should've finished reviewing hours ago. Even if words turned from fuzzy to legible and I marked that one contract complete, there were dozens more waiting—a never-ending hamster wheel of work. I was sinking. Fast. Gasping for life in a sea of paperwork. The only thought dragging my head above the worries I was drowning in was Eden. It felt like a lifetime since she'd smacked my arse and sent me out the door to work this morning.

Shit.

My eyes searched the clutter on the desk for my phone. I hadn't messaged Eden back. I'd promised her that I'd get better at keeping in touch, but tonight, her timing couldn't have been worse. Michaela had been too close. *Personal lives stay personal.* No one could know about Eden. Not my boss, who still looked at me like he was worried my sanity would snap any second. Certainly not Michaela, who was probably only using me as a tool to coax Chris's attention back on her.

Screw this.

I snapped the laptop shut and pushed away from the desk. Shrugging on my jacket, I typed a quick message to Eden on my phone.

Zach

> It's a wait-up night. xo

Exhaustion sunk like concrete in my bones. Barangaroo wasn't far—maybe ten minutes from the business district—and it was quiet this late. No tourists. Almost no traffic. Usually, the walk was a circuit-breaker between the grind and home. My listening skills were piss poor, but the walk helped me to at least manage a smile by the time I opened the front door.

My phone buzzed in my pocket.

A dopey smile spread across my face.

Please be Eden.

For the first time in months, I might make it home early enough for her to chuck on the new TV show she'd been raving about. I was six episodes behind, but I remembered enough of the characters' names to keep up as she gasped through the latest twists and turns.

I glanced at my phone. Not Eden. Michaela. I stopped dead in my tracks. A taxi screeched to a halt in front of me, and I waved a quick apology at the driver as I jogged to the other side of the street.

Mac

> Can I tempt you to reconsider?

I snorted so loud a woman walking on the street whipped a frantic look at me before hurrying to the other side.

What the hell was Michaela playing at? Why wasn't she taking the hint?

I'd already hit the red cross to delete her message when my phone buzzed again. Reflex dragged my eyes down to the screen.

"Shit!"

A dry retch of shock jolted through me, and my phone flew out of my hand, plunging face down into the gutter with a crack. I didn't care if the screen was smashed. If I never saw that photo again, it'd *still* be too soon. A shudder rippled over my skin.

Naked. So much...*naked*.

I bent over, my hand shaking as it curled around my phone. Fighting the puke burning a path up my throat and one eye squeezed shut—as if that somehow limited the possibility of seeing anything I shouldn't—I frantically jabbed a finger at the screen until Michaela's photo disappeared.

Gone.

I've never typed a message so fast.

> Zach
> Mac, this is a work phone. Keep it professional. First and last warning.

My finger hovered over the block button. Should I? *Could* I?

Michaela was on the financing side for most of my clients. How much of a shitstorm would start thundering if I deleted her or if I took it a step further and refused to work with her altogether? It was a no-confidence motion. She'd be in Chris's crosshairs, and with his engagement announced, maybe she was already treading through risky territory. He might be looking for an excuse to fire her and keep the drama to a minimum. It wouldn't be the first time. He'd fired people for a lot less.

Sighing, I shoved my phone back in my pocket.

I'd worry about how to get rid of Michaela tomorrow.

· ♥ · ♥ · ♥ · ♥ · ♥ ·

I EASED OPEN THE front door. A smile cracked the frown off my face. Eden's boxes were gone. She'd unpacked.

Day thirty-four.

Finally.

Every light in the apartment burned. Chuckling, I followed my usual routine, wandering through the rooms, flicking off the switches, and searching for Eden's final hiding spot for the night. My hand hovered over the switch in the bedroom. This was the last room, but...

Where was she?

I walked through each room again, ducking into the ensuite to use the bathroom. I paused. The vanity was spotless. The potions Eden used for her bedtime skincare routine were missing. My stomach plummeted when my gaze landed on the cup with only one toothbrush in it. I forced a smile and tried to brush the dread away. She'd probably gone on one of her cleaning frenzies. She did that sometimes. Usually, the day or two before her period, but that wasn't due yet...was it?

I swallowed heavily, not sure if my skin was burning up or freezing cold, and tugged a hand through my hair.

Where *was* she?

I was overreacting, getting myself worked up over nothing. Eden was okay. She was probably out with the girls and lost track of time. It was Friday night. Yvette was constantly scoping out new nightlife around the city. It wouldn't be the first time she'd dragged Eden and Andie out to a club at the last minute. Yeah, that was probably what happened.

I sent Eden a quick message.

Zach

> Miss you, Denny Dee. Let me know if you want me to pick you up. xx

I waited. No blistering reply. No little dots.

Anxiety wound so tight around my chest I struggled to breathe. I tugged off my tie and tossed it on the kitchen counter as I walked to the fridge. I grabbed one of the fancy juices Eden kept stocked on the top shelf, twisted off the lid, and swigged a sip. My foot hit the pedal for the bin. A flash of colour caught my eye. Brows furrowed, I bent over.

The remnants of ripped photos sat on top of Eden's uneaten toast crusts from breakfast. Photos of her and me that had been stuck to the fridge with colourful fruit magnets when I'd left for work this morning. A panicked look darted to the fridge. All the photos were missing. So were the magnets.

Adrenaline pumping, fire igniting tired muscles enough to run, I rushed back to the bedroom. Not even bothering to snap on the light, I threw open the door to the closet. Empty clothing rails. I yanked out every drawer. Eden's were empty. My heart slammed against my ribs. Sweat clung the cotton business shirt to my skin.

This...this isn't...happening.

Eden's clothes were gone.

The throb of my headache split through my skull.

Was Eden pissed off that I didn't answer her messages quickly enough? Maybe I'd forgotten I was meant to be somewhere. It wouldn't be the first time...or even the fifth. Work piled up, and chasing my tail to get on top of one email ended up being a cycle of 'just one more' that lasted for hours on end. But she understood how important this promotion was to me—to us—didn't she?

The apartment spun. Forcing one step in front of another back into the kitchen was almost impossible. My eyes stung, but my heart was obliterated. No matter how many breaths I tried to force in, none reached my lungs. I braced my hands on my knees.

And that was when I saw it.

The fluffy cat keychain on the kitchen counter.

My heart twisted. My stomach quickly followed. The juice was out and on the floor in seconds. I couldn't pretend anymore.

Eden was gone.

And she wasn't coming back.

6

She didn't say, "You make me weak."

Eden

Stalker mode activated.

Bundling the chunky woollen blanket tighter, I sank into the sofa, leaving just enough space to prop up the essentials—my phone and the tub of ice cream I'd stolen from Andie's freezer.

I snuck a guilty look over my shoulder. The living room was deserted. No rustling in the kitchen, either. Andie was nowhere to be seen.

I grinned.

It was time to devour every scrap of information the internet had to offer. The Worley and Stone website was my first stop, but it wouldn't be my last. Scrolling down the 'Our Talent' page, I scrunched my nose. Who'd curated these mugshots? The black and white photos popping up one by one convinced me that being a lawyer was the most serious—and *boring*—job in the world.

You want a smile? Let's add that to your bill.

I stifled a giggle under the blanket, but my grin dulled when Zach's photo stared back at me. A serious scowl in black and white worked for him. The man certainly knew how to rock tall, dark, and brooding. What talents would the firm list for him? Real ones, like warm hugs, enthusiastic about eating pussy, and skilled at breaking hearts? I doubted it. I kept scrolling.

Bingo.

A woman. Blonde hair. I squinted. It was impossible to tell if her eyes were blue or hazel, but that was her. The homewrecker.

Michaela. I twisted the lid off the ice cream tub, dug in the spoon, and kept reading. *Macintosh.*

I snorted. What kind of name was Michaela Macintosh? It sounded like a pair of sensible shoes marketed to grandmothers for wearing on their weekly shopping trips. Was that what attracted Zach to her? She was the sensible shoes you could wear every day, and I was the designer stilettos that pinched your feet so much you only bothered with them on special nights out?

My phone was yanked from my hand.

I whipped around. "Hey!" An incriminating spoonful of chocolate ice cream hovered at my lips.

"I left you alone for two minutes," Andie said. "What's all this?" She waved a hand at the disgrace I'd created on her sofa.

I tipped my chin and smiled sweetly. "I'm wallowing in self-pity, thank you very much. I'm told it's a rite of passage for betrayed women like me."

"Told by who, exactly?"

"The caring folks of the internet."

"And this?" Andie flipped around my phone. Michaela's black and white mugshot glared at me. "You're stalking his side piece? It won't make you feel better to learn a single thing about her."

"I plan to learn *everything* about her." A bitter edge cut through my voice. I jabbed my finger into the back of my phone.

"See her hair? Didn't I tell you? Whoever did that balayage should be blacklisted!"

Sighing, Andie flopped on the sofa, manspreading like she always did with a lazy arm stretched over the backrest. "You, ah..." She slid an uneasy glance at me from the corner of her eye. "You wanna talk about, um, how you're...*feeling?*" She grimaced.

Emotions had never been Andie's thing. Lucky for her, tonight, I was more than happy to ignore the advice of every therapist I'd ever seen and bury mine.

"Nope." I dug the spoon into the ice cream and wrenched out an even bigger scoop. "I want to stay angry. I'm going to make that man wish he was never born!" I stuffed the spoon in my mouth. Big mistake. With one eye screwed closed, I choked out, "What is this?"

"Vegan ice cream."

I forced myself to swallow. Mud, with the hint of twig and the crunch of disappointment. "Boo, whatever this is"—I jiggled the tub—"it ain't ice cream." That didn't stop me from digging out another spoonful and shovelling it into my mouth. The second bite went down just as rough.

"So, how long does the rite of passage last?" Andie asked.

"Um." How the hell would I know? Before Zach, I'd been the one doing the dumping. Sydney wasn't exactly short of new dicks to bounce around on if a man turned out to be a disappointment—and they always did. "Tonight? Maybe the weekend? I dunno. How long did it take you to get over the girl with the hair?"

Andie lifted a shoulder. "A few months."

"A few months! Sorry, no."

"Ed, you can't rush this."

I scoffed. *Please.* "When have I ever rushed anything?"

Andie scratched her chin, one brow slowly lifting.

Okay, maybe she had a point. Sometimes, I rushed into things blindly. When it came to the salon, I was a machine, planning and executing every detail to the last love heart I used to dot my i's. But my personal life? That was a well-travelled road to chaos.

"Zach isn't the only man out there," I said, my voice pitching up, more defensive than strong.

"True, but that doesn't mean you need to find his replacement straight away."

"Can't hurt."

Andie chuckled. "You've got a lot to learn about relationships, Ed."

"I think I'm officially retiring from relationships."

"Yeah?"

I nodded. "Maybe I'll take up a class or something. I heard they're running some cooking classes in Surry Hills again—"

Whomp! Whomp!

The front door rattled under the power of the knocks pounding the old oak. I threw the blanket over my head and disappeared into the sofa.

"Gee." Andie's voice dripped with sarcasm. "I wonder who that could be."

Whomp! Whomp!

"Andie!" That was Zach, alright. "I know you're up!"

I inched the wool down to glare at Andie. "He can't see me like this."

Andie slapped her hands on her knees before pushing up off the sofa. "Guess I'm getting rid of him, then."

Her footsteps pounded away.

A snap—she'd flipped the lock. A creak—she'd opened the door.

"What do you want?" Andie growled.

"Eden."

I lowered the blanket, scrambled down the sofa, and craned my neck to peek through the gap down the hallway. My heart stuttered. Zach looked wild. Had he run across the city? His chest heaved, and his hair flopped over his forehead. Sweat prickled on his brow. Fog clouded the bottom of his glasses. He usually only looked that unpolished—that *undone*—when he was, well, *fucking*.

"Eden's not here," Andie said.

Zach's palm landed flat on the door to stop her from slamming it in his face. "Really?" His laugh was hollow. "Funny, those boxes sure look familiar."

"You the box police now?"

"I kicked my toe on *that* box this morning. The label says 'kitchen,' but I know for a fact Eden stores clothes to donate to the women's shelter in it."

"Cool story. See ya." She pushed her weight into the door, but Zach pushed back.

"Slam the door in my face if you want," he said, "but I'm not leaving until I see Eden. I'll keep knocking all night if that's what it takes. Just try me."

Andie threw a helpless glance back at me.

I held up my index finger. Girl code: *I need a minute to make myself presentable.*

Andie dipped her chin in a nod and turned back to the wild man. "Wait there," she said. "Step one foot through that door, and I'll introduce you to my fist before I call the cops. Got it?"

I didn't hear Zach's response.

I tossed the blanket, tumbled from the sofa, stripped off the ugly cardigan, and unbuttoned my blouse until just enough eat-your-heart-out cleavage peeked through. I up-ended my handbag and chased the lipstick rolling into the kitchen to swipe on a fresh coat. A quick scrunch of my hair, a spritz of gardenia-scented mist, and then I strutted down the hallway like it was a runway and my entire world hadn't turned upside down.

My stomach fluttered to see relief weaken Zach's knees. He wouldn't get that same reaction from me.

"Oh, it's you," I said, slouching against the doorframe and folding my arms like his being there was no big deal. "What do you want?"

"Please come home."

I snorted a laugh. Home? Where the hell was that? Certainly not where I'd grown up. Not where I'd lived with him, either. "No, but thanks for stopping by." My fingers curled around the edge of the door, getting ready to slam it shut, but Zach's shoulder butted into the wood to stop me.

"Talk to me, Denny Dee."

He had no right to use that achingly low voice on me. He was trying to peel my armour off. The earnest look on his face, the step he took to crowd the doorway until I could only smell his cologne—it was too much. I needed to be stronger.

"I'm surprised you had time to stop by," I said.

"Work's full-on, but—"

"Work." I scoffed. "Please. We both know what's actually been keeping you so busy." I smiled sweetly. "I believe her name is Michaela."

A deep line creased between his brows. "Michaela?"

His innocent act was adorable, but he wasn't fooling me. "I saw you with her. In your office. Tonight."

He shook his head, still ten steps behind. "Wha—that's—how?"

"I let the security guard have a little peek."

"Pardon?"

"You heard me." I ran my finger along the sharp placket of my blouse, making sure he saw the cleavage framed with delicate white lace. "A li'l peek."

Zach's nostrils flared, and laboured breaths made his chest jump. He glared at my buttons as if he was about to snap every last one back into place so no one could see what used to be his. He was seething with jealousy. I grinned. Petty revenge was a delight.

"My visit was supposed to be a surprise," I said, "but it turns out the biggest surprise was for me. Who would've guessed my man was nothing but a cheating bastard?"

The accusation made Zach's eyes blow wide. "I've *never* cheated on you. I wouldn't even—that's not—" He tugged a hand through his hair, only making the mop a bigger mess. "God, I'd *never* cheat on you."

"You told her she could put her hands on you."

His grimace was almost convincing. "I was distracted by some work. I didn't realise Michaela was going to do, well, *that*. As soon as I did, I told her to get the hell out. I literally shoved her out the door. You saw that, right?"

I swallowed. No, I hadn't seen that. I'd panicked. I'd run. But I wasn't about to admit how weak he made me.

I hiked my chin. "And when she promised there'd be no crowds this time?"

"She asked me out for a drink a couple of nights ago. Some bar on the harbour. I can't tell you which one because I didn't care. I said no." His lips curved. "I was on my way home. Nothing in the world is more important than seeing you."

My shoulders sagged. My resolve withered under self-doubt. Had I made the worst mistake of my life? Maybe my old therapist had been right. My relationship with my father had primed me to think the worst of men—*this* man. I stared helplessly at Zach. I'd lost count of how many times I hadn't felt like an essential part of his life, let alone the *most* important, but maybe I'd rushed into—

"Eden, whatever was going on between Michaela and me—"

I cut him off with a brutal laugh. *Here we go.* "Whatever *was* going on?" There was always more to the story.

"It's been over for a long time."

And to be 'over,' they needed to have started, which meant... "You've fucked Michaela?"

Zach's hesitation told me everything I needed to know.

I hadn't rushed a damn thing.

I'd been right.

"You've fucked her!" The words flew out of me with too much emotion. Zach couldn't see how much he hurt me. I forced down a deep breath. "All the times you stayed at work late, the weekends you went into the office to help her out—" I flattened my lips and wrestled my anger under control. "How *convenient* that you forgot to mention you used to be in a relationship with her."

"It wasn't like that!"

"Then explain to me *exactly* what it *was* like!"

"Eden, when I was with Michaela..." His head bowed, but his fist clenched by his side. He was fighting to hold himself together. When his eyes lifted again, they were clouded, misty.

No, no, no.

"You were in love with her?" I choked out. That was it, wasn't it? He'd said those words to her. Not me, but to *her!*

"No!"

"Then what? What's all this?" I waved at him. The feelings he was battling were almost tipping him into tears. He'd never been particularly emotional over the times he'd let me down. Maybe he'd muttered a few half-arsed apologies and promised to try harder next time, but nothing as raw as this. Not even close.

"It's...it's...nothing," he said.

"Liar."

Zach flinched but didn't deny it.

"We're *done*."

And he didn't knock again when I slammed the door in his face.

7

She didn't say, "I cried when no one was looking."

Eden

"Well, well, *well*," Yvette said. *"Someone* has some tea to spill."

Her puffed marshmallow sleeves blocked the back door to the salon. Sneaking past was impossible unless...

I darted a look down the alley. I could make a run for it. The odds were in my favour. The catering boxes crooked under my arm weighed me down, but Yvette would never catch me in those stilettos.

She stood firm, fists on her hips. "Don't even *think* about it."

I was still considering running when I pushed past her with an unconvincing laugh. "Good morning!"

It was time to dial up the sunshine.

I was her boss. *The* boss. I wasn't the pathetic little missus who'd been lied to and left without a scrap of affection. I'd left that pathetic piece of myself at Andie's place. All weekend, I'd waited for Zach to crawl back and make it all better. He hadn't.

No more visits. Even before I'd blocked him, no calls. Silence. The wad of scrunched-up tissues I'd guiltily stuffed in the bin on the way out the door was the only proof my life had been torn apart.

I blinded Yvette with my best smile. "I'm loving this outfit. Is it new?" A sideways glance allowed me another peek. I wasn't sure the scraps of pink and white gingham would pass as a dress. There was more fabric in the sleeves than anywhere else. "Andie's going to flip when she sees that dress."

"Don't try distracting me with the promise of a good time." Yvette's eyes narrowed. "I'm *so* onto you."

The catering boxes under my arm wobbled, the aroma of rich cheeses and freshly baked pastries reminding me I'd skipped breakfast...and dinner the night before. *"Moi?"* The indignant tone was convincing. "I've got no idea what you're talking about."

"Ra-ha-healy? Here I am, innocently assuming you've ditched me all weekend because you've finally dragged your man away from his desk for some baby dancing, but no-oh-oh. Care to explain these?" She shoved a fan of heart-shaped sticky notes in my face.

My eyes bulged. Whoa. That was a tonne of phone messages.

"Well?" she said. "What do you suppose these are?"

"Dunno." Even without seeing the neatly blocked capitals spelling out 'Zach' at the top of every note, it wasn't exactly a lie.

"Oh, but I think you do. Your sweet nerd has been calling every ten minutes on the dot since seven o'clock this morning."

I pretended to be busy sorting through parcels. "Nothing unusual about that," I mumbled.

"Sweetie, we both know Zach isn't usually tripping over his pointy black shoes desperate to talk to you. In fact, he's never called here or dropped by. Makes sense, though, when he can just—I don't know—see you at your place? Hmm?"

I shrugged.

"Spill it, Deenie."

"Um..."

Andie strode into the kitchen, her hands overloaded with coffees. "Yvette," she growled. "Put some damn clothes on."

Silently, I sidled along the counter to sneak my coffee from the pile. As long as those two were bickering, I was in the clear. I inched closer to the doorway.

Yvette slipped the incriminating phone messages down the front of her dress and shook out her blonde curls. "I'm afraid I have to disappoint you, Andrea, my dear."

"You did *not* just call me—"

"You've seen these beauties, right?" Yvette hiked up the front of her dress. "One hundred percent natural. You know what that means?"

Andie suddenly seemed very interested in fiddling with the lid of her coffee. "I'm sure you're about to explain it to me," she grumbled.

"It means I've got another five years tops before these girls start their ill-fated journey to my knees," Yvette said. "I need to make sure they get the attention they deserve."

"Nobody here's interested in looking at your damn boobs." But even as Andie lied through her teeth, she was sneaking another peek.

Sipping my coffee, I rolled my eyes. "When are you two going to get a room and get this over with?" Hopefully soon. This flirting nonsense had started well before I'd poached Yvette from another salon a year ago.

"Wha—what!" Yvette squawked.

"G-Gross," Andie spluttered at the same time.

"Uh-huh," I said. "Keep proving my point." My grin grew wider the more they kept trying to deny it.

The front door chimed.

Andie puffed out a sigh of relief.

I bent over the kitchen counter to peer around the corner. I couldn't quite see who was at the door.

A delivery?

Appointments didn't start until nine, but the luxury experience we offered needed hours of meticulous preparation before the doors officially opened each day. Extra fluffy robes and towels, aromatherapy for the ultimate relaxation, five-star catering, and more alcohol than the bougie bar down the laneway made Voom tick. Our stellar reviews and a nine-month waiting list didn't happen without supporting local businesses. We were always fielding deliveries.

I strolled into the waiting area. Stopped. My jaw hit the floor.

A woman teetered from side to side as she headed for reception. I guessed it was a woman by her faded denim skirt and ballet flats. The wall of roses trimmed with a floppy red bow hid the rest of her.

"No tea to spill, huh?" Yvette laughed behind me. "Someone's been a bad, bad boy."

My eyes narrowed. That bunch of poison had better not be for me. Was I imagining the sneeze tickling my nose and the itch clawing at my throat?

He seriously couldn't have forgotten my allergies...could he?

"I'm looking for Eden," the delivery girl squeaked.

He forgot.

Andie stormed across the salon. "What the fuck was he thinking sending these here?" She grabbed the bouquet and signed for the delivery with the ridiculous mess of flowers propped on her hip.

Yvette's chin tipped in my direction with a smug grin. "Care to explain?"

I absolutely didn't, so I examined my nail polish instead.

Andie glanced around the salon, searching for somewhere to dump the flowers. "Eden caught him with his pants down."

There was no sugarcoating my humiliation. The truth was just...there.

Yvette's eyebrows shot to the roof. "Say it isn't so?"

I sighed. "It's true."

"I wasn't expecting anything like that." She cocked her head, humming as she thought the news over. "Now, there's no doubt Zach's a catch. Rich, gorgeous, and a hot bod. He could pull some serious pussy if he weren't so damn shy—"

"Is this helpful?" Andie snapped. "What's your point?"

"My point," Yvette shot back, "is that despite all his selling points, Zach's so socially awkward it's a miracle he bagged one babe, but juggling two? Come on. When would he even have the time? The man's chained to a desk."

"It helps the side chick's chained with him," Andie said.

"He said they weren't"—I waved a hand around, searching for the word—"dating." Or fucking. Same, same.

"Anymore," Andie added.

That reminder was worse than an elbow in the ribs. My eyes zeroed in on the roses dumped on the counter. A pink envelope was tucked in between the green stems. I grabbed the card, running my finger along the sharp edge, my pulse kicking into gear.

I didn't want to admit it, but the words on the paper meant something. Oh, who was I kidding? The words Zach had written on the card meant *everything*. An explanation, a promise, an apology—I wanted them all.

The card was light, a feather, air even, but somehow, the weight of the thin paper was enough to almost buckle my knees. I couldn't read it.

I flicked up the card. "You read it," I said to Andie.

She hesitated before plucking it from my fingers. "You sure?"

I nodded.

Frowning, Andie scanned whatever was written inside. She grimaced.

Yvette peered over Andie's shoulder. Her eyes darted over the words. "Yikes on bikes," she murmured under her breath.

"It can't be that bad," I squeaked. "Can it?"

"Ah…" Andie said.

"Well…" Yvette said at the same time.

I snatched the card from Andie. The message was typed because Zach couldn't even be bothered to write a message himself. I read the card.

I MISS YOUR SMILE.

There had to be more. There *had* to be. I flipped the card over. Nope. The other side was blank.

Anger exploded in my chest. "That's it?" I scrunched the card in my fist and pitched it across the room. It hit the wall and dropped to the floor in a crumbled pink mess.

No one dared to say a word. I rarely lost my shit and certainly never over a man. The only sound in the silence was my scratchy breaths. My chest was tight. I wanted to punch something. Yell at someone. No. Just one person. Zach.

The shrill chirp of the salon's landline broke the silence.

Yvette cackled and tugged the wad of phone messages out of her cleavage. "I wonder who that could be!" She fanned the messages in my face before she strolled over to pick up the phone.

Andie was watching me closely. "You okay?" she asked gruffly.

"No."

"He's a thoughtless dick."

"Yeah."

"Told you we should've taken out the TV."

I laughed.

"The offer's still there to torch his place," Andie said. "I'd do time for you."

I bumped my shoulder against hers. "Right back at ya."

Yvette waved us over to reception, the phone cradled in the crook of her neck.

"Zach, I swear I'll pass on your messages the second Eden gets here," she said. "Uh-huh. Sweetie, I'm *totally* writing this down." She quirked an eyebrow at me, not writing a word. "Mmhmm. Okay, so you'll be in a meeting for the next two hours, but you're going to call Deenie the second you're back. Got it. Toodles!" Yvette hit the button to end the call and propped her hip against the desk. "He sounds like shit, by the way."

"Good," barked Andie. "He'll sound a lot worse if I get my hands on him."

"Should we arrange a catch-up?" Yvette smirked. "A special lunchtime delivery of Andie's right hook?"

Andie chuckled low. "Ed?"

I stood bolted to the spot. My mood was bouncing somewhere between murderous rage and complete devastation.

How had I lived with that man? Didn't he know me at all? And what the hell was that note? *I miss your smile.* Generic. No thought. No explanation about why he'd hidden the truth of his precious *Mac* from me. No apology. Our six months together hadn't even been worth a simple sorry.

I fought the tears stinging my eyes. My friends deserved better than seeing me crumble like a soggy old cookie, and I'd never give Zach the satisfaction of making me cry. Voom was my domain. My second home. He didn't get to destroy me at work, too.

A diabolical smile twisted my lips.

A new scheme started spinning in my mind. I was channelling evil genius with a petty revenge side plot.

Zach was about to find out exactly who he was dealing with.

8

He didn't say, "I'm sorry."

Zach

THE BOARDROOM ECHOED WITH the restless drum of Chris's fingers.

"Zach, I'm not angry," he said. "I suppose I'm...well, disappointed."

My jaw clenched. The air in the room was claustrophobic, stale from the scattered coffee cups and untouched pastries, and the tension that sucked the walls closer. But if Chris was waiting for me to offer an apology, he was about to be even more disappointed.

He'd seduced the clients through the door with his movie star smile, a firm handshake, and a fairytale timeframe to deliver what they wanted. I'd served up a heavy dose of reality by telling them how long it'd *really* take to settle their bullshit deal. No amount of free coffee and movie star smiles undid that kind of damage.

Had Chris expected me to give an obliging nod? Agree to work impossible hours when my universe was collapsing? Probably. There was precedent. I'd done that before, hadn't I? I'd always worked my arse off to make the firm—him—look good. I'd delivered.

Not today.

Chris's incessant tapping stopped. "Maybe it's my fault. Maybe I expected too much of you." He shook his head, a blonde hair spilling across his forehead until he tucked it neatly back into place. "I fooled myself into believing you were ready to step up this time."

My attention snapped away from the wall. I met Chris's gaze head-on, even though his words had torpedoed in my gut. "I'm ready."

"Is that why you just embarrassed me? Yourself? Because you're ready?"

"I—"

"You're distracted."

I couldn't deny it. I was. I needed to speak to Eden. She'd been dodging my calls all morning. Had she received the flowers? We'd left so much unsaid—

"Distracted." Chris sighed. "We've talked about this. Partnership is a privilege, not a right. You need to earn it—"

"I've *earned* it. I'm the highest fee earner for a reason."

"Leadership is about more than how much you bill. I pulled you out of the gutter, Zach. I took a chance on you, and yes, you're one of the best property lawyers in the city, but no one is bigger than the firm. Personal lives *stay* personal. Don't make me the monster again. Don't force me to tell the other partners you're heading down the same path you were two years ago."

Shame ripped through me. My eyes, my chin, my whole body just…dropped. "I…"

I couldn't apologise. I could barely breathe. Did Chris think I'd forgotten the day he'd summoned me to the boardroom? The partners—the people I respected most—had stared down their noses at me, shaking their heads with disgust while he'd presided at the head of this very table, spitting out the long list of ways I'd failed the firm. He should've saved his breath. I'd known I wasn't performing my best. It was no secret I'd let everyone down.

But what other option was there?

Mum's diagnosis had sent everything off the rails. One day, she'd been pottering around the kitchen. The next, she'd been sitting in front of an oncologist. Breast cancer. Stage three. Dad hadn't coped. He'd struggled to manage all of Mum's appointments, her recovery from surgery, and the nights when she couldn't even keep down water. The chemo had made her *so sick*. And what if the treatment had failed and Mum had—

Shit.

My hand fumbled for the water sitting on the table. I gulped a few sips, my hand squeezing around the glass, fingertips turning white, my resilience cracking. The script the therapist had taught me ran through my mind.

Count to ten. Count the blessings. Mum's okay. She's in remission. Everything's okay.

The frantic beats of panic slowed in my chest. I loosened my grip on the glass.

When I glanced up, Chris's lips were curved. I blinked, shaken off-kilter. That couldn't be right. My mind was playing tricks on me. I blinked again. The smile I'd imagined was replaced with a look of concern.

"S-Sorry," I said.

Chris dipped his chin in a nod. "Take your time."

No, no more weakness. Not in front of him. "I'm fine."

He smiled. This time, it stuck. "Good to hear." He leant forward, hand reaching out but never actually touching me. "Zach, I'm on your side. You know that. I wouldn't have invested so much of myself in you if you didn't have a future here." His head cocked, thinking for a moment. "Thinking ahead, I'd like you to attend more client events. A couple of networking functions. You need to get your face out there, instead of only being the man hidden behind the desk."

"Okay." I'd rather stick a fork in my eye. "I can."

"And speaking of good impressions... Should I call back the client to let them know we've reconsidered our resourcing and can meet their deadline?"

"Ah, y-yes." I forced a smile. "If you think it's the best option."

"Trust me, Zach. It's the best option for you, too. You'll see."

·▼·♥·♥·♥·▼·

Michaela waved.

Could this day get *any* worse?

I pretended not to see her and walked even faster down the corridor. She could buzz off. Everyone else, too. I wanted to get back to my desk and shut out the whole damn world, except for Eden.

From the corner of my eye, I noticed Michaela snatch an oversized red folder from a paralegal before charging down the corridor after me.

"Hi," she huffed, struggling to keep up beside me. "Where's the fire?"

"Under Chris's arse."

Her eyes bulged. The man was basically my idol. I never spoke about him in a tone that harsh. "The meeting with the new clients didn't go well?" She smirked.

I ignored her.

"Hey, we should catch up about the sale of the building on York Street," she said.

"Everything's sorted."

"The buyer had a question about—"

"Sorted."

Michaela sighed. "Zach." She ushered me to the side of the corridor and lowered her voice. "If this is about the other night…"

I responded with a raised brow.

"Okay, it is. I just wanted to say I'm sorry." Her voice dipped even lower. Michaela knew the firm's rules. She played by them better than anyone—most of the time. "Everything that's happened with Chris… It's hard, and I…" Her smile was thin. "Honestly? I never really recovered after you ended it between us. I miss hanging out with you. I probably should've just said so, but it's hard to break through all the noise with you."

"No more late-night pop-ins, okay?"

Michaela hesitated a step, not used to me being so blunt, but she nodded.

"And no more photos either," I said.

"No more photos. Strictly professional in the office." She tilted her head with a smile. "What about outside the office? Let's have a drink after work."

"I don't think so."

"Zach, if this is because I used to say we were only casual—"

"Don't. Just don't. I can't do this right now, okay?"

Or ever.

I left Michaela standing with her chin on the floor. I shut the door to my office, yanked the chair out from behind the desk, and collapsed. Finally, I'd returned to the safety of my concrete prison. My fingers flew over the laptop. I'd lost two hours in meetings and had a flood of missed calls to check. I scanned the list and sighed. Eden's name wasn't there.

With a frustrated groan, I reached for my desk phone.

"Knock, knock!"

My executive assistant's timing couldn't have been worse.

Sue's bobbed grey hair popped through the gap she'd wedged in the door. "Hey, boss." She bumped her hip against the glass until there was enough room to wriggle through with a stack of files cradled in her spindly arms. "I rounded up all the leases for the shopping centre purchase."

"Thanks." I pointed at the monitor. "Sue, are these the only phone messages?"

"Not enough for you?" She laughed. "Waiting to hear from someone in particular?"

"Eden."

"Eden...from...?" Sue dumped the pile of folders on my desk. "Is she part of the hotel chain merger? The dickhead with the accent has been calling. *He's waiting.*" She rolled her eyes.

"No. Eden. My girlfriend." The word came out strained. Girlfriend didn't feel right. Partner? Sweetheart? Soulmate? I ignored the dark whisper in the back of my mind reminding me to add 'ex' in front of every option.

"You have a girlfriend?" Sue stopped, her eyes on the ceiling, thinking it over. "Huh." She shrugged.

Huh?

I'd always carefully followed Chris's example and mastered keeping my worlds separate. Whatever label was slapped on my time with Michaela, I'd never let it impact our work. I rarely overshared details about my life or blurred the lines, but I must have at least *mentioned* Eden, right?

"No," Sue said. "Can't say I've heard from her, but I'll pop her straight through if she calls."

"Thanks."

My eyes flicked between the phone and the red reminders of how much I needed to catch up. Chris's words echoed in the void. I was so close to all the years of hard work finally paying off. I couldn't blow my chance...and...well... Eden wouldn't know I was back from my meetings yet. With a defeated sigh, I adjusted my glasses and got typing. One email was sent. Another. Two minutes turned into twenty.

I was about to hit send on a response to a tree dispute when Sue stuck her head through the door.

"Ah, boss." Her tone was cautious. "There's, ah, well..." She grimaced. "There's a delivery for you."

Distracted, I kept reading my screen and muttered, "Who from?"

"Eden."

My head whipped up. Relief shot a dopey grin on my face, and I started scrambling from my chair.

"Hold that smile," Sue warned, pointing her finger for me to sit back down. "I'll bring the, er, *delivery* in."

An uncomfortable itch of anxiety niggled at me, but I shoved the feeling out of the way.

Eden must have received the flowers I'd sent. She'd realised there'd been a communication breakdown between us, and she was bridging the gap with a thoughtful gesture. She was sweet like that. Always had been.

Maybe the roses hadn't been such a terrible idea after all.

My finger had hovered over the buy button for an eternity. The same itch of anxiety had whispered in the back of my mind, but no matter how much I'd tried to turn up the volume, I couldn't quite hear the warning. It had to be paranoia. Eden loved flowers. I'd surprised her once with a hand posy of daisies—small, cheap, wrapped in brown paper, and nothing special—and she'd beamed at me like I'd given her a diamond.

But daisies didn't exactly scream, "You're the love of my life. Please come home." And Mum's suggestion certainly hadn't helped.

Mum

> Flowers stolen from your neighbour's yard just because you were thinking about her.

Useless.

My mind had gotten stuck on needing something bigger and better. And you couldn't get much bigger or better than roses. All the websites said so.

The grimace on Sue's face told me everything I needed to know. The purchase I'd made at two in the morning would haunt me for the rest of my life.

My jaw dropped.

Sue carried a glass vase crammed with the charred remains of three dozen roses. The blackened tips of the petals were fragile, crumbling to ash as she made her way to the desk. Barely a drop of the red flowers' former glory still bled through.

"Wha-what happened?" I choked out.

"I'm thinking she set 'em on fire." Sue slid the vase onto the desk. She gave the roses another look over, her grey brows pinched together. "You *sure* she's your girlfriend?"

I battled the sting in my eyes with a clenched fist.

Personal lives stay personal.

This was my fault. I'd blurred the lines, but I refused to bawl like a baby in my office. Everyone always underestimated me. They called me weak and teased me for being shy or reading books. But I was also a grown man. I settled multi-million-dollar contracts every day. Some of my clients had billions. I could sort out some flowers without losing my shit.

"There's a card, too." Sue's slim fingers held out a white envelope.

I hesitated. This wasn't going to be good. After a deep breath, I took it, flicked off the tab, and pulled out the card. I chuckled. It was a cartoon ginger cat licking its butt with the words, "Giving Zero Fucks." Another shaky breath. I opened the card. Eden's looping handwriting spelt out a simple message.

I MISS YOUR STREAMING SUBSCRIPTIONS.

I tossed the card on the desk. I wasn't angry at Eden—her card was genius. The rage was all directed at me. I'd screwed up. Again. Monumentally. Somehow.

I wasn't risking another misstep. The phone was already in my hand. "Sue, give me a minute, okay?"

She nodded. "Good luck." Before shutting the door, she muttered, "You're gonna need it."

I jabbed the redial button. A few rings bleeped before Yvette's voice greeted me for the hundredth time that morning.

"Hi, sweetie," she said. "We thought we might hear from you."

"Put Eden on."

"She's a little busy."

She hadn't been too busy to send her special delivery. "I'm going to call back every minute until she's free," I warned. "I need to talk to her. No more fobbing me off, Yvette. I mean it."

Silence.

The awkward echo of nothingness dragged on, and I glanced down at the phone to make sure the call was still connected. A rustle. Some whispers. Finally, I heard the voice I'd ached to hear.

"Did you get my delivery?" Eden asked.

Except that wasn't *my* Eden. Eden's voice was usually high and sweet, melting my insides like butter on toast. The voice talking was ice, so cold and sharp it plunged between my ribs and snicked my lungs. I couldn't breathe.

"Stop calling here," she said.

"We need to talk. Not like the other night, Denny Dee. Properly this time. I tried to give you space over the weekend to cool off, but God, everything we have together is worth at least one more conversation, isn't it? *Please.*"

"I..." She paused. "Um."

"Can we meet somewhere? Anywhere." I didn't even bother hiding the desperation in my voice. "I'll do anything. I'll stop calling. I promise I'm not trying to get you in trouble with your boss."

"My boss." The sweet uncertainty in Eden's voice disappeared, and the arctic wind was blasting back down the line.

Unsettled, I stammered, "Y-Yeah."

"You don't want me to get in trouble with *my boss*." The bitter crackle of Eden's laugh wasn't a sound I'd heard before. "Yeah, we better not piss off my boss. She's a real bitch."

The call went dead.

A growl of frustration bellowed out of me. I smacked the phone down and threw myself back in my chair. Tired eyes searched the ceiling for answers I knew I wouldn't find.

Even though I didn't understand why, I knew my call had just made everything so much worse.

9

She didn't say, "It's easier to be angry than hurt."

Eden

Just my luck.

I'd grabbed the shopping cart with the wobbly wheel. My hands rumbled under the cart's red handle like I was holding onto the world's most boring rollercoaster, and the annoying clackety-clack announced my arrival down every aisle.

Heads turned. Strangers stared like startled cats.

Fan-freaking-tastic.

I wasn't shy. I loved the limelight. But who'd want an audience as they grabbed tampons off the shelf in aisle four? No one. Not even a D-lister craved that kind of attention. I tossed the box in the cart, kicked the wheel into gear, and pushed on.

This was all Andie's fault. I could've avoided my late-night excursion to the supermarket if she'd stocked her fridge like a normal person.

My best friend was a riddle. She was a talented barber and a budding mechanic. She'd even renovated her terrace into an edgy show home after only watching a few video tutorials. The fact that the same set of hands capable of so much had once set a bowl of mac and cheese on fire in the microwave defied belief. Being that bad at cooking was truly a talent.

Andie's unique talent also meant she'd made it to her thirties surviving off an empty fridge and hideous drinks she tried to pass off as *shakes*. Sorry, no. Scoops of powder shaken with water that smelled worse than a cat's butt weren't on any food pyramid I'd ever seen.

As much as I loved her, five days of camping out on Andie's sofa was my limit. I couldn't soar through life if I was hobbling around using my best friend as an emotional crutch. Life needed to start again. Big changes needed to be celebrated—and with tastier snacks than the limp carrot and mouldy wedge of cheese in the back of Andie's fridge.

And I had a lot to celebrate.

Keys jingled in my handbag as the shopping cart bumped along. I smiled. The paperwork for my new place at The Rocks was rolled up in there, too. The apartment was too modern, too much like Zach's, but securing a lease was another step in the right direction. The familiar soap and cologne of the man who'd forgotten me wouldn't be lingering on brand-new pillows or unboxed sheets. I had my own big bed again. I had a fridge to fill. Tonight, Andie's. Tomorrow, my own.

The cart's wonky wheel clackety-clacked as I headed down the next aisle. The wheel jammed.

"Stupid fu—"

I shoved the cart, but it stalled in protest. Aisle five was officially the end of the line.

"Great." Another push, but the cart didn't budge. "Just *great*."

"Eden?"

My gaze snapped up.

I knew that voice. I expected the dark eyes behind black-rimmed glasses to stare back at me, but I still wasn't prepared. Butterflies battered my stomach. Zach was perfectly polished in his suit, his hair combed back, and his tie knotted *just so*. His sweet, uncertain smile was the same, too. The only difference was the betrayal stinging in my chest.

I wasn't ready to see him. Not yet. It was too soon.

I took a step back.

Zach lowered his grocery basket to the floor. "Eden." He raised his palms, creeping forward like he was trying not to spook me.

Too late.

I spun around. Four-inch stilettos wouldn't stop me. I forgot the shopping cart, abandoning it in the middle of the aisle. My eyes frantically searched for an exit to avoid confronting the boot stomping on the little bug of my dreams again.

"Eden! Wait!" Zach's footsteps followed. "You forgot your bag!"

Hesitating, I glanced over my shoulder. Zach had scooped my handbag out of the shopping cart. The strap swung from his outstretched hand, but he stood there, frozen, waiting for me to make the next move.

I stalked down the aisle and snatched my bag. "Aren't you supposed to be chained to your desk?" I snapped.

No 'hello.' No 'how are you?' Right into battle. And Zach didn't know what hit him.

"I, um..." he stammered to an awkward stop. I used to think that was adorable. Not tonight.

My eyes narrowed on the basket he'd dropped by his feet. A tub of chocolate ice cream, fancy tea bags, crackers, and a pot of smoked salmon dip I could've eaten by the truckload—and had done exactly that the day before my period had started. Zach didn't eat a thing in the basket. Begrudgingly, he might drink a cup of tea. Were these treats for his secret office viper? Was he planning to spoil her after she'd dug her fangs into him again?

Zach noticed my eyes on his groceries and rubbed the back of his neck. "It was supposed to be a surprise," he said. "I was going to drop a basket by your salon tomorrow morning."

"Wha—what?"

"You always said gifts are better in a basket. I wanted to have a go at making one with a few of your favourite snacks to, um, you know..." He shrugged. "Make your day better."

Hope tickled my aching ribs. Zach was finally acknowledging me. *Trying*. But was this how desperate I'd become? Settling for *snacks?* Screw that. Screw him.

Defiant, I lifted my chin. "That's the best you can do?"

He winced. "I deserve that."

"You *deserve* a good kick in the balls."

"The roses?" His Adam's apple bobbed on a nervous swallow. "I remembered you have allergies. It hit me around four o'clock this morning." To the flecked-concrete floor, he muttered, "Sorry."

The *floor* got his apology? The *audacity* of this man! "The flowers are a symptom of a bigger issue, don't you think?"

"Michaela?"

"Getting warmer." I huffed a laugh. "I bet she was ecstatic when you told her I'd moved out." Little homewrecker.

"Oh, uh..."

I stared at him, my jaw somewhere on the floor with his half-arsed apology. "You told Michaela I moved out, right?" Dread crept over me, tossing me back in the shadows outside his office, remembering how he'd shoved his phone across the desk. Out of sight, out of mind. "She knows about me...right?"

Zach's lips flattened. Whatever he was about to say, he didn't want to say it. "Eden, you need to understand. My boss has drilled into me—God, everyone at Worley—personal lives don't exist—"

"I don't *exist?* You haven't told *anyone* at your work about me? Like I'm—" A strangled sob threatened to choke my words. "I'm *nothing?*"

"No, of course not. You're my universe, Denny Dee."

"Except for work. Except for the fact you don't know anything about me!" My chin wobbled, devastation crawling up my neck in a hot flush. I clenched my fist to fight the tears. "You didn't even remember I own my salon! Strangers queue up around the block just to get a photo of it...and you forgot about it...like...it didn't matter at all!"

Zach's fingers speared through his hair, his shoulders slumping under the weight of realising what he'd done—or *not* done.

"I came from nothing," I shot at him. "I had no one on my team except Andie. I'm so proud of what I've achieved, and you stand there and reduce it to nothing...because you think I'm..." I gulped. "You think I'm *nothing*. You said I was *no one*." Just like my father. "Even though I gave you everything."

The pain softening his dark eyes hardened. "Did you?" The words were ice.

"You know I did."

"You never even bothered to unpack!"

"I—I was busy."

"Bullshit, Eden. Bull. Shit." His words, spoken so calmly, were brittle. "You've had one foot out my door since you moved in. You were just waiting for an excuse to leave." His eyes widened, almost like he was shocked the accusation had spewed out.

But he was right, wasn't he?

He'd seen more than I'd realised. He'd peeked through the cracks in my dazzling smiles to see the lost girl underneath, but he'd said nothing. Not a word.

Was that how little he cared?

Or was that how *much* he cared?

My spine didn't want to hold me up anymore. I wanted to collapse, curl into a ball on the supermarket floor, and for Zach to drop beside me. I wanted his arms around me. I needed him to promise he'd erase all the nights I'd spent alone before him...and with him.

That thought kept me upright.

The nights alone.

The nights he'd forgotten me. No messages. The occasional bunch of flowers or mumbled apologies about how he'd try harder but never did.

Maybe Zach was a good man in some ways, but I was nothing to him.

"I didn't need any excuses," I snapped. "You gave me a hundred reasons to leave you. See this?" I dug the rental paperwork out of my handbag and shoved it in his face. "Now, I've got *both* feet out the door. And I'm *never* coming back!"

It was so much easier to be angry than hurt.

It was so much easier to walk away than stay.

10

He didn't say, "I want a lifetime, too."

Zach

THE BELL JINGLED.

Habit lifted my gaze off the spot knotted in the hardwood floor. I'd watched the door at Brew Haha for months, hoping to catch a glimpse of Eden. I'd only stopped my daily habit when she'd started walking into the coffee shop with me. We'd join the line. She'd smile, wave, and dole out the charm, and I'd sneak a kiss on her neck.

"Stop that," she'd whisper, even though she'd arch her neck for my lips to find the soft spot below her ear.

These days, Eden floated through the door alone.

She didn't hesitate when she spotted me through the crowd. She flipped her ponytail over her shoulder, smiled, waved, and doled out the charm like always...but not to me. She was proving a point. I hadn't hurt her. No. I didn't even exist.

Eden set a cup on the counter. White with—I adjusted my glasses—roosters. The rose gold mug she'd used every other day for the last three months sat beside her fluffy cat keychain on my kitchen counter. The only two things she'd left behind, and probably on purpose. I'd bought her both.

The cashier beamed the special smile she reserved just for Eden. "New mug?"

"New me."

"Cute chickens."

"Roosters," Eden corrected, her grin turning sly. "A woman can never have too many c-o-c-k-s." She winked at the cashier, but her head swivelled, her lips curved. She was making sure I'd heard her. She wanted to see my reaction.

If she turned a little more, she'd see my frown and the jealous eyes tinged with the misery of missing her. If anyone with a c-o-c-k dared to go near her, I wasn't sure what I'd do. Something stupid, probably.

Eden stuffed a ten-dollar note in the tip jar and waved a few hellos. It didn't take her long to start a conversation with a woman bouncing a baby on her hip. Eden avoided looking at the little blob with his mop of red fuzz, but he was determined to get her attention. He gurgled a laugh, and the moment his chubby fist squeezed her finger, her gaze found me across the room. I saw the flash. Pain. Just for a second. She screwed her eyes shut, and her throat bobbed hard when she swallowed.

Did Eden want...a...baby?

We'd never discussed it. Family was a no-go topic. She'd teared up the few times she'd mentioned her mother's passing with a vague story about a car accident. Any mention of her father was instantly shut down. I hadn't pushed. We had a lifetime to share our stories...or so I'd thought.

Had she wanted a baby—a lifetime—*with me?* Even though she'd never unpacked?

I stepped away from the wall.

Eden's eyes rounded.

Please give me another chance.

I'd silently confessed how much I loved her a hundred times. More. Why had I taken her for granted? Why hadn't I said the words? Even if she never came back, I still wished I'd told her I love her at least once.

I want a lifetime, too. A hundred little blobs with mops of fuzz.

I sidestepped through the crowd.

Eden's head turned left and right, eyes wild, her forced smile cracking into full-blown panic. I paused. Raised my palm and took a slower step. She dived for the gap. She was on the run.

Shit.

The bell jingled.

Shit!

Eden was gone.

·♥·♥·♥·♥·♥·

My coffee sat untouched in the cupholder when I pulled up outside my parents' place. The rooster mug was in the slot next to it. Eden never came back, and I couldn't just leave it there.

I glanced out the windscreen at my parents' split level. The modest orange bricks were darker in the shadows of the apartment buildings that had sprung up all around. Developers had offered them ludicrous amounts of money to sell up, but they'd said no. They clung to the suburban life and the idea of a big backyard for grandkids they may never have.

I scrubbed my palm down my face and breathed.

One...two...

Eden was supposed to be with me. My mother was about to fire questions at me I wasn't ready to answer.

Three...four...

No point delaying the inevitable.

Mum must have heard me walking up the driveway. The front door flew open, and she burst outside.

"Hello! We're so excited to finally—" Her smile vanished.

I avoided seeing her disappointment by pulling her against me in a hug. "Morning, Ma." I kissed the top of her head. Her hair smelled just like it did when I was a kid—a bit heavy on the floral. Her once-treasured auburn curls were only wisps of soft silver barely touching her ears now, slowly growing back after finishing chemo.

"Where's Eden?" Mum lifted her glasses and peered over my shoulder. There was nothing to see but my car parked out front. "Did she forget something?"

I shook my head.

"Oh." Mum's face fell. "It's just you?"

"Afraid so."

"Zachary, you promised!"

Zachary. Ouch. I was in trouble. "Sorry, Ma." I followed her inside, flinching at the snap of the front door closing behind me.

"Your dad even wore his nice shirt with the collar. He grumbled the whole bloody time he was buttoning it up!" Mum glanced at me over her shoulder as she marched through the living room. "Did Eden end up having to work today? The poor girl's flat out! You know I follow her salon on the DL—"

"The...DL?"

"The downlow. Our neighbour's little granddaughter taught me. Not important. Anyway, Eden does a tonne of celebrity weddings. She's booked out for months!" Mum excitedly rattled off some names I vaguely recognised. "And Eden has such incredible taste in fashion. Did you see how her outfit for the gala dinner went viral? Best dressed! I wanted to get her opinion on my new sandals." Mum popped her foot out to model a black sandal with strappy bits up to her ankles.

Too much information was flooding in. When did Eden go to a gala dinner? Oh, and sandals. "I like them, Ma."

Mum snorted. "You wouldn't notice a decent sandal if one hit you on the head!" She paused at the kitchen sink, her hand landing on her hip, studying me from head to toe, always seeing too much. Her eyes narrowed on my fidgeting hands. "Will Eden have time to pop over next week?"

"Ma..."

"It doesn't have to be lunch. If she's busy, we could all catch up for breakfast. There are so many charming spots near your apartment. I could convince your dad to drive into the city—"

"Ma, Eden's not..." I shook my head. "She's not coming."

"Now? Or...?"

Never.

I couldn't say the word out loud.

Whatever emotion Mum saw on my face made her gaze drop to the sink. She nodded, swiping at her nose. She knew.

My heart dropped. My screw-up had made my mother cry. "Ma—"

She waved me off. "Everything's under control for lunch." She sniffled. "Why don't you go help your dad with the barbecue?"

It wasn't a suggestion. It was an order. Mum didn't want an audience when she stood over the sink crying about how I'd ruined my life. I bent down and pecked a kiss on Mum's head. She flashed me a watery smile and then shooed me outside.

I pushed open the screen door. Potted herbs cluttered the deck, leaving just enough room for the oversized outdoor table, chairs, and the barbecue where Dad kept himself out of trouble. His hair was threaded with more grey than brown these days, and for once, it was neatly combed back. Along with wearing the collared shirt he kept tugging at, Mum had bribed him into doing his hair, too.

Dad's thick brows knitted when the screen door snapped shut. He sent a questioning look past me into the kitchen, wondering why he wasn't being introduced to Eden, but he shook off the confusion. After a quick hug to say hello, he returned to the barbecue.

"Thought you'd be helping with the salad," he said.

A fair assumption. I usually spent more time in the kitchen with Mum than daring to interfere with Dad's expert hands on any form of protein. He considered cooking meat an art form. He watched TV shows about it and everything.

"Apparently, you need a helper," I replied.

"Do I? Sounds like your mother's interfering again."

"She means well, Dad."

Dad chuckled. "Her agenda begins and ends with getting you down the aisle and buying a minivan to cart around all your kids. Don't think I'm joking. She made me walk around the dealership last week." He held up his beer. "You want one?"

He didn't wait to see my nod before bending over, opening the mini fridge, and grabbing a fresh beer. He popped off the lid and passed it to me. "Cheers?"

What was there to celebrate? "Not today, Dad."

He tapped his bottle against mine anyway. "Every day's a blessing, even if it's not turning out how you want."

We didn't say much after that. We sipped beers. Shared a bit of small talk. Mum disapproved. I'd caught glimpses of her craning her neck, trying to hear what was happening, getting closer and closer to the door as the minutes ticked on.

The screen door snapped open. Mum sailed onto the deck carrying a bowl of sliced onions. She'd had enough of us wasting time.

"John," she hissed. "Talk some sense into him, will you?"

"About what?"

Her eyes narrowed. "About Eden." She dropped the bowl beside the barbecue. "She's not coming."

Dad tugged at the collar of his shirt. "You're telling me I wore this itchy thing for nothing?" He grunted. "Figures."

"That's what you're worried about? Your shirt?"

"You seemed pretty worried about it when you made me put it on."

"John!"

"Come 'ere, Maz." Dad wound his arm around her waist and pulled her close enough to plant a kiss on her cheek. "You're getting yourself all worked up. I'll sort it. You know I will. Head on back inside."

Nodding, she sniffled and showed Dad her other cheek. Dutifully, he pecked a kiss there, and Mum disappeared back into the kitchen.

"So, what happened?" Dad didn't look at me, preferring to keep a close watch on the steaks, tongs ready. "You know, with Eden?"

I sighed. "I wouldn't even know where to start."

"You two have a fight?"

A fight was something you had over who took out the rubbish. Our problems were much worse. "There's this...woman...at work..." Our problems were bigger than Michaela, too, but it was a starting point.

Dad's lips thinned. The tongs clattered onto the metal grill, and he turned to face me. "I raised you a lot damn better than that, young man."

Does he think I...? "Dad, I didn't cheat on Eden!"

His chin lifted to inspect my face, and coal-black eyes drilled into mine. He nodded. A decision. Hopefully, he wasn't about to disown me.

He threw his head back and called out, "Maree!"

"Yeah?" The screen door opened, and Mum's head poked out.

Dad nodded at the barbecue. "Keep an eye on the steaks for me, yeah? I'm gonna show Zach the new veggie patch we put in."

A smug smile stretched across Mum's face. She knew Dad's code.

'Showing me the veggie patch' meant he wanted to talk to me—one of his awkward man-to-man talks. When I was twelve, 'showing me the new fence' led to the most uncomfortable conversation ever about sex. Two years ago, 'showing me the new lawnmower' meant Dad breaking down because the doctors had found a lump in Mum's breast. I'll never forget that day. It was the first time I'd ever seen my father cry.

Dad was down the back stairs and in the yard in a second. I followed him, but even at thirty-five, my steps were tentative on the lawn he kept greener than a golf course with his shed full of tools and contraptions. He stopped by the raised garden bed lining the back fence and gestured at the buds of green sprouting out of piled sugarcane mulch. Tomatoes already flowered nearby.

"Looks good, Dad," I said.

"Your mother wanted it." He bent over to flick out a weed and stood tall again, sweeping his gaze over the yard, as awkward about the conversation as me. "Why didn't you tell me things weren't good with your girl?"

"I'm not sure I was ready to admit it to myself. And after everything that's happened with Mum—"

"Now, hold up. Your mum getting sick doesn't mean you and I stop talking."

"It wasn't as important."

"If it wasn't important, your girlfriend would be standing in the kitchen with your mother right now." He found another weed to pluck out. "And this other woman?"

"Someone I work with. We..." I grimaced. I wasn't about to tell Dad any of the gory details about Michaela. I wanted to leave those days firmly in the past. "Look, that woman is a non-issue. Eden misunderstood a situation she saw at work and thought I was cheating. I wasn't."

"That's a trust thing. Women who know their men love 'em don't misunderstand situations like that."

"She knows how I feel."

"Does she?" He grunted. "You're not always good at using your words. You tell her?"

"N-No."

Dad frowned. "You *showed* Eden how you feel? You need to *be* there, mate. And not just in your body. The sex—"

"*Dad.*" I still hadn't recovered from his last round of sex advice.

He raised his palms. "I'm just saying, the physical is good. You need that. But you need your brain there, too."

Well, if that was the benchmark, I was a failure. My brain was always dialled into the office, and Eden knew it. "I haven't even come close to showing her." My shoulders slumped from the guilt of admitting it out loud.

"Work?"

"Yeah."

Dad sighed. "You're always working too much. Always reaching for more. I can't blame you. I know we never had much when you were growing up—"

"We had plenty."

"Nothing like that apartment you've got on the harbour. Or that nice car you've got parked out front."

"That's just stuff, Dad."

"Just stuff, huh?" He smiled. I'd just proven his point. "You've got to stop to enjoy what you've achieved. Your prick of a boss sells you a dream—a better life, money to splash, accolades, and so-called respect. But there's no point in earning all that if you've got no one to share it with."

I sighed. "Eden's already gone, Dad."

"Yeah." He patted my shoulder. "Maybe it's for the best. Gives you some time to focus on getting your promotion sorted. I mean, if it was important enough to let her walk outta your life—"

"I didn't let her walk out! Yeah, maybe I didn't have the balls to admit the whole 'I love you' deal yet, but Eden knows how I feel."

"Oh, so that's why she left?"

"Dad! Seriously? What the hell?"

"I think you're missing my point, mate. You might not like talking, but your girl's not a mind reader. What I hear you saying is that you didn't tell her how you feel, didn't show her, didn't prioritise her over that fuckin' job of yours, or give her enough faith in you so she wasn't threatened when some other sheila came sniffing. Yet, you're standing there, surprised she left." Dad grunted. "Can't say *I'm* surprised. Honestly, I'm shocked she stayed as long as she did."

"Thirty-four days."

"Eh?"

"Eden lived with me for thirty-four days." I sighed. "She never unpacked."

"What's that about?"

"I don't know. You'll be shocked to know we never discussed it." I laughed, but it was sad. "She's got so many secrets. I assumed I'd have more time to get her to open up. Now..." I sighed. "Dad, she hates me."

"How much?"

"You know those flowers I asked Mum about sending?"

"If you ended up going with the three dozen roses, you overdid it."

"You might be right. Eden set them on fire. She had the ashes hand-delivered back to my office and everything."

"She's a keeper." Dad chuckled. "Let me give you some advice, mate. The opposite of love isn't hate; it's indifference. If she was done with you, those roses would've ended up in the bin, and you wouldn't have heard a peep. If she's upset, she still cares somewhere under all her anger. Keep trying."

"How Dad? She wants nothing to do with me."

"You can't rush her. You need to give Eden enough space to heal, but not enough for her to forget how you feel about her—once you bloody tell her."

"Easy as that, huh?"

"Nothing about loving someone is easy. But mate, if you find the right person, one smile is worth all the fuckin' hard stuff."

11

She didn't say, "I'm not over him."

Eden

The beefcake's eyes bulged bigger than the muscles straining in his arms. He dropped his dumbbells on the mat. Smiled. Posed. Flexed to show me what he was packing. An unspoken offer to hook up if I'd ever seen one—and I'd seen plenty.

In your dreams, honey.

Grinning, I tossed my braid over my shoulder and bounced past the weights room, heading for spin class. My new fuchsia workout combo was magic. Yvette had tried to veto the bike shorts with a horrified, "Oh *hell* no," but she'd been wrong. I twisted around to peek at my booty in the mirrored walls. Scorecard? Killin' it.

A crowd of regulars huddled around the spin studio door. A commotion. I grinned. Sign me up.

"Accountant?" one of them asked in a whisper.

Another woman laughed. "I'd let him balance my books, if you know what I mean." She winked.

I refused to be left out of the action. If there was eye candy to gobble up, I wanted in on it. I elbowed my way to the front but got stuck in the crowd.

"Ladies." I popped onto my tiptoes. Ugh. I still couldn't see a thing. "Is there a new guy in the class?"

"Doubt it in the sexy suit," one of them giggled.

Sexy suit?

My stomach plummeted. *Heaven, help me.* I was about to suffer through Zach's Shit Gift Attempt 2.0. I just knew it. Laughter threatened to burst out of me. Men were so predictable. Zach had been a ghost when we'd lived together. Forever at the office. After I'd moved out—whatta ya know—he was everywhere.

My high-tops squeaked on the shiny wooden floor as I threw a few more elbows to get to the doorway. I peered through the gap. And there he was. The heartbreaker.

"That's no accountant," I snipped.

Zach was about to wish he'd never been born.

With my head held high, I charged at him. "What are *you* doing here?"

Zach scrambled off the bench and stood tall, his shoulders too stiff. His shaking hand smoothed out the invisible wrinkles of his jacket. He straightened his tie. Smiled.

"Well?" I snapped.

"Oh, you know," he said, trying to play it ultra cool. "Manly man things. Working out. Getting buff."

I put a hand on my hip. "In a three-piece suit?"

"A gorgeous woman once told me a man in a suit is never overdressed."

Me. I'd said that. I narrowed my eyes.

"I stopped by because I wanted to give you this." Zach twisted around to grab his gift off the bench. The oversized pot in his hands burst with green—not flowers this time, but herbs. Basil, mint, and what was hopefully parsley and not cilantro. "It's a housewarming present."

I blinked.

"I know it's not much," he said. "I was at my parents' place on the weekend, and Mum was tidying up her herbs." He thrust the pot closer with a shaky smile. "I made it for you."

My heart bounced a beat. Zach made me a gift. He'd been thinking about me enough to make me something. I couldn't stop my hand from fluffing the green leaves sprouting from the dark, earthy soil. I inched closer to steal a sniff.

"Eden." His eyes pleaded with me. "I'm trying."

He was, and I hated it. Why couldn't he have made this effort months ago? "It's a bit late, don't you think?"

He shook his head. "Not until you tell me it's hopeless." He turned his cheek, his lips flattening. Was he bracing himself for the impact of my stinging words? I was tempted to smack him with a few home truths. My gaze shifted back to the pot. But I wanted his gift so much more.

"There's a card, too." He nodded his head at the envelope hiding in all the green.

"I don't know if I'm ready for another one of your cards," I mumbled, plucking out the purple square. With one eye screwed shut, I opened it. Huh? The card was blank except for a lazy 'Z' written with his fancy fountain pen. There was one more thing inside.

I held up the stem of delicate purple flowers. "A sprig of lavender?"

He grinned. "It's proof."

"Of…?"

"My trip to Apartment 14C."

"Oh." I cleared my throat, my eyes darting everywhere. "Apartment 14C, you say?"

"You know what I'm talking about, little villain." Zach chuckled with so much warmth my cheeks heated. "The old lady knocked on my door the morning after you left. She handed me a pair of her kitchen tongs and a garbage bag and instructed me to collect all the undergarments befouling her lavender. I did. Using the tongs. They're my tongs now. Then her yappy little fluffball peed on my shoes. Twice."

"Twice, huh?"

He grinned. "I found the lavender yesterday when I was catching up on some laundry. It was a good reminder of what she said to me when I left."

"And what was that?"

"She told me I was a damn fool for not treating you right."

"What did you say?"

"I agreed with her."

· ♥ · ♥ · ♥ · ♥ · ♥ ·

I BREEZED THROUGH THE back door into the salon's kitchen. I was Sparkles the Unicorn, prancing over rainbows, nothing but smiles, holding a tray of coffees.

And Andie wasn't buying it.

Her mocha on almond milk remained untouched in the cardboard tray. Frowning, her eyes locked on the pot of herbs sheltered in the crook of my other arm.

"What's all the green shit?" she asked.

"Just some herbs." I ducked past her laser eyes and slid the tray of coffees on the counter. The pot was next. I couldn't resist rearranging the stems and fluffing the green leaves until they were picture-perfect.

"Did you stop by the markets this morning?"

"Ah, no."

Andie's eyes narrowed on the envelope stuffed in the leaves. The neat capital letters on the front were a dead giveaway. She'd seen enough of Zach's shopping lists stuck on the fridge to recognise his writing.

"You saw the suit," she said.

"He was at the gym."

"You've got yourself a bit of a stalker." She nodded at the card. "What's it say?"

"N-Nothing." I turned my body to shield my little pot of broken dreams.

"Tell that to your face."

"Please. The gift, the card—they mean nothing. I'm totally unmoved."

"Ed—"

"What?" I snapped. "My whole life turned upside down a few weeks ago. Do you want me to act like a robot? Pretend like I never cared about him?"

"I want you to stop pretending he cared about you!" She raked a hand through her hair. "*Sorry*. I just want you to remember why you left. Zach's always working. *Always*. Even if we forget his side chick, think about why you schemed your way into his office in the first place. You were always running around after him. He hangs around the coffee shop a few times, gives you a jar of green shit, and you're a heartbeat away from running around after his stupid arse all over again."

"You make me sound like some dumb teenager."

She scoffed. "You're a lot damn smarter than most people give you credit for," she said. "Ed, you've been running from some of these feelings for years—"

"Do not go there."

Her lips flattened. "I'm just saying..." She sighed. "There's nothing wrong with admitting you want to settle down and have a family when you never had one of your own. I get it. More than anyone, you *know* I get it. But that doesn't mean you should let Zach walk all over you because he might treat you right one day."

"I left him. Without a second thought, *I left*."

"You were in shock and hurting really fucking bad. We both know leaving is the easy part when people treat us like shit. It's the weeks—the fucking *years*—after that matter. Don't lose yourself again because Zach's finally decided to notice you. You're worth so much more."

The two of us stood on opposite sides of the kitchen with matching folded arms, glaring at each other. I hated this was happening between us. My frustration should never be directed at the woman who was truly my ride or die. That didn't mean my stubborn pride would let me apologise, though.

Yvette wandered into the kitchen. She waved, all smiles, dumped her oversized bag on the counter, and plucked her coffee from the tray. Beats passed. She shot a questioning glance over the top of her coffee, first to me, then to Andie, and then back again.

"Totes awkward energy in here, ladies," she said.

Andie grunted.

Yvette cocked her head at the pot. "Where'd that come from?"

"The suit," Andie said.

"Finally stepping up, is he?" Yvette smiled. "I thought he might."

"It doesn't matter," I said.

Yvette snorted a laugh.

Andie shook her head. "You're not over him, Ed."

This *again?* "What else do I have to do? I've got my own place. I'm volunteering extra nights at the youth centre. I even tried that pottery class on the weekend!" My voice rose in full-on defensive mode. "I barely think about Zach at all."

Yvette cackled. "Sweetie, you're not convincing anyone in this room you're over your big ol' nerd."

"Amen," Andie muttered.

"I'm *totally* over him," I said. "Just watch." I whipped my phone out of my bag and opened the app store. My fingers whipped over the keyboard to type 'dating.'

Yvette squealed with horror. "What are you doing?" Her hands snatched at the air, trying to grab my phone.

I dodged out of the way and hit download. "Zach isn't the only man with a big dick in this city." And I was counting on it. Some bedroom action with a suitable alternative might be the only way of grinding him out of my memory.

"Deenie, the idea has merit. The *means*, however." Yvette scolded me with a *tsk*. "A woman like you doesn't fish in the cesspool of a dating app. You're a celebrity. A queen needs a king, not a, uh... Okay, I have no idea what sort of blob is dwelling at the bottom of a cesspool. Whatever it is, it's stinky and ugly, and you should avoid it at all costs. What you need is a friend with connections."

"Strongly disagree with this plan," Andie said. "Jumping straight into another relationship is a bad idea."

I laughed. "Who said anything about a relationship?" I wasn't risking the brutal reality of intimacy again. I'd been onto a winner with short and casual. No strings meant *no* strings—no feelings, no false promises, no future. Just the way I liked it.

"Let's test the water with something low stakes," Yvette suggested. "How about a coffee or maybe a drink after work?"

"No," Andie said.

"I'm suggesting a drink with a handpicked, eligible gentleman." Yvette snorted. "I'm not telling Eden to bang the Australian cricket team or anything."

"Let's start with low stakes," I said to Yvette. "You go ahead and fix me up with one of your kings. The sooner, the better."

Andie threw her hands up.

I added, "No cricketers. Absolutely *no* lawyers."

Yvette bounced on the spot, clapping her hands. "Actors? Crypto bros?"

"No to crypto bros." Ninety percent of those guys were scammers or did nothing but talk about crypto. Snooze.

"Finance? Sports? What about rugby or tennis? I happen to know a *very* hot doubles player who's just landed in the country." Yvette waggled her eyebrows. "Thighs for days."

"Choose whoever the hell you want," I said. "Just make 'em hot and not dumb."

Somewhere in the city, my old therapist was shaking her head. I was falling back into the same pattern of chaos, but anything was easier than facing reality.

Andie was right.

I wasn't over Zach.

12

He said, "I'm not proud of how I treated Eden."

Zach

"What the fuck are *you* doing here?" Andie stalked across the salon until the tips of her boots almost touched mine. "Well?" One eyebrow rose.

"I..." My finger trembled as I pushed up my glasses.

The murder flickering in Andie's eyes was a sign I was a dead man. Dropping my gaze to the spot where my feet were stuck wasn't the answer, though. That was the Zach who'd let Eden walk out the door. I needed to do more. Try harder. Learn from my mistakes.

Today, I wasn't just going to push past my comfort zone; I was going to obliterate it.

I lifted my chin and forced myself to confront Andie's glare. "I want to see where Eden works."

"You've seen it." She pointed a black fingernail across the room. "Why don't you take another look at the door on your way out?"

Except for the quick shake of my head, I didn't budge. "I want to learn more about Eden's job. What she does. So I can support her better."

"Or, you know, *at all*."

"Fair. I'm not proud of how I treated her, Andie. I know I made these last six months all about me. I didn't listen. Eden must've talked about her salon a hundred times, but I'd decided for my own stupid reasons she was putting on a brave face 'cause she was working for some dive."

"A dive? You think this place"—Andie's arms spread wide as she motioned around the salon—"is a *dive?*"

I grimaced. The ridiculousness hit even harder when I stood smack bang in the middle of what a viral influencer called 'luxury meets comfort.' Mum had swiped through photo after photo for me to see on her phone, and none had done Voom any justice.

Eden's salon was high-end, but every inch looked warm and cosy—exposed brick, overstuffed white chairs, delicate wooden edging, and drooping greenery, all offset with a whiff of fresh citrus.

"So, you're here trying to weasel your way back into Ed's life?" Andie scoffed. "Wanna earn yourself some brownie points?"

"This isn't about point scoring," I said. "I'm honest about wanting to learn about the salon. You don't even have to tell Eden I was here if you think it's best. I know she's working on location for a TV show today."

I'd learned that information thanks to my mother's call barking at me, "Hashtag so much eye candy, Zachary!"—whatever the heck that meant. And, maybe, also because I'd developed an awful habit of checking for Eden's updates via the social media account I'd vowed never to create.

Heels tapped across the floor.

"Well, well, well. Look who's here." Yvette never just walked anywhere. She pranced past me. "Colour me shocked." She didn't look shocked. Her smirk and the way she popped her hip when she stopped beside Andie suggested she expected to see me standing there.

"Um, h-hi," I said.

"Hi?" Yvette giggled. "Isn't he the sweetest little morsel of nerd?"

"Nope," Andie said.

"Aw, don't be such a grouch." Yvette poked a finger in Andie's side. "Look how nice he's dressed up! Forget everything Deenie said about the eye candy on set." She examined me lazily from head to toe. "I think we've got our own distraction right here."

"Uh." Confused, I glanced down at my faded jeans. Andie had on nicer trousers than me. Even her sequinned tank top was fancier than the white T-shirt I'd yanked on.

"Turn around," Yvette instructed.

"Why?" I asked suspiciously.

"We need to check out your butt in those jeans."

Embarrassment blazed a fiery trail up my neck. "Y-You can't say stuff like that—" I gulped, not sure where to look. "E-Eden..."

"Sweetie, allow me to be the one to break it to you," Yvette said. "Our fearless leader has drooled over your butt plenty of times. *More* than your butt. Our clients know *all* about you."

"Let's not objectify the man," Andie said.

I beamed. "Thanks."

"I'd rather keep down my breakfast," Andie added.

I cringed.

Yvette cackled a laugh. "So, what brings you uptown, Mr. Lawyer Man?" She peered with interest around the salon. "More peace offerings? Geez, I hope you've bought some nice chocolates. It's my damn luteal phase, and I'd literally kill for sugar right now."

"He's here to learn about the salon," Andie said. "Allegedly."

Yvette nodded. "I approve."

One down. One to go. I turned to Andie to plead my case. "I can be useful," I said. "I'll do anything you want."

An evil grin spread across Andie's face. "Anything we want, huh?"

My stomach plummeted to the hardwood floor.

Maybe this was a bad idea...

To my surprise, Andie agreed I could stick around for the day, but she didn't waste a second putting me to work. She barked orders like a drill sergeant.

Hang this. Stack these. Fluff that.

She explained preparation was the key to running a successful salon, and it started well before the doors officially opened. There were luxury robes to hang and freshly laundered towels to unpack. Inventory in the trolleys and shelves needed restocking, and the day's catering had to be carefully stored for serving later. Even the cushions and magazines in the waiting area required extra special attention.

More staff trickled in as the morning went on. My head spun, barely able to keep track of all the new names and faces. Two girls hovered around the basins and giggled whenever I glanced in their direction. A barista in his late teens hung out in the kitchen, helping with the food and preparing the salon's famous artisan coffees.

Maddie wandered in last. She hoped to become an apprentice and earn her place by fussing over the clients, tidying up, and keeping the trolleys cleaned and restocked. Usually. She spent her morning perched on the stool at the front reception, sometimes answering the phone but mostly tapping away at some app as she sipped a fancy coffee.

Andie reassigned all of Maddie's jobs to me.

I also learned more about what everyone did. Eden specialised in colouring and was renowned for fixing the impossible. Andie was all about edgy cuts, and Yvette had a knack for something called blowouts.

She called me over to her station every time she spun around her client for their final reveal. Everyone crowded around to *'ooh'* and *'aah'* at the woman beaming at her transformation in the mirror, the big, bouncy waves rivalling the women in shampoo commercials on TV.

Yvette leant her hip against her station, watching me with an amused smirk as I ran through the list to restock her trolley.

"Will you be gracing Worley's corporate box with your presence tonight?" she asked.

"Maybe." Suspicious, my eyes narrowed. "Are you fishing for an invite?"

"I'd rather stick a hot curling iron in my eye than spend my night with a bunch of lawyers pretending to understand sport." A coy smile danced on her lips as she ran her finger along the edge of her trolley. "I kinda thought you might be the same?"

I lifted a shoulder. "I watch the games with my dad sometimes, but yeah, I usually avoid all the bullshit work functions."

"Why are you going then?"

"My boss told me I had to go."

"Chris Stone, right?" She snorted a laugh. "What a prickly pear he is."

"You know him?"

"Sweetie, he makes himself known to a lot of women despite the clueless fiancée he's trapped."

The bite in Yvette's voice zipped up my spine. Made me stand up taller. "Lola's...nice."

"She's positively delightful. There are plenty of rumours, though, that Chris isn't." Yvette shook out her curls, her sneer disappearing into a smile. "Are you taking a date to the stadium?"

"What the hell? Of *course* not. Eden's the only one for me."

"Ain't you sweet."

I shrugged. "Just being honest."

"I approve. Be gone with you, little peon." She waved me away from her trolley. "I'll finish taking care of this before my next appointment arrives."

"O-Okay."

I glanced at Yvette over my shoulder as I grabbed the robe and towels. I didn't know her well, but that conversation was weird, even from what little I'd seen.

The stench of bleach and wet towels burned my nose when I opened the door to the laundry room. After I stuffed a pile of robes in a dry-cleaning bag and tossed some towels in the wash, I slumped against the scratchy, ancient bricks and groaned.

The salon was brutal.

The noise. The people. There was nowhere to hide. I regularly clocked eighteen-hour days at Worley, but long days—and nights—in the office were a cakewalk compared to the salon. My feet screamed. My calves ached. There was no time for breaks. Yvette had ducked out to the bathroom maybe once, and I'd kept one of Andie's appointments amused long enough for her to chug a shake for lunch.

How did Eden work in conditions like this and bounce through the door every night? She'd never complained. Not once. And I'd let her dote on me, cook for me, and take care of me, with barely even a 'hello' some days.

If I ever won her back, all that needed to change.

Footsteps approached from behind. Not Yvette's clicky heels. These steps were purposeful. Like a soldier. I'd been waiting for Andie to come for me. The intense glare she'd shifted in my direction throughout the day hinted a confrontation was coming.

"Slacking off in the laundry, huh?" Andie said, chucking a towel across the room to hit the top of the pile. "You wouldn't be the first."

"I was putting on another load of laundry. You guys go through a tonne of towels."

Andie's gaze didn't stray, eyeing me like I was a puzzle she was trying to solve. I stuffed my hands in my pockets, ready for the lashing I was about to face.

"Zach, what was today really about?"

I sighed. "I'd be lying if I said I didn't want your approval. You and Eden are a package deal."

"We are. Do you understand why?"

"Bits and pieces. Eden keeps most of her past from me." That comment got a deep frown from Andie. "I know you've been friends for a long time," I quickly added.

"Ed's more than a friend to me. She's the only family I've got." Sighing, Andie mussed her short hair. "I was worried she wasn't being honest with you about her past. I love her, but..." She shook her head. "Not my story to tell. Just know there's more."

"There were some clues," I admitted. "Does the story have anything to do with her leaving all the lights on?"

Andie's eyes rounded. "Shit, I thought she'd gotten over all that."

I shook my head.

She scrubbed a hand over her chin. "Look, I can't break Eden's trust...but..." Another sigh. "We escaped pretty shitty families and a life barely off the streets. The first few years were rough, but we made something of ourselves. Together. So, if you think I'll stand by and watch you keep treating Ed like an afterthought, you've got another thing coming. She deserves better."

"I know I made mistakes. I put my career first, and I shouldn't have. But Andie, everything I was doing was for us—for her—so we could have a better life together. I never meant to hurt Eden."

"What did you think her reaction was going to be when she caught you fucking around?"

"I know how it might've looked to Eden that night, but I've *never* cheated on her."

"Prove it."

"I want to, but how can I?"

"Unlock your phone and give it to me."

Without hesitating, I slipped my phone out of the back pocket of my jeans, unlocked it, and passed it to Andie on an open palm. Shock flashed across her face—she obviously didn't think I'd do it—before she snagged the phone.

She swiped through the screens, her heavy brows pinched together. "Where are all your apps?"

"I don't like too much clutter," I replied. "And I don't do much on my phone. I mostly use it for work."

"Glazed and Confused Doughnuts?" Andie smirked.

"My executive assistant likes snacks," I explained weakly. "Sue needs to be happy if I want any work done."

Andie scrolled through my messages. "Damn. You only get texts about boring shit."

"Yeah, mostly organising settlements or meetings."

"You text your mum and dad *a lot,*" she said, her eyes still on the screen. "And all these texts to Eden... You know she blocked you, right?"

"Yeah, but I like to text her every morning and every night just in case she changes her mind. I don't want her to think I've stopped thinking about her."

Andie's head tilted. She watched me for a few beats before she dropped her eyes again. "Michaela... Michaela... Where is she...?" she muttered as she kept tapping. "Mac. Gotcha!"

Gotcha? Hardly.

Michaela was a colleague. Nothing more. I'd already put her on notice to keep it professional, and she was on testy waters with Chris after their breakup. She couldn't risk me telling him about the photo. No new ones had followed. The looks she sometimes shot me were confusing, but I was enjoying the quiet space she'd stopped crowding.

Andie scrolled through Michaela's texts. *"The bank says it's off until five... Where are the guarantees... That dumb shit paralegal forgot the land title searches..."* I cringed hearing the last one as much as I had the first time I'd read it. Totally unprofessional. I hope Andie saw my scathing follow-up. "What is all this shit?"

"Michaela's a senior associate in the banking team," I explained. "She runs the financing side for some of my transactions."

"Besides work, nothing's happening between you two?" When I shook my head, Andie asked, "But you didn't block her?"

My eyes turned to the laundry ceiling as I blew out a long breath. "It's like I said. Michaela and I work together on some transactions. She needs to be able to contact me in case something goes wrong. It would raise a lot more eyebrows if I blocked her than if I just kept things professional. That's all it is. Professional—and barely that. I keep her very much at arm's length after what happened."

Andie nodded slowly. Then, her lips curled into a grin that chilled me to my core. I took a step back and hit the washing machine.

"Photo time!" she said.

Wow, she was about to be *really* disappointed.

"Get excited for all the fishing memes I send to my dad," I muttered.

Scrolling through the photos, Andie's eyebrows popped up. "Why the fuck do you have all these pictures of bread?"

My face flamed. I'd forgotten about those. "I've, um, well..." I rubbed the back of my neck. "I've been teaching myself how to bake sourdough. The first few loaves were a write-off, but the last couple have been pretty good." I attempted a wobbly smile. "Edible, even."

Andie was still staring at me like I was nuts. "You know you can just buy bread, right?"

I lifted a shoulder and kept the rest of my stupid plan to myself.

Right after Eden had moved out, I'd decided if she ever gave me a second chance, I wanted to cook her dinner. Eden loved Italian, so I'd spent my spare time perfecting a menu—a Caprese salad, bread, lasagne, and tiramisu. Everything homemade. The tiramisu needed some work because I'd dug in my heels about making the Savoiardi from scratch instead of using store-bought, but everything else was coming along nicely.

Mum was fully invested in my dinner plan. She got a real kick out of my bread updates.

Andie held out my phone. "You're literally the most boring person I know. You don't even have any nudie pics on there."

Raising a brow, I asked, "People don't really do that, do they?" I took my phone and slipped it into my pocket.

"A nude selfie? Sure."

"Um... Are you saying... *You?*"

"What? Fuck. No!" She pushed her palm into my shoulder. A playful jibe. "Gross, man. Yvette's got loads."

"Had a peek, huh?"

Andie's cheeks turned hot pink. "No, I just—" She shrugged. "I *heard*."

"Uh-huh."

She recovered from her embarrassment by squaring her shoulders and putting her usual grim frown back on. "For what it's worth, I believe you when you say you didn't cheat."

"Thank you."

"But I'll still never tell Ed to take you back."

The air whooshed out of my lungs. Knowing Eden's best friend would never accept me was a blow I wasn't ready for. "Why?"

"Why? How long have you got? How about all the times you missed Friday night drinks? Or the time you couldn't make it to the picnic Ed planned for weeks? Or the time you were late to the premiere? You never prioritise her."

Andie paused, waiting for me to deny all the times I'd let Eden down. I couldn't. She was right.

She stabbed the knife even deeper between my ribs when she said, "What about how Eden had a panic attack at your work bringing you dinner because she'd never see you otherwise? How many times did you bring her dinner?"

I could only defend myself with a mumbled excuse. "I can't always control my work—"

Andie barked a laugh. "Yeah, *your work*. We all know about your fucked-up priorities. How far down your list is she, exactly?"

"Eden's number one," I bit back. "Always."

"Maybe right now, she is. You lost her, so you're panicking, pulling out all the stops to win her back."

"It'll never be like it was before. I understand—"

"Zach, that is such bullshit, and you know it. Maybe everything will be great for a week. Maybe even for a month. But eventually, I know Ed will be calling me because she's back at the end of your list. I can't watch my best friend lose herself again. I won't." Andie paused to take a shaky breath, chest heaving. "Zach, I know you're not a bad person. After today, I actually think you're pretty okay, but work will always be your number one priority, and I'm sorry, but Ed deserves better."

"You're right. She does."

And it was time I started proving that to Eden.

13

She said, "What's the matter, jealous?"

Eden

Yvette was my fairy godmother.

My eligible bachelor's name was Sam...*Something*. I mean, really, who cared about his surname? Crew-cut blonds who played professional rugby weren't usually my type, but Sam was all kinds of rough and pretty to look at. A blocked jaw. His black blazer stretched across heavily muscled shoulders. Tall enough to tower over me, even though I strutted through the stadium beside him in four-inch stilettos.

His enormous paw rested in the curve of my spine. A gentleman. He guided me through the crowd supporting some team playing some sport, but the innocent touch didn't help settle my stomach. This man would be a fine notch on my bedpost. Why wasn't my body getting the memo?

Sam punched the button for the elevator to the corporate box and turned to me. One of his eyes was so fat and purple it was like he ended every smile with a wink.

I waved a hand at his face. "What happened?"

"Copped a knee to the eye, babe." Sam's chest puffed out enough to strain the buttons of his black shirt. "Got flattened after making a break for a try."

"Um." Was he speaking English? What the hell was a 'try?' Was that when his team scored? I had no idea, but I couldn't keep blinking at him like a doe-eyed debutante, so I nodded and said, "Cool."

"Damn straight. Now, show me this dress. Give us a twirl."

I spun around and jiggled my hips to model the vintage designer gown I'd rented at the last minute. "You approve?"

"I'm givin' you another damn straight. This dress is doin' it for me." He snuck an extra-long peek at my booty—with his one eye—and gave an appreciative nod. "You're a class act, babe."

The grin eating my face also ate up some of the pesky guilt.

Kisses to Yvette for playing fairy godmother. She'd truly outdone herself by helping me with my rebound dating scheme. *Not a cricketer?* Tick. *Hot?* Not my usual type, but the man was too perfect to be anything less than a big tick. *Not dumb?* Welp, I wasn't holding out much hope after he'd wondered if limes were unripe lemons, but two out of three wasn't bad.

Sam's broad shoulders crowded most of the space in the elevator. I squeezed in beside him, trying my hardest not to smoosh my boobs into his brick wall of a chest even though that might've been his plan.

"So, what's this shindig?" I asked. "You were vague on details. Some corporate function?"

"A booze fest with the sponsors. Coach likes us to keep 'em happy when we're not on the field. It'll be a few dudes from an insurance company and some law firm."

I groaned. "Lawyers?" I'd had enough of one particular lawyer to last a lifetime.

"Those uptight bastards aren't so bad once you get some booze in 'em."

My lip curled. Maybe that was where I'd gone wrong—not getting Zach drunk enough. "I'll take your word for it."

"Babe, listen 'ere. I don't want you gettin' all pouty. We're here to make an appearance. I'll shake a few hands, and you'll shimmy your sexy rear around enjoying all the free champagne. Then, we'll fuck off somewhere fun."

"Promise?" I clasped my hands under my chin. "Yvette's getting together a few people for margarita shots at El Diablo Cantina later."

"Lock us in, babe."

Two guys in suits fell over themselves when we walked through the door. Heads turned. More people rushed over. Sam was a Big Deal. Deep voices boomed, and there was a lot of shoulder slapping and congratulations for last night's 'amazing fucking game.' Sam shook off the praise and proudly introduced me as 'his special friend,' which led to round two of shoulder slapping.

What a bunch of drongos.

"Sam," said one suit. "The line breaks you managed last night—"

Cue my exit.

Let them talk about boring rugby. One remotely interesting group of people drowning in the sea of suits needed rescuing; I just had to find them. My polite smile faded as I scanned the room.

A group chatted in the corner with some guys stacked like Sam. Boring. The women huddled near the bar appeared to be having about as much fun as me. Maybe they were my people? My eyes fell on another group by the windows overlooking the stadium. I didn't notice the game unfolding on the other side of the glass or the thousands of thundering cheers.

Why, hello there, gorgeous.

My greedy eyes found a new home appreciating the man wearing a navy suit. Dark hair barely tamed. Tall. Broad shoulders. A veiny hand wrapped around a glass of...hmm, probably scotch. Rich lawyers always sipped scotch. Zach did.

The man across the room had a commanding presence. Sexy supervillain vibes. My new partner in crime—if he was lucky. My libido burst back to life with the swoop of my stomach.

Oh yes, this man would be the perfect distraction.

When I dragged my gaze away from how nicely this new gentleman filled out his trousers, the old guy next to him locked eyes with me and grinned.

Busted.

Old Guy leant over and whispered something to his companions, pointing across the room at me. I rolled my eyes. The group whispered with the subtlety of a group of giggling teenagers. My handsome stranger's head started to turn, seeking me out over his shoulder. Dark, stubbly jaw...a serious scowl...and...familiar brown eyes blazing behind black-rimmed glasses.

My hand balled into a fist by my side.

Some fairy godmother Yvette turned out to be. What the hell did she think she was playing at?

Mr. Supervillain was none other than Zach.

I stepped back, the familiar flutter of nerves in my feet urging me to run, run, run! Flustered, I stumbled, but before I fell ungracefully on my butt for the first time in my life, Sam's arm weaved across my back to steady me. His big hand clasped my shoulder. Instinct. He didn't even stop chatting.

My heart raced. I pressed my hand to my chest, took a deep breath, and dared to lift my gaze. I expected to clash an awkward look with Zach, but his slitted eyes were locked on the hand Sam had left draped lazily over my shoulder.

Oh.

Power surged through my veins. Jealous, was he? The evil bitch inside me awakened. It was time to up the ante and make Zach suffer.

I shimmied close enough for my hip to knock into Sam. "Want a drink?" I feathered my fingertips up his side, hoping one particular set of dark eyes watched my every move from across the room.

"Babe, you read my mind." Sam flashed me his winking grin. "Surprise me with somethin' that knocks my socks off more than that dress."

I blew Sam an air kiss as I sauntered away. What a show. I could feel Zach's eyes follow the swish of my hips as I walked to the bar.

And I only needed one guess for who edged the empty glass on the marble counter beside me. Zach must have downed his drink on his way to the bar. Dutch courage? Was he worried I'd create a scene? *Please.* I had more class than that. But I refused to acknowledge him. I couldn't. My skin was too flushed, burning up, and my pulse still pounded. I wouldn't give him the satisfaction of seeing the effect he had on me.

"Do you believe in coincidences?" Zach's voice was lower than usual. Intimate.

I kept my eyes fixed on the jumble of bottles behind the bar. "No," I said. "This has Yvette written all over it."

Zach sighed in agreement. "I knew she was acting weird when she kept asking me about my plans tonight."

"You talked to Yvette?"

"Ah, well... Yeah? She didn't tell you?"

"Not a peep. Where'd you run into her?"

"At your salon."

My eyes rounded. Had Zach dropped off Apology Present 3.0? Was it awful of me to wonder what his latest gift was? "I'd advise you against stopping by for a haircut." I turned to smile at him ever so sweetly. "Andie has been itching to practice her barbering skills on your balls."

He grunted. "I'd rather take my chances with Andie than see you here with *him*." A glare shot in Sam's direction.

"Aw, what's the matter, honey?" I fluttered my eyelashes. "Jealous?"

"Yes."

Zach shifted a step. Just one. He was so close. He'd always been too close. The familiar tickle of his cologne and the memory of warm hugs heated my cheeks. Every breath I dragged in pinched my chest.

Zach took up even more space when he dipped his head and whispered into the crook of my neck. "I'm losing my mind I'm so jealous. You look so..." His fingertips grazed along my wrist, sparks shooting up my spine. "So stunning. But then, you always do, don't you?"

My heart pummelled my ribs. I was a sucker for a compliment—especially one delivered with Zach's shy smile. But I wasn't about to let him have the upper hand.

"I bet you're sorry now you never brought me to one of your functions," I said, scorn dripping from my voice.

Zach's lips flattened. "Just so we're clear, I never usually go to these stupid kiss-arse networking events. My boss said I need to be more visible." He lifted a shoulder. "A partnership expectation, I guess."

I scoffed a laugh. Zach had once politely refused to go to a food festival with me because of the crowd, but when his boss said, "Jump," suddenly he was out networking. It shouldn't have hurt as much as it did.

"Convenient," I said.

Zach had the nerve to huff out an exasperated breath. "Eden, it's not like that—"

"Jesus." A blonde woman fell out of the crowd, crashing against the bar. "I didn't think I'd escape the leech with the comb-over. He just tried to grab my arse."

Michaela leant over the marble counter in her Saturday night finery, waving for the bartender. I scrutinised her from head to toe. She wasn't tragic. In fact, she'd put herself together rather nicely in a blushed pink cocktail dress. My eyes narrowed. But she was standing far too close to Zach. She relied on him. Sought him out when she had a problem with some creep. Another reminder that those two had too much history.

I laughed. "The gang's all here, huh?" I said to Zach.

He frowned. Not at me. At Michaela.

Hazel eyes turned in my direction. Did Michaela know who I was? I lifted my chin but didn't smile. Her eyes widened. Oh yeah, even if she didn't know my name, she knew who I was: competition.

Zach cleared the awkwardness from his throat with a cough. "Mac, can you please give us a minute?"

I snorted. Still with the whole Mac thing. Cute.

A scowl scrunched Michaela's face into too many sharp points. She didn't want to give us a minute. She was more tempted to take a shot at clawing my eyes out with her French tip manicure.

"Sure," she said. The smile that followed was basically a sneer. "I can give you a minute."

A tense silence filled her place at the bar when she left.

"Eden." Zach's voice was urgent, desperate to drag my attention off the woman sauntering across the room. "This is *not* what it looks like. I'm not here with her. I mean, I am, but not like—we're not—" He forced in a breath to calm himself enough to get the words out. "I didn't *bring* her. She isn't my date, and she's absolutely *not* my girlfriend."

"Just your fuck buddy?"

His jaw clenched.

"And you're still calling her that adorable pet name," I said. "I love how you guys rhyme. Zach and Mac. Total couple goals."

"Everyone calls her Mac!"

"Is that what you call out when you come?"

Zach's eyes bulged. *"Eden!"* He growled my name. "I keep my personal life *personal*." He'd never glared at me like that before. Agitated, almost angry, like he had something to lose—and it wasn't me. "I don't broadcast my business for the whole bloody stadium to hear!"

"No, of course not. No one can know about your dirty little secrets."

"Eden, you weren't—"

"No, I wasn't even your secret, was I? I was no one." My laugh was dark. "It takes one to know one, right?"

"What's *that* supposed to mean?"

"Does your pride burn to see me here with a *real* man, Zach? Sam's a big deal in this city. Notice how your colleagues fell over themselves to shake his hand? And who are you? Some half-baked lawyer?" I snorted. "Not even a *partner*."

Zach's face shuttered. Did he think I'd let him stonewall me? I wanted his anger. I wanted him to argue back. I wanted him to tell me in a fit of rage why I'd never been good enough. So, I stooped even lower into the filth to get a reaction.

"I can't believe I ever settled for someone as pathetic as you," I said, my voice edged with cruel.

A soft whimper of shock was torn out of Zach, as if I'd reached in and ripped his heart out. I clapped my hand over my mouth. I regretted letting my pain take hold of me, wrenching those ugly words from my throat and spewing them into the world. I knew he was sensitive about his work...himself...how quietly he moved around in the world. *I knew.* And I'd said the words anyway.

"Z-Zach, I—"

"I can't believe you chose me, either." He jerked his chin down in a nod. "Enjoy the rest of your evening."

There was nothing sweet about my revenge...or watching the shattered shell of the man who walked away.

14

She said, "You were never there."

Eden

Flashbulbs crackled like white-hot fireworks.

"You ready, babe?" Sam grinned.

He didn't shy away from the paparazzi; he ate up the attention. He slung his tree trunk arm around my waist and charged us through the defensive line of cameras crowding the entrance of El Diablo Cantina.

Cocktail bars in Sydney didn't get more exclusive than the Cantina. Tucked underground, it was edgy and vintage and all kinds of cool. Mahogany walls, rich suede leathers, oversized chandeliers, and everything soaked in luxe. That place was the shit. The real deal. People—celebrities—went there to be seen.

The suited giant guarding the door nodded and lifted the red velvet rope. Sam and I didn't need to be on his list. We were known. We were in.

But the Cantina was the last place in the world I wanted to be.

My big, lonely bed was calling. I wanted to curl up under my doona with a packet of Tim Tams, watch an endless stream of cats squishing their butts into boxes on my phone, and pretend the night never happened.

My revenge hadn't gone to plan. I hadn't acted like the bigger person. I'd stooped so low—so *very* low—to hurt Zach. Why had I let such ugly words spew out of my mouth? By the time I'd gulped down enough champagne to bravely step into my big-girl apology pants, Zach had left.

Guilt churned in my stomach.

I stole a look at my phone. His number lit up the top of my blocked contacts. My thumb hovered over the screen.

Should I...?

No one had taught me the right things to say or how to navigate all the confusing paths in a relationship—certainly not my father. Therapy had helped, but that was all theory, no practice. When life forced me into a corner, I came out swinging. I'd been hurt too many times not to fight for myself. But I needed to make this right.

I swiped my finger to unblock Zach's number and opened a new message. I stared at the blank screen.

What should I say? *Sorry, I was a bitch even though you treated me like shit.* That wasn't an apology. *Sorry, I couldn't behave like an adult after you told me no one knew I existed.* Probably not.

Maybe all I needed to say was...*sorry*.

Before I could start tapping out a message, Sam whooped out a cheer. "Crew!"

I glanced up from my phone. The silhouettes crammed around the dark table glowed amber under the chandeliers. Rugby players. Women I vaguely knew from the social scene.

An arm stacked with rows and rows of clinking gold bangles shot into the air. Yvette beamed like a disco ball in her sequin dress and patted the empty stool beside her. Andie slumped on the other side, shoulders rolled over a tall glass of beer, her customary all-black invisible in the gloom. A row of empty glasses lined the table in front of her.

My phone disappeared into my clutch. My apology to Zach would have to wait.

Showtime.

I pushed my shoulders back, pasted on a smile, and dodged through the gaps to take up the spot between my friends.

I smirked at Andie. "I guess the party started without me."

She grunted.

I nodded at the line of glasses. "How many of those have you knocked back, exactly?"

"Not enough to drown out her"—Andie pointed at Yvette—"and all the crapping on about bridesmaid dresses. Navy blue, off-the-shoulder, in case you're wondering."

"Call me an optimist," Yvette cooed. "But you never know who you might run into at one of those corporate events."

I narrowed my eyes. "Oh, I think you knew *exactly* who'd be there."

Yvette didn't look remotely guilty, but her life was spared when Sam's head popped in between us.

"Girlies." He beamed his half-winking grin. "How about some drinks?"

"Maybe a cantarito for me and Vettie?" I fumbled with my clutch to pass him my bank card. "A beer for Andie."

Sam put his meaty paw over my hand. "My shout for this round, babe."

I studied my hand as he lumbered off into the crowd. No tingles. No little zings like when Zach had touched my wrist at the stadium. Nothing.

Yvette turned to me. "Isn't Sam a doll? You two will make such beautiful babies." Her smile was sly. "Unless, of course, someone else caught your eye? Someone tall, dark, and scowly, perhaps?"

"It's super cute you think you can interfere in my love life," I said. "There's just one little problem with your scheme."

Yvette cackled. "Oh, sweetie, I don't think so—"

"Michaela was there," I said.

Yvette's jaw dropped.

"Are you fucking kidding?" Andie growled. She was already pushing off the stool when my hand clutched her arm, pulling her back. She tried to shrug me off. "Let go."

"Not a chance," I said, shoving her back on the stool.

"I know where the suit lives," Andie said. "After all his bullshit today, I'm going to kill him if he thinks he's making a fool outta me."

"One of you better tell me what the hell is going on," I demanded. "Zach mentioned he saw Yvette at the salon but not you." I groaned. "Please tell me he didn't drop off another one of his scary-as-shit special deliveries."

Andie threw back a gulp of beer and, grimacing, said, "Zach worked at the salon today."

Yvette's enormous gold hoop earrings bounced as she nodded. "He wanted to learn about what you do, so we gave him the full experience. Honestly, we should fire Maddie's butt and put Zach on full-time. That man has a serious work ethic."

"It was a fucking con job," Andie sneered. "He's just getting desperate trying to win you back, Ed."

"Well, *duh*." Yvette rolled her eyes. "For the record, I'd like to add that Andie was a total bitch to your man, and he didn't complain once. Not once! Not even when she made him clean the bathrooms."

"But we don't touch the bathrooms." I shifted confused eyes between them. "We have professional cleaners for that."

"Yeah." Andie smirked. "But Zach doesn't know that."

"He was a total cutie with his yellow rubber gloves on," Yvette added. "He even spritzed a little eucalyptus in each stall when he was done. I didn't even know we had any!"

Yvette kept gushing about how they'd kept Zach busy all day, but my gaze dropped to my lap, my fingers flicking restlessly at the clip on my clutch.

On. Off.

On. Off.

My mind spun. Zach had worked all day at my salon to learn more about my work. He was a big-shot lawyer, but he'd let my friends boss him around. He'd cleaned *toilets*.

Zach did all that for me, and how did I repay him for his efforts? I'd told him he was no one, not a real man. The guilt of all the ugly words I'd said to him at the stadium still stained my soul. No matter how much he'd hurt me, I never should've lashed out at him.

I gnawed on my bottom lip.

Don't cry.

"Ed, you okay?" Andie's voice was gruff.

Nodding, I tried balling my fists to stop the tears instead. "Yeah," I choked out. "It's just been a big day, that's all."

A buzz vibrated on my lap. My phone. I didn't care what the notification was—telemarketers, nonsense updates about some clothing sale. Bring it on. Any distraction would work until Sam came back with enough booze for me to numb the guilt.

I flicked my clutch open and took out my phone. A devastated breath whooshed out of me. I locked my phone again, but it didn't matter. Zach's message was already burned in my memory.

Zach

> Even when you hate me, you're still the most beautiful woman I've ever known. Sweet dreams, Denny Dee. xo

·♥·♥·♥·♥·♥·

My hand shot out to push open the door signed *'Bonitas.'* I didn't speak a lick of Spanish, but even in a drunk haze, I was certain that was El Diablo Cantina's fancy way of signalling the women's restroom.

Wobbling from foot to foot, hands out, trying to keep myself balanced, I stumbled inside. The mishmash of black and white tiles and blood-red doors made my stomach lurch, but my shaky legs reached the free stall at the end. I slammed the door shut, but it took two attempts for my fingers to fumble the lock closed.

My eyes darted around the tiny, suffocating space. What now? My escape plan had never gotten further than getting my booty to the bathroom. I had to get away from Andie and her judgemental eyes. She was always asking too many questions: *You okay? Maybe that should be your last drink.*

Andie's eyes had almost bugged out of her head when I'd chugged down my first cantarito in record time and then demanded a second. She'd even had the nerve to rain all over my pity party by trying to ban Sam from getting me any more drinks after I'd downed my third.

Well, the joke was on her because I'd stolen sips from Yvette's glass when she wasn't looking. My head was numb. Drunk as a designer-clad skunk. A wave of giggles escaped me and bounced around like a whole party was crammed inside the tiny stall with me. The distraction only lasted a second. There was no party. It was just me. Sad, lonely me.

Why couldn't Zach just stay away like all the men before him? Why did he keep trying? Locking up my feelings and pretending I hated him would've been much easier if he'd stayed away. And he *should* stay away. I hated him, didn't I?

I leant against the stall door, closed my eyes, and let all the regrets, the shame, just drop away until the world was blissfully black.

That message...

I pressed my fist into my chest.

I should respond to his message. He deserved my anger for the way he'd treated me, but not my cruelty. I needed to make it right somehow. I'd start by saying sorry.

My fingers fumbled on the clip of my clutch, and with a sharp tug, my phone was out without spilling my makeup and tiny perfume all over the tiled floor. When I looked down at my messages, my brain spun. I squinted, but the letters on the screen spun, too.

Whoa.

"Okay," I grunted, "maybe no messages."

I jabbed my finger to press the call button before I could change my mind, and my hand shook as I pressed the phone to my ear. Maybe this wasn't such a great idea. The phone trilled for a beat. What the hell was I doing? This definitely wasn't a great idea. I couldn't—

"Eden?"

My heart thumped against my ribs. My strappy heels were too flimsy to hold up my wobbly legs, so I flipped down the toilet seat lid with my knee, the loud crack rattling my nerves. I sat down in a puffy black lump of guilt.

I gulped a breath. "H-Hi."

"You unblocked me?" Zach's voice was low and heavy, like a sad but relieved sigh. "It's so good to hear your voice."

It was good to hear his voice, too. When we'd first started dating, he'd loved chatting after sex. He'd prop himself up on his elbow, trace lazy fingers over my skin, steal kisses, and share a hundred stories about the kayaking and hiking trips he was planning. His words had been murmured in a deep, sleepy voice that comforted me to my bones. Not that he ever went on one of those trips. He was always too busy working.

"I, um..." I sat in dumb silence, gripping my phone so hard to stop the shaking my fingers were about to snap off.

"Denny Dee? Are you okay?"

Everyone kept asking me that. I always lied. *Yeah, sure, I'm peachy. Couldn't be better.* But there was no one with me in the toilet stall to bother painting on a brave face. Maybe it was okay to admit the truth for once.

"No," I whispered.

"Are you safe?" My foggy brain registered that Zach's words were clipped, hurried. Was he worried about me? That was a first. "Where are you?"

"Oh, I'm just here...hiding out with the *bonitas* at El Diablo Cantina." My voice sounded so *sad*. "You... You like the *bonitas*, right?"

Silence stretched.

"I'm still here," Zach said. "My verbal prowess is limited to English, and the online translator took forever. It means beautiful...I think?" Another pause. "Eden, you know there's only one woman who I think is *bonita*."

"Michaela?"

"Never. You hear me? *Never.* It's only ever been you."

I gulped in another breath. My nose itched, and tears brimmed in my eyes. "But I wasn't enough for you."

"You were always enough." The big liar sounded so sincere. "Since the day I first saw you at the coffee shop."

"Then w-why didn't you—" My throat seized. I forced in a shaky breath, but the more I fought the wave of emotion swelling inside me, the more it wanted to crash through my chest. "Why d-didn't anyone know—"

Why didn't anyone know about me? Why did you keep me a secret? Why were you ashamed of me? Why am I good enough to fuck, but not to love?

Humiliating tears dribbled down my cheeks. I clapped my hand over my mouth, but a strangled wail still escaped.

"Oh, Denny Dee... Oh, love..." Zach's voice cracked. "I'm sorry you're hurting so much. Cry it all out. I'm here."

"You're not. You *never* are." The restroom was so cold. So lonely. I dragged up my knee and hugged around it with my free arm, resting my cheek on the scratchy tulle of my skirt. I hiccupped through the sobs. "Why didn't you want anyone to know about me?"

"I want everyone to know about you," he insisted. "I do."

"Michaela didn't know about me."

"No, she didn't."

"But you've told her about me? After we met?"

Zach sighed. "No."

His admission stabbed through the last of the patchwork armour I'd slapped over too much past hurt. I screwed my eyes shut. "Oh." There was nothing else I could say.

"I didn't tell her about you because she's not a part of my life. She doesn't deserve to know anything about who I'm with. If you want me to tell her, I will. In a heartbeat." When I said nothing, he added, "Michaela's just a colleague. Nothing more."

My laugh was brittle. "That's a lie."

"It's not. She's just—"

"She's not *just* a colleague," I snapped. "You've been *inside* her, Zach."

He exhaled sharply. "Shit, Eden, I can't change that. I would if I could. A thousand times over. I'd never ignore my values like that again. Believe me."

"Is she the only one? At your work?"

"Yes."

Was that better...or worse? "Personal lives stay personal except for Michaela?"

Silence.

"She was worth bending the rules, but I wasn't?"

Silence.

Why did that hurt so much? I had no right to be upset about who Zach had been with before we were together. I was no doe-eyed virgin when we'd met. No, *women like me* got around. I'd bet good money the notches on my bedpost outnumbered his ten to one, and I'd never cared about body counts with anyone else I'd been with. History of screwing around? Have at it. You do you. So why did I care about Michaela?

The ugly whispers of childhood echoed in my mind.

Because you love him, and he doesn't love you. He chose her *first.*

Fresh tears popped into my eyes. I hugged my knees again to dull the sobs echoing in the tiny toilet stall. The numbing effects of all those drinks were a long-lost memory.

"Zach, what did I need to do to make you love me?"

Silence.

Agony made me restless. Why didn't he say something? Shout at me? Anything? I couldn't stand it.

But maybe...

I eased the phone away from my ear. I broke apart all over again when I looked down. The screen was blank.

Zach had hung up.

15

He said, "I'm sorry I didn't see you."

Zach

El Diablo Cantina was a dead zone.

The dodgy phone reception was no surprise—that hipster hellhole was literally buried underground—but I'd still been tempted to hurl my phone when Eden's call had dropped out.

I barrelled down the stairs two at a time, sidestepping the maze of people blocking my way, and landed with an ungraceful thud at the bottom. I screwed my eyes shut. I had to. The Cantina was an introvert's worst nightmare. I couldn't hear my heart pounding in my chest over the wailing music bombarding me from every direction, and it was impossible to breathe when the air was suffocated by alcohol, old wood, and too many nameless faces.

What was I even doing here? Eden had always been out of my league. A celebrity. She deserved the kind of man who commanded respect—not the bumbling nerd who snuck looks at her like a love-struck teenager.

She settled.

I glanced at the escape beckoning me at the top of the stairs, but my feet refused to budge. I wasn't leaving.

I grabbed my phone out of my jacket pocket and hit redial. *Call failed.*

I sighed.

Eden had called me, so there was reception...somewhere. I took a deep breath and made my way into the bowels of hell. Silhouettes crowded the bar, the dance floor, and intimate booths of button-tufted leather lining the walls. Everywhere was a hiding place.

As I weaved through the swarm, I spotted a familiar face. Yvette was impossible to miss. Her gold dress twinkled under the chandeliers, and her head was thrown back, laughing, utterly oblivious to the meathead rugby player perving at her tits.

I stopped. That bastard. My fist clenched.

I glared a dark promise at the rugby player across the bar. Once I'd found Eden, I'd take care of him, too. He wasn't going to disrespect Eden. It hadn't been on my bingo card to get beaten up by a famous rugby player after failing abysmally to defend my woman's honour, but at least Dad would be proud. I'd always feared he thought I was too soft and didn't stick up for myself enough. He'd said so in the hospital two years ago, hadn't he?

My lips quirked up when I rounded the corner and saw the sign slapped on the door that said *'Bonitas.'*

I didn't think twice before barging inside.

The wailing music dulled to a low thump when the door swung closed. My heart stuttered. Eden's solitary figure hunched over a basin, her phone clutched in a death grip in one hand and a wad of paper towels stuffed in the other. The tip of her nose was red, and rivulets still streaked her cheeks.

"Denny Dee." I was surprised I got the words out without a stutter. Seeing her cry was a punch in the chest.

She bolted upright, spinning on her black heels to face me head-on. "What are you doing here?"

"Did you really think I wouldn't run straight here?"

Of course she would. I'd let her down a hundred times before. Slowly, tentatively, like she was a skittish kitten I didn't want to spook, I crept forward. Eden took a step back. The paper towels fluttered from her hand as she leant her hip into the basin to steady herself, her chest heaving and her eyes never leaving mine.

I took another step.

"I thought you hung up," she said.

I took another careful step. "Never."

An ache gnawed in my chest, plunging me forward, begging me to get close enough to run my fingers through the little curls that had slipped loose from her bun. I wanted to touch the blotched skin on her cheek and whisper everything was going to be okay, but I forced my hand to stay by my side. Eden's lips quivered. She wrung her hands, and her eyes darted frantically away from mine—to the door behind me, around the room, everywhere but me.

She was going to run.

"I promise I won't hurt you," I said.

"You already did."

My gut clenched. I had. Too many times.

The woman standing in the bathroom with tear-stained cheeks wasn't the brave force against nature who'd battled me at every turn. I'd always guessed Eden protected herself behind walls of sparkle, but I'd never seen it. Not like this. No bluster, no anger, only raw and real emotion.

I shouldn't have, but I bundled her in my arms. She didn't hug me back. Her arms stayed stiff by her side, but her nose burrowed into my chest, and her shoulders started to quake with silent sobs, a wet patch blooming around my collar.

"I want to hate you so much," she whispered.

"I'm sorry, Eden. I'll never forgive myself for not showing you how important you are to me."

"You never treated me like I was important."

"I'm seeing it. I am. I've been lying to myself for a long time, saying I was working so hard for you...and I was, but..."

"Your work has always been about you."

"It is. *Was*. Tonight, at the stadium, when I snapped at you, I felt it"—I slapped my palm over my heart—"right here. My insecurities, my goals, just how much I've been putting them first. Dad's been telling me for years to stop and notice the good things in my life. I didn't, Eden. I didn't see the best thing that ever happened to me until you walked out my door."

"Just more words."

"I'll prove it to you," I said. "Actions."

Eden eased back. Her lips pressed in a fine line. "More gifts?"

"Whatever you need. Anything you want."

Her chin lifted. "Beg me." Her glare was defiant. "On your knees."

My gaze bounced off the checkerboard tiles. "Eden?" I grimaced. Sparkling basins and the slightly offensive smell of too much air freshener, and I'd guarantee this place was cleaner than the men's, but it was still a bathroom.

Eden scoffed at my hesitation. "So, *not* whatever I need?" She peered down the end of her nose at me, one brow lifting in a challenge.

I didn't always say much, and when I did, it usually stuttered out of me, but I'd never begged a day in my life.

And yet...

My joints protested with a hot squeeze as I sank to my knees. When Eden's slender fingers speared through my hair and yanked back my head, forcing me to look her in the eye, her smile was feral.

"How many times did you see me on my knees in front of you?" she asked.

So many. "You were beautiful." She was.

"You liked it, Zach?"

Was there any point in lying to her? "I loved it."

"You like being in control?"

"Yes."

Eden's head cocked. "Me too." She scoffed a noise. "Too bad I can't act like you and just take what I want."

I reached out, my fingertips brushing the smooth skin of her ankle. "You can."

Bone-aching *want* flared in my chest. The barometer of Eden's mood was shifting—cool, detached. She wanted to take control. I'd let her. She could coax me into a stall and demand I lift her dress. I'd welcome it. I'd push her knickers aside, tug her leg over my shoulder, and press my face between her thighs. I'd groan when her rough hand threaded in my hair as she ground her hips against my face. *Fuck yes.* I'd crawl across a festering truck stop for that.

Hell, I'd beg Eden simply for a smile.

Her attention.

Anything.

Acid leached in my gut. My hand fell from her ankle.

This persona of Eden—the Ice Queen—had never been about sex. She flipped the switch when the balance of power shifted between us in those moments when she'd been thrown out of the pilot's seat and was still flailing midair, not quite on the ground, not sure how to land.

I'd never shown her. And that was my job.

I'd forgotten her so many times she felt like she needed to beg for my smile, my attention, my *anything*. The realisation punched me in the gut.

I lifted my gaze, and when our eyes met, I hoped she saw mine weren't filled with lust. Only regret. True remorse.

"I'm sorry." I didn't intend to whisper, but the shame curling around my throat wouldn't let me speak any louder. "I'm so sorry I didn't see you. I prioritised my work. I didn't listen and brushed you off with too many promises I didn't keep. I convinced myself it'd all be fine because I'd be someone you looked up to...who provided for you..." I laughed at how blind I'd been. "But that's never what you wanted from me, is it?"

Eden shook her head.

"You just wanted me to be there for you? Notice you? Make you my number one?"

She nodded.

"I can do that. I'll prove to you I can. Please, give me another chance."

"I've already given you another chance."

"A *final* chance."

Her fingers toyed with the fluffy frills of her dress. "I...can't."

"I was yours the first day I saw you, Denny Dee. I'll wait until you can."

She snorted. "You'll be waiting forever."

"Okay."

Just like that. Easy as pie. What was the point of life without Eden in it? I'd read enough books to know nothing good ever came from turning your back on the woman you loved. You'd be miserable alone, sure, but you'd go mad trying to replace something priceless with anything—or anyone—else.

She folded her arms. "As if."

"Try me."

"Zach, be serious."

"I'm on my knees in a club I vowed never to step foot inside. It doesn't get more serious than that. You're it for me, Denny Dee. It's you or no one. If you want to parade me around for everyone to laugh at, do it. I've got nothing to lose. If you're not by my side, I've already lost everything."

"I'm just not—" She puffed out a breath. "I can't waste anymore of my life wondering when you'll come home...who you're with..."

"Let's take it back a few steps," I said. "I'm not asking you to move back into my place or take me back. I *want* that, but I won't push for it. Right now, all I'm asking for is the chance to prove to you I see you. I just want to be a part of your life. Any way you feel comfortable. No matter how small."

She was shy when she quietly said, "Messages."

My heart leapt out of my chest. "You're okay with messages?" A small step was still *something*.

"Just the goodnight messages."

I grinned. "I've been sending those for weeks. If you keep me unblocked, you'll keep getting them."

Eden dipped her chin.

I pushed my luck a little more. "How about the occasional cute cat meme, too?"

She giggled, exaggerating an eye roll. "I *suppose* we can stretch the new rule for cute cats."

My gaze found its favourite safety net on the floor, but my cheeks burned, unused to stretching from such a wide smile. I ghosted a touch to Eden's ankle.

Messages.

It was a start, and any small step was better than it being the end.

16

He said, "There's someone else."

Zach

Paperless office, my arse.

The leather chair groaned when I leant back to survey the damage.

My desk was ground zero. The in-tray in the corner was a long-lost memory, buried under the piled ruins of contracts and client files long ago. My electronic filing system was worse. My inbox was nothing but red flags, and Sue had plastered so many yellow sticky note reminders around my monitors they resembled a kindergartener's craft project of a rather gloomy sun.

How had I ever seen this mess as a badge of success? It used to be proof I had value and was worthwhile, but these days...

These days...

Everywhere I looked was just *more work*.

Frustrated, I torpedoed my pen into a lopsided mountain of papers, an avalanche of white spilling over the desk. I couldn't concentrate. My mind twisted in a loop.

Eden... Eden... Eden.

How could I focus on soulless concrete buildings when the delicate whirl of her perfume had faded from my bathroom? There were never leftover crumbs to wipe up anymore, and nights were sleepless, never-ending, hopelessly wishing the shadows on the ceiling would blot out the nightmare I'd invented. I tortured myself for hours imagining Eden pinned under the rugby player, moaning her encouragement in his ear, urging him to "Come... *Please* come..."

I tossed my glasses on the desk and pressed my palms into overtired eyes.

Personal lives stay personal.

I needed to shake this...didn't I? My career, twelve years of my life, teetered on the brink of collapse, and Eden was with the rugby player. Sam. The internet gossip said they were 'dating.' Nothing punched me in the gut quite like seeing the woman I loved smiling for the cameras while hanging off the arm of another man. But when I peered closely at the photos of her, I *knew* that smile. Polished. Perfected. Fake. Not *my* Eden.

She hadn't blocked me again after El Diablo Cantina. Sometimes, she'd even responded to my goodnight messages or the silly meme I'd flicked her during the day. My chances of winning her back were still in the toilet, but she hadn't flushed me totally out of the picture. A one percent chance was *still* a chance. And I wouldn't waste it.

But things needed to change.

Now.

I pushed back the chair and yanked my briefcase out from under the desk. I'd already made a decision that morning. When I'd rolled out of bed, I'd chosen to take the wooden frames off the nightstand, and now, I swept aside a pile of contracts to put the photos on my desk instead.

The first was of my parents, smiling back at me, all loved up on their fortieth wedding anniversary. I let my eyes linger longer on the second photo of Eden and me at her birthday party. My lungs filled up with sunshine. I breathed a little easier with reminders of why I came to work every morning.

My shoulders squared. I picked up my pen. I got back to work.

"Knock, knock!"

Sue didn't wait for me to answer before heading into my office. A pile of folders crashed onto the desk. A wrapped sandwich dropped unceremoniously on top, but she used more care to plop the coffee in front of me. Was it lunchtime already? Time had a habit of slipping away once I got busy.

"I'll start printing off those letters as soon as I'm back from Pilates—" Sue froze. "Are you deliberately trying to piss off Chris?" She jerked a nod at the frames on my desk.

I downplayed it with a quick wave of my hand. "It's just a couple of photos."

Sue snorted. "Tell that to Riley Rodriguez."

"Who?"

"Exactly." Squinting, she bent over to peer at the photo. "Is she the little lady who chargrilled your roses?"

I couldn't help but smile. "Yeah."

"She looks...familiar." Sue's grey brows pinched together. "Wait, wait, *wait.*" She snatched the frame and studied the birthday scene. "Your Eden is *Eden Phillips?*"

"Yeah." I sounded love drunk, and I didn't even care.

"Huh. I thought she was dating Sam Simmons."

I grunted. "He wishes." Maybe. One percent.

Sue neatly arranged the frame back on the desk. "Zach, hon." Her smile was uncertain. "She's real pretty. A good sort, too, from the stories I've heard about how much time she puts in helping kids living rough. But are you sure you want to risk pissing off the boss?"

"This won't affect the promotions." My voice wavered. I didn't sound so sure.

Sue didn't look so sure, either. "You're close. People want to see you succeed this time." Her hand landed on my shoulder. Squeezed. "Think it through."

I was still staring out the window five minutes after she'd left, weighing up the options, my mind ticking through the pros and cons.

I made two more decisions.

The photos stayed.

The next decision was long overdue but probably going to bite me on the arse.

With a weary sigh, the weight of my collapsing career heavy in my bones, I pushed off the chair. It was time to see how much more I could risk in one day.

Michaela's office was on the other side of the floor, but the walk through the winding, busy corridors was still too quick. I paused to take a deep breath and then tapped my knuckles on the glass. Michaela's eyes stayed locked on her computer screen as she stuffed a bite of sandwich in her mouth. I guess I wasn't the only one who worked through lunch.

I took a tentative step inside. Michaela always wore too much perfume, and an overdose of floral clung to the walls. My empty stomach retched. I didn't take another step. It was safer to hover close to the door and keep as much distance between us as possible, anyway.

I cleared my throat.

Her eyes darted across the room, brows popping up. "Daafght a shamoth?"

I rubbed my jaw. I wasn't exactly fluent in Mouthful of Chicken Sandwich.

Michaela chewed frantically and grabbed the glass of water by her keyboard. "Sorry!" She gulped down a couple of sips and flashed me a sheepish smile. "Did I forget a settlement?"

I shook my head.

"Oh." Her hand fluttered around the desk to swipe a tissue. She dabbed at her mouth and then balled the tissue in her fist to point it at the empty chair across from the desk. "Do you want to...?"

Sit down? No way. I wasn't staying. I shook my head again, standing rigid by the door.

What do I say...?

I should've written some notes down on palm cards or planned an agenda. I wasn't good at impromptu deliveries of bad news. I stuffed my hands in my pockets, eyes dropping to examine an invisible scuff on my shoe.

"Zach, don't be nervous."

I flicked my gaze back to Michaela.

"I'll save you the angst," she said. "I accept."

"You...?" *Accept what?*

"Drinks. Dinner. Dessert." Her laugh was almost breathless. "But I know you prefer indulging in the last option at my place." She attempted a wink but didn't quite stick the landing.

No. "Ah..." *Absolutely not.*

My mind screamed at me that the conversation was already derailing, hurtling towards oblivion, so why was I standing there, saying nothing? I needed to find my voice. I needed to find my *spine*. I couldn't have the remnants of this—God—*arrangement* hanging over my head or ruin my one percent chance with Eden.

"You need to stop," I said.

Thin brows knitted together. "What?"

"You need to stop. We work together. We—"

"Fucked." She smiled innocently. "In case you forgot."

I sighed. "I wish I could."

Michaela's spine stiffened. The comment hit her harder than I realised it would. "You want me to stop showing an interest in you?"

I nodded. "There's...someone."

Michaela stared at me, not blinking. "Someone."

"Someone special."

"How special?"

"I'm in love with her." Relief painted a smile on my face so big it hurt my cheeks. It felt so right to admit my feelings for Eden aloud.

Michaela's arms folded across her chest, her fingernails drumming against the sleeve of her blouse for a few beats before she dug them into the fabric. "You're in love."

"Yes."

"Since fucking *when?*" She spat out the words, her voice pitching up with anger.

One step, and my hand was on the door. A soft click, and it was closed. No one else needed to hear this—for Michaela's sake, as much as mine. *Personal lives stay personal.*

"Michaela, you need to understand that Eden—"

"Are you fucking *kidding* me? Eden Phillips! You've only known that social-climbing bitch—"

"Watch your damn mouth."

"Zach, you met her a week ago!"

"I met her nine months ago."

"What?" Michaela ran the math, lining up the dates in her mind. "Nine months? But...that's right after..." She slumped in the oversized leather chair until she almost disappeared.

She'd figured it out. Nine months ago, I'd ended it with her. The day I'd first seen Eden at Brew HaHa.

No one existed in the world except for Eden from that point on. It hadn't mattered that it took me another month to suck up the courage to peel myself off the coffee shop wall and move to the front. My courage had earned me my first smile from Eden. A month later, I'd earned a heap of smiles and a first date. And another month after that, I'd made love to her all night long...and the next morning...and after lunch.

The only decision I regretted was hooking up with Michaela. Four times too many. Nights in Michaela's bed had left me hollow. I'd walked out of her place even emptier than when I'd walked in. A shell. Every time with Eden had fed my soul. Lifted me up. Made me want to move mountains. Corny, but true.

Michaela's eyes widened. How many of those thoughts could she see playing out on my face? Enough to make her smack her palm on the desk and stand up.

"I don't want casual," she said.

I sighed. Old ground, and I had no interest in stomping in that void of regret again.

"Zach, I never really wanted casual. Not with you." She started pushing out from behind the desk, but I raised my palm to stop her. "We're good together. We make sense."

"We make *zero* sense," I said. "Just yesterday, you felt the need to remind everyone in the boardroom I drove a bloody Toyota Corolla when we went to university. I was never ashamed of that car, but you seem hell bloody bent on making sure I am. You still want to tell me how we're great together?"

"You're going to be a partner soon."

"Oh, so suddenly I'll be good enough for you?" I laughed. "I still come from Campsie. My parents still live there. We didn't all grow up in mansions on the northern beaches, Michaela. Maybe you could bring it up at the next division meeting? Have a good laugh about it?"

"I never meant to make you feel bad."

"Like fuck you didn't."

She bristled. "How else was I supposed to get your attention?"

"Pardon?"

"How else could I get you to notice me, Zach? You've got tunnel vision. The only thing you care about is work. You don't see or hear anything else."

"You say those awful fucking things to me to get my attention?" I laughed. "Michaela, come on. You said that garbage even after you started seeing Chris."

She laughed even louder. "Newsflash—I've been screwing Chris for years, Zach."

Shock jerked me back a step.

"Yeah, that's right, golden child. *Years.*" She lifted a stubborn chin. "And what choice did I have? I started in this firm the same time you did. A few months earlier, actually, considering you chose to yack all over the floor trying to *do good* in the world first. I work the same hours you do. I settle the same deals you do on the financing side. Yet, you got promoted to senior associate *two years* before I did."

"I deserved that promotion. I worked my arse off!"

"Me too. Me *fucking* too. And until I sucked Chris Stone's dick, I was never going to get the same opportunities as you. Not just this firm but any firm."

"I'm sure that's not true—"

"Where are the women partners, Zach? Fucking *nowhere*. I used whatever advantage I had to even the odds, but when Chris put a ring on the doctor's finger, it ended my chance for promotion in this firm." Her fists landed on her hips, and she blew out a long, steadying breath, stamping down her anger. "That's not your fault. You're not like that, and I love that about you. You're going to be an excellent partner." Her smile was thin. "In and out of work, you're an excellent partner."

"Not with you."

"We're *good* together."

I shook my head. "There's no *together*. No *us*. No *me and you*." My hand curled around the door handle, and I pushed it down, ready to leave. "I'll treat you fairly, Michaela, but if you ever drag my name again because of where I came from, or if you say one damn thing about Eden, you can guarantee you won't be a partner under my watch either."

17

She said, "I want you to keep trying."

Eden

THE SIMMONS SQUAD HAD been summoned.

Their call to action? Little ol' me.

Sam's online group of devoted fangirls was in meltdown. Was Sam finally settling down? Was I 'the girlfriend?' Post after post dissected every photo the Squad dug up, and the paparazzi were only too happy to feed their hunger with fresh content.

I'd become news. An even bigger deal.

But frustration tugged my stomach into knots. I'd dated celebrities and powerful men before, always quickly shaking off the gossip, but the comments about Sam annoyed me. Too many people deemed my long list of achievements as finally being worthy because the owner of a famed penis was standing beside me in a few photos. So much for feminism.

"You will *not* believe this," Yvette said.

Groaning, I sank into the leather chair. I bet I *could* believe it. Thank God Yvette scored us this booth in the corner of the bar.

At least my misery was safe from prying eyes and photographers. I scooted up to peek over the upholstered wall blocking us from view. *Hopefully* safe.

Andie leant over to get a better look at Yvette's phone. Her beer stayed hovering at her lips. Her eyes went wide. "Ah..." She grimaced.

Was the latest photo that bad? I squeezed my eyes shut. "Just tell me," I said. "Get it over with."

Yvette's cackle peeled across the bar. "The paps got one of you leaving the laser clinic."

"Seriously?" I groaned. "Can't a girl get the hair on her vajayjay zapped without it becoming national news?"

Nope.

When Yvette flipped her phone around, I was rewarded with the headline: IT'S SILKY-SMOOTH SAILING FOR NEW COUPLE.

I groaned even louder.

Yvette patted my hand. "If it makes you feel better, there's also a nice write-up about your work with the youth centre."

That didn't make me feel better. "I don't want people taking pictures of me doing charity work," I hissed. "I don't do that for clout or likes. That's..." *Personal.*

Andie's hand landed on my shoulder. She understood.

"This is a disaster," I said miserably into my cocktail. I twirled the little umbrella stuck in the side. Nope, still miserable. I sighed.

Andie's gaze turned sideways. "Maybe it's time to stop stringing along a first-grade rugby player?" She swigged her beer.

I glared at her. "I object to the use of the term 'stringing along.'"

Still the picture of innocence, she asked, "So you're *not* just using him to make Zach jealous?"

"Of course not." Maybe a little. It wasn't the type of behaviour I'd bothered to indulge in before or felt entirely comfortable with now.

"Uh-huh."

"Since when do you care about Zach's feelings?"

Andie shrugged. "The suit's growing on me." She hid a small smile behind the foamy top of her beer. "I haven't decided yet if he's like a boil or a cute li'l freckle." She was chuckling as she took the sip.

"Wait"—Yvette's palm went up—"so despite all the dates, the movie premiere, the party where the cops got called in Longueville, you *haven't* taken the hunk for a test drive?"

"Um..."

"Sweetie, if the rumours are true, Sam knows how to bend for the curves...if you know what I mean." Yvette winked.

Andie almost choked on her beer. Who could blame her? I was close to puking myself. The idea of touching someone—sleeping with someone—other than Zach made the plantain chips I'd scoffed wage a war in my stomach.

Something was wrong with me.

The only time I'd been this hung up on a man was a misguided crush at the ripe old age of nineteen. That guy had been a dirtbag. Father 2.0. After spending thousands on therapy, it wasn't a mistake I'd made again. Opening my heart to Zach was a new kind of mistake. I didn't want therapy to make it better, but I couldn't have what I wanted. I wanted to live in an alternative timeline where Zach was a lonely monk who'd never touched or even thought about another woman until I'd waltzed into his life to corrupt him. A shiver of pleasure tingled between my legs. *That* was a fantasy I'd indulge later.

I twirled the umbrella in my cocktail. "The lack of bedroom...er, *activities* with Sam is by mutual agreement." Basically the truth.

Yvette's eyebrows shot up. "Say what now?"

"He said to me"—I hulked my shoulders and deepened my voice—"'Gotta be honest with you, babe. I wanna bang you like crazy, but we gotta wait 'til the season's over.' Or something like that." And I'd never been so relieved.

"Why is banging off the menu until the season's over?" Yvette asked, sipping her cocktail.

I shrugged. "Something about keeping enough rage simmering to knock everyone's head off on the field."

Yvette's face screwed up. "Erm, weird much?"

"Right?" I laughed.

Yvette and Andie exchanged a look.

"What?" I asked.

Andie's eyes disappeared to some invented spot of interest on the other side of the bar.

Yvette smiled sweetly. "Oh, *nothing*." Her laugh was anything but sweet. "Andie just owes me fifty bucks."

·♥·♥·♥·♥·♥·

Zach

> Do you have time to talk?

I CHEWED ON MY lower lip. This message wasn't like the other goodnight wishes from Zach.

Last night, he'd sent, "May your dreams be filled with the softest feathers and the sweetest honey." He explained in a follow-up message it was from one of his favourite books when he was a kid, *The Secret Garden*. I'd seen the movie yonks ago but didn't remember that line.

I stared at my phone. This new message wasn't anything like the one before.

We *needed* to talk. We were hopeless at communicating. Zach had shut me out, and I certainly couldn't pretend I was perfect—I'd shut him out, too. There was so much he didn't know about my past. There was also still a part of me that hoped Zach could do something big enough—some grand gesture—to make the past few months hurt less. That part of me knew we needed to learn how to talk to each other. A message like 'time to talk' was rarely a simple conversation, but when had we ever done things the easy way?

I hit the button to video chat.

One beat.

Two.

Panic shot through me. Zach wasn't answering. Was he giving up?

I breathed again when Zach's face filled the screen. He waved, then propped his chin in his hand, dark circles hanging from his eyes. I didn't have to ask where he was. One disastrous visit had been enough to memorise every detail of his office, including the row of fancy certificates on the wall behind him.

I glanced at the time. Past midnight. And Zach was still at work?

I scuttled my mind back to all the hours I'd put into opening my first salon. Double shifts to save up the down payment. Painting the walls on the weekends. Scavenging antique mirrors and dinged wooden furniture from garage sales. Bringing Andie plenty of snacks and beers because she had the talent to refurbish all my bargains. Having support was the only reason I'd made it. I understood the grind to achieve your dreams, but was Zach's promotion worth the exhaustion in his eyes?

"Hey there," I said gently.

"Hey." Even his smile was tired. "I wasn't expecting a video call."

"It's so much nicer to chat face to face."

"Says the extrovert."

"Too much?"

He shook his head. "I want to see you. Your hair." His finger swirled around the screen. "It's a blowout, right?"

"Yeah! You know some styling?"

"Yvette was in her element when I helped at your salon."

I bounced one of the curled waves. "She styled this."

"I was instructed an acceptable response is an appreciative but not fake 'Ooh,' but...can I tell you...you look beautiful?"

My cheeks heated. "Also an acceptable response."

Zach smiled.

"So..." I twisted a wave of hair into a tight ringlet around my finger. "What did you want to talk about?"

"Oh. I, um..." A deep breath rose in his chest. "I saw the photos. Of, you know...you and..." He waved a hand as if that filled in the rest of the details.

He was talking about Sam.

"You stalking me on the internet?" My tone was teasing, but the question was genuine. I wanted him to be interested in what I was doing. I twisted the ringlet tighter around my finger.

"No, not exactly." He winced. "I did sorta create an account to follow your salon."

A fact I'd already known. I concealed the smile threatening to burst across my face. The glasses avatar of MisterPaigeTurner had stood out when it popped up in my notifications. His confession was sweet, though.

"I can't categorically promise my mum isn't stalking you." Zach chuckled. "She was the one who sent me a photo of you and Sam having dinner together, along with many outraged texts demanding to know what I planned to do about it."

"Yeah? And what do you plan to do about it?"

"Eden, I..." He dragged a hand down his face. Paused. Took a big breath. He was planning to say something serious. "I don't want to give up on us. I want to keep fighting to prove I'm the right man for you."

"I sense a *but* coming."

"If you're serious about this guy—I dunno—it doesn't feel right for me to keep bothering you. Am I crossing a line? Do you want me to stop trying?"

Everything suddenly felt too real. I turned away from the screen to examine the pearly polish on my nails for any tiny fault.

Was that what I wanted?

I trusted Zach to respect the boundary if I scratched that line between us. If I told him once and for all there was no chance, he'd step back. He'd be gone. Possibly...forever. I blinked away the prickle of emotion stinging my eyes.

"No," I whispered. "I don't want you to stop trying."

When I was brave enough to lift my gaze, Zach was waiting. Water swam in the corner of his crinkled brown eyes, and he rubbed the tip of his nose, relief written all over him.

"Then I won't," he said.

·♥·♥·♥·♥·♥·

For once, I planned to handle my personal life with maturity instead of chaos.

Okay.

Big breath.

Okay.

I headed for the salon, dashing down the narrow laneway, sensible loafers thunking on the cobblestones, my phone pressed to my ear.

The first hitch in my mature plan: Sam wasn't picking up.

Not entirely unexpected at 8:00 a.m. Even less surprising after Yvette had sent me a photo of him on the dance floor—allegedly last night—surrounded by a group of grinning women. Righto. Sam was a great guy. Fun. Chill. So, I wouldn't be on his bang roster when the season ended. Who cared? But it was time to end the shenanigans once and for all.

Andie explained to me there was a certain etiquette for breakups. Apparently, I'd 'dated' Sam too long for my preferred option—ghosting—and we hadn't kissed, so he wasn't getting the obligatory breakup over coffee. He'd earned himself the minimum of a heartfelt text breakup. I was going one better. A call. We'd have a pleasant chat over the phone.

I rehearsed it again as I turned the last corner for work.

"Thank you for including me in your life. I've had a lot of fun getting to know you, and I think you're a cool guy. But I've had to be honest with myself about what I want for my future, and I think—I think—" I groaned. Maturity was overrated. This sucked. "I think I'm stupidly head over heels for another man," I mumbled.

Saying those words out loud was a mistake.

The universe hadn't just heard me but decided to hand-deliver the man twisting me into knots right to the doorstep of my salon.

Zach was the poster child for swanky lawyers in his finely tailored suit, but I did a double take at the dainty lunch bag clutched in his big hand. Colourful cartoon cats dotted a dusky pink background. Cute as a button, but not quite vibing with the rest of his corporate wear.

He nodded a shy smile my way. "Good morning, Eden."

If the universe wanted to test me, bring it on. I swallowed my nerves and lifted my chin to give him a playful smile. "Hey, stranger."

"It's Wednesday."

I arched an eyebrow. Zach was acting even more socially awkward than usual. "Yeah?"

His face brightened. "This is for you." He thrust the bag at me. "I made you lunch. I might have gone a bit overboard, but everything in there is great if you're on the go. I know getting a proper break can be hard for you."

Almost giddy because my heart was fluttering so fast, I lifted the bag from Zach's outstretched fingers. The rip of the Velcro made me cringe when I peeled open the top to peek inside. A neat stack of clear containers was filled with all kinds of yummies—strawberries, spongy chocolate cake, finger sandwiches with what I hoped wasn't tuna but probably was, and a quaint but wonky home-baked quiche. Curse him. I adored everything he'd packed in the kitty cat lunch bag. I loved that he'd taken so much time to make me something special.

"This is thoughtful of you." I fought to keep the emotion from my voice. "Thank you, Zach."

He stuffed his hands in his pockets, dropping his chin so I wouldn't see the blush forming around his smile. "I also wanted to see if you're free on Friday night."

I hummed thoughtfully. "Friday?" Where was he going with this? Should I keep him guessing?

"Maybe we could have dinner together," he said. "Andie mentioned a new restaurant you liked the other day. The French place. I can book a table."

My heart skipped a beat. The two of us sharing French food over candlelight was a dream, but I couldn't look too eager. "I think I might have something on with Sam…"

"O-Oh."

"I mean, I'd have to check…"

"Yeah." Zach forced a smile. "Sure." His head snapped around at the sound of footsteps. "Speak of the lucky devil," he muttered.

What?

I turned. Sam swaggered up the laneway, his sweatpants and T-shirt stretched taut over bulky muscle and his cropped hair glistening with sweat. He'd lost the winking grin now his black eye was only a smudge, but he was still all smiles.

What the hell is he doing here? Had he messaged…?

I quickly fumbled my phone out of my bag.

Oh no.

I slapped my palm against my forehead. My phone recorded a connected call—two minutes and twenty-three seconds of me rehearsing a breakup speech for a man I was technically maybe not even really seeing.

Zach stepped in front of me. "I hope you meant what you said last night." His chest lifted, his nostrils flared on a big breath in, and he nodded like he'd made some kind of decision.

"Hey, crew!" Sam waved.

"Mate, mind if we step over there?" Zach said, jerking his head away from the salon. "We need to have a word."

Sam's eyebrows shot up. "Yeah. Sure, man," he said. "If this is about last night..."

Head down, he lumbered after the lawyer, which was...weird. Maybe Zach's words were Bro Code for something like, "We have a problem here."

The two men huddled a few steps from the salon, face to face, tense words passing between them. Sam stood a head taller, but Zach squared his shoulders, braced his hands on the hips of his expensive trousers, and lifted his chin. Powerful. Completely in control. Absolutely no fear.

"What on earth..." I muttered to myself.

Sam's head cocked to the side. A confused look darted in my direction but transformed into a smile. As the conversation went on, Zach's eyes slid to me. He ignored Sam throwing his head back, laughing, and he didn't acknowledge the friendly slap on his shoulder or the wave goodbye. Zach's eyes never shifted away from me.

I nibbled nervously on my bottom lip.

I was in big trouble.

Zach beckoned me with a short, sharp wave. I walked over to him, my legs wobbling almost as much as my smile.

"So." He drawled the sound so casually, but his eyes were razor thin. "Forget to mention something?"

"Um." I played with the Velcro catch of my cute new lunch bag. "No?"

"Sam said he was here to explain the photos of him dancing with some girls. Ring any bells?"

"Not even a ding-a-ling-ling."

"He thought maybe that's why you broke up with him. I suppose you forgot to mention that part, huh?"

"Must have slipped my mind."

"What else slipped your mind, I wonder?" Zach cocked his head, a slight tug to the corner of his lips. "Perhaps how you told him you're head over heels for another man?"

"M-Maybe."

"Maybe." He grunted. "You've had your fun making me jealous, Denny Dee. This isn't a game I want to play all the time, okay? I know you're beautiful. I've always known I'm not your only option."

He was right. I had plenty of options to be lonely, dance to the same old tune, and chase chaos. I hiked up my big-girl pants. "Zach, I'm sorry—"

He raised his palm to stop me. He wasn't fishing for an apology. He wanted us to be honest with each other—and he was already light-years ahead of me.

"I'd like to renegotiate our terms," Zach said.

Smirking, I flipped my hair off my shoulder. "You going all bossy lawyer on me?" My stomach fluttered. Now, *that* was a sexy thought. Even sexier than Zach, the uncorrupted monk.

"The. Bossiest." A playfulness bounced in his eye I wasn't sure I'd seen before. "If it's you and me, it's *just* you and me, okay? No more rugby players."

I blasted him with my best finger guns as confirmation.

"No other men you or Yvette dream up to torture me either, agreed?"

"Agreed. Anything else?"

"Yes." He beckoned me with his finger. "Come here."

I glanced left, then right, and took a hesitant step.

"Closer, little schemer."

A shaky smile curved my lips, and I took another step.

"Turn around."

I slowly rotated on the spot. "Why do—"

A firm but gentle smack landed on my booty. I squealed, and with my brows speared down, I snapped a furious look at him over my shoulder.

He grinned. "Now, we're even."

18

He said, "I'd give anything to kiss you."

Zach

The suit was too much.

I glanced around the restaurant. The intimate space was crammed to the ceiling, people talking over the jazz floating in the background, a melting pot of different styles, but a couple of guys were suited up. Okay, I wasn't overdressed, but I could take it down a notch or two. Keep it more casual. Maybe that would help with the nerves.

Who was I kidding?

Nothing was going to help with the nerves.

I shucked my jacket, yanked down my tie, and folded my sleeves to my elbows. I fumbled open another button on my shirt, and another, and attempted to lounge back in the chair, my ankle propped on my knee. Better. *So* casual.

But my calm veneer vanished when I spotted Eden at the door. I jumped to my feet, bumping the table, water sloshing out of the glass and snaking along the wood until I sopped up the mess with a napkin.

Eden arrived in front of me with a raised eyebrow.

I laughed nervously, rubbing the back of my neck. "H-Hi." I cringed even as I said it. I was *definitely* at risk of screwing up again if that greeting was the best I had to offer.

"At ease, soldier." Eden's huge smile eased my nerves…just a bit.

I pulled out her chair and hesitated, stuck on what to do next. Usually, I'd kiss her cheek, but I pulled myself back. We weren't up to kisses yet. This was our first official date—no, *re-date*. We weren't at the beginning. There was even more pressure now—I knew what I was risking if I screwed up.

I settled on saying, "You look crazy beautiful tonight."

Eden waved away my compliment. "Oh, this old thing." The edge to her laugh seemed nervous. She sat across from me, smoothing her palms down her thighs to erase the wrinkles in her pink wool dress. I tried to smile at her, but she stared back, not even blinking.

"Should I not have said that?" I touched my hand to her knee under the table.

Eden almost jumped out of her seat. "N-No. It's, um, *nice*." Her eyes lingered on my shirt, her tongue darting out over her lips as her gaze dropped lower.

I touched the spot on the buttons she seemed stuck on and glanced down. Was there a stain, or…?

She grabbed the menu and flicked through the pages. "Did you come from work?"

"Straight out of a settlement and into a taxi," I said. "What about you?"

She shook her head. "I helped out at the youth centre tonight."

"The one in Belmore?"

"Yeah, you know it?"

"Sure. I grew up around there. I'm from Campsie, remember? My parents still live there." I skimmed the menu. French. I couldn't read a damn word. "I didn't know you volunteered at the centre until a couple of weeks ago when Mum saw some pics of you. You, um...never mentioned it."

Eden's eyes only flitted off the menu for a second. "It's not something I do to brag about. It's incredibly personal to me."

What the hell? We'd *lived* together. "Obviously." My tone was sharper than it needed to be. I flipped through the menu, not even reading it, just needing the distraction.

"I—" Eden cleared her throat. "I help there because I feel it's important to give back to the community that helped me. I didn't grow up like you, Zach."

"Poor?" That was how I grew up.

"It doesn't matter what suburb you live in. No one's poor when they have a family and a proper home."

"You didn't have that?"

"I lived in a house with a man who called himself my father. He didn't act like one, except when he got the belt out to teach me a lesson or two in manners." She spoke without any emotion and kept her eyes trained on the menu. "I needed a lot of lessons."

My heart broke. My family was my haven. They were the people I could count on when I couldn't rely on anyone else. The people who'd never hurt me. I couldn't imagine what Eden went through growing up if she didn't have the same safe space to call home. The way she talked about the abuse was so matter-of-fact. Pain barrelled into my lungs and knocked the breath out of me, but I couldn't just sit there and say—or do—nothing.

The wooden chair scraped on the floor when I jostled it to sit closer to her. I wanted to hold her. Was I allowed to do that yet? Probably not. Instead, I put my hand back on her knee.

"I'm so sorry that happened to you." My words seemed meaningless years later. "You...left?"

She nodded. Her fingers curled over my hand, and she squeezed until I thought they might snap off. "I ran away. Andie came too. She's always right behind." Eden forced a sad smile. "We lived rough for a couple of years, jumping between different share houses and hostels. It was hard to scrape money together during our apprenticeships, but at least we were living on our own terms. No belts for me. No bigotry for Andie." She squeezed my hand even tighter. "Anywhere was better than where we came from."

There had been moments in my life when I'd wanted to lash out, punch a wall, yell, but this was the first time the swirl of so many emotions had paralysed me. That man. Some father. Why hadn't Eden told me? Another emotion crammed in the fractured gaps. *Shame.* She hadn't told me because I'd never listened to the small stuff. A truth like this needed to be heard, never ignored. She hadn't trusted me...until now.

I dropped my voice to a low whisper. "Is that why you didn't unpack your boxes? You thought I'd be like your father?"

Tortured eyes lifted to meet mine.

"Is he why you're too scared to turn all the lights off?"

Eden's head bobbed up and down, and her chin wobbled.

"Come here, Denny Dee."

I reached for her, but she was already scrambling off her chair, crawling into my lap, and burying her face in my shirt. I wrapped my arms around her.

"I'm never going to be the reason you're afraid like that," I said, trying my hardest to keep my voice low and comforting. "I know I hurt you. I know one day I'm going to slip up, say something dumb, do something stupid 'cause no one's perfect, but I'll never hurt you. Not like that."

"I know." Her sniffle was muffled.

"Thank you for telling me."

This woman, she was something else. I hated that Eden had lived through hell, but I was beyond proud of her for surviving. Strong in a way I never could be. Perfect in her imperfection. Familiar words threatened to tumble out of my mouth again.

I love you.

Now wasn't the right time. That would put too much pressure on Eden when she was only just learning to trust me again. We were only minutes into our first re-date. Shit, and we were going off like a firecracker, too.

I glanced around the restaurant. More than one couple's eyes quickly dipped back to their dinner plates when I looked up.

"How do you feel about sticking around?" I asked.

Eden's head lifted off my chest, her smile sheepish. "Wanna grab burgers instead?"

·❤·❤·❤·❤·❤·

"So," I said, "for our second re-date—"

Eden's eyebrows popped up. "Re-date?" She dipped a couple of fries in ketchup and wolfed them down.

"Yeah, that's what I'm calling my second chance to woo you." I sipped my shake. "It's in the terms of our agreement."

"Well, if it's part of the *agreement,* please proceed, your grace."

"Thank you. As I was saying, for our second official re-date, I have somewhere a little less, um, well, actually a *lot* less fun in mind."

"Intriguing...continue."

"I wanted to ask you if you'd go to this boring charity art gallery work thing as my official date. Super official. Name stickers and everything."

"Boring charity art gallery work thing?" Eden laughed.

I groaned. "You know I hate networking stuff."

"Try harder to sell it to me before I say yes."

"Exclusive, strictly black tie so you can get all frocked up, a quartet, French food that we'll actually stick around to eat this time, and an open bar where they do custom martinis—or so I'm told."

"Other than mingling with all those boring suits again, it sounds like it might be fun."

"Fun isn't the word I'd use. Pretentious? Unbearable?" I grunted. "But I'd love for you to be there experiencing hell with me."

Eden's gaze dropped to where her burger sat untouched on the tray. "Will she be there?"

"If you mean Michaela..." And of course she did. "You don't have to worry. She won't be there. My boss told her she'd be sitting this one out."

"Convenient."

"For Chris, yeah, it was. I think he's trying to avoid any awkward conversations between his fiancée and his ex-girlfriend about the dubious timing around their respective relationships."

Eden's eyebrows rose with interest. "Sounds like quite the office scandal."

I lifted a shoulder. "None of my business. The less I know about those two, the better."

"Because you still have feelings—"

"Because I have *zero* feelings for Michaela, and I'd rather stay on my boss's good side by avoiding all the damn drama she's trying to stir up." My stomach roiled, and I pushed my shake away. "I've got some seriously conflicted feelings about how a man I respect has cheated on his fiancée. Everyone else just brushes it off like a joke—Michaela included." I balled my napkin and pitched it onto the tray.

"Hey." Eden reached for my hand. *"Hey.* I'm sorry."

"Don't be. We need to talk about these things, and after what's happened, you have every right to ask." I dragged a hand through my hair. "The situation with Chris and Michaela is just something I struggle with, you know?"

"You admire your boss?"

"He's almost like an older brother to me. He's been there for me for my entire career, and he's a damn good lawyer, but..."

She squeezed my hand. "Maybe not a good person?"

"Maybe." And that knowledge sat in the pit of my stomach like a boulder. "For what it's worth, I told Michaela about you. I told her how I feel about you and how important you are to me."

"And what did she say?"

"Honestly? She lost her shit, and I didn't care. Not one bit. Michaela was never important. I can't change the fact she works in the same office, but I'm limiting my contact with her and keeping it strictly professional. I swear to you, Eden."

"Okay."

That was all she said. *Okay.* Didn't she believe me? Uneasy, I took a few bites of my burger, watching as she chewed, thinking over whatever was circling around in her head.

"When is your boring work charity art gallery thing?" Eden asked.

"Next Friday night."

"Perfect! I've got enough time to source an awesome dress to rent." She grinned, already scheming. "I'm thinking niche Australian designer. Something chic. Black. Definitely silk—"

"Let me buy you a dress."

She rolled her eyes. "I don't need you to buy me a dress."

"I *want* to. It's okay if you can't afford—"

"Zach. *Seriously.* You've seen my salon, right? There's no mortgage on my space. I own it."

"Then why are you out there renting dresses?"

She lifted a shoulder. "I love designer clothes, but I'm not wasting three grand on something I'll only wear once." She grinned and dipped some more fries in the sauce. "Frugally chic, Yvette calls it." She happily munched away.

I smiled and dodged the hand she swatted at me when I stole one of her fries. "You like to keep people guessing, huh?"

"Most of the time." She frowned. "Not you, though. I should've been more honest with you about...me...all my *mess*. I was scared if you knew you'd—" She clamped her mouth shut.

I scooted closer to her in the booth and slipped my arm around her shoulders. "Will you tell me? Whisper it if you want to."

The returning glance was dubious, but Eden took a big breath. "I was afraid...you'd think...I'm too much." She admitted it so quietly I strained closer to make sure I didn't miss any words. "I was afraid if you saw who I truly am, you wouldn't want me anymore."

That took some serious courage to admit. "There's never been a second I didn't want you," I reassured her. "The woman I see is confident and caring and maybe, yeah, sometimes a little schemer who keeps me on my toes, but Eden... I've seen hints that you were holding something back from the start. It never made me want to walk away. I only ever wanted to bring you in even closer. I'm not always good at doing that, though. I've got a lot to learn about relationships."

Eden snorted. "At least you've done this before."

"A relationship? No, not really. I'm selective about who I sleep with, and I've had a couple of longer-term girlfriends, I guess, but I've never had what we have with anyone else. I've never lived with anyone before. This is all new to me, too. That's why I can be so confident I'll do something stupid to stuff this up again." I rested my chin on her shoulder and absently twirled a wisp of her hair to keep my lips off her cheek. "I'm glad we talked tonight."

She started nodding, but her bright smile fell away.

"What happened then?" I nudged my nose into the crook of her neck. "Already dreaming up an excuse to get out of the boring work charity art gallery thing for our second re-date?"

I wouldn't blame her. If Chris hadn't told me I had to go, it certainly wouldn't be how I chose to spend my Friday night.

"You really don't want to see me again for a whole week?"

A crack splintered through my chest. "I was trying not to be too pushy," I admitted softly. "I want to see you every day."

Every day. Every night. I wanted to bundle Eden up, park her on my lap, and never let her go. I wanted to curve my hand around her big belly when our baby was in there. I wanted to hold her hand when we watched our grandkids playing in our backyard.

I didn't want much—only *everything*.

Eden's eyes skimmed my face. "Zach." She caught her bottom lip with her teeth. "Tell me what you're thinking."

Cautiously, my finger explored the chunky knit cables crisscrossing her sleeves, gliding over the ridges, wondering how honest I should be. I was standing with my toes curled around the edge of the cliff. Vulnerable. Eden was trying so hard. When she'd already admitted her fears, hurtling over the edge, the least I could do was leap after her.

"I was thinking how much I want to see your face every day of my life," I said.

Her head swivelled just enough to show me the smile curving her lips. The pretty sight was enough to fuel my thumping heart with more courage. I scooped more of the wisps of hair springing from her ponytail behind her ear.

"Now," I whispered, "I'm thinking I'm the luckiest bastard in the world to even have a chance of being yours again."

"You want to be mine?" Eden's breath was coming quicker.

"Only yours." I lowered my hand to the curve of her hip, letting it sink into the fluff of pink wool. A new hope urged me to dig my fingers in deeper. "And now..."

"Y-Yeah?"

I leant close enough to smell the strawberry shake hinted on her breath. "I'm thinking I'd give almost anything for you to say I can kiss you." But not her. I'd never give her up.

"You can," she whispered.

I scanned the diner from the corner of my eye. "Here?" A teenager was gaming on his laptop in the booth behind us. Two guys at the counter were having a heated discussion about interest rates. Not much of a venue for a sexy kiss.

I didn't imagine Eden leaning into my grip. "Even a re-date needs a first kiss, right?" She whispered the words huskily along my neck.

Was I dreaming? After everything I'd done, after the torture of the last few months, was this happening?

The tip of my nose bumped hers. I waited for her to change her mind, to push me away, but she didn't. I pressed my lips to her jaw.

Eden let out a huff of frustration. "You know I like *proper* kisses."

"Yeah," I said, dusting another kiss on her cheek.

"So, what are you waiting for?"

"You."

A quick kiss landed on my chin. "Your turn."

I smiled. "Oh, is it? You want something like"—I brushed my lips over hers—"that? Or..."

I breathed through the nerves curling from my toes before sealing my mouth over hers in a soft, sensual kiss. My fingertips pressed into her neck, thumb soothing her cheek, coaxing her closer, tempting her sweet mouth open to slip my tongue in to savour her even more.

Eden responded with as good as she got. She was juicy watermelon lip gloss and urgency. Her fingers clung to my shirt, and as she kissed me back, she pressed the pink wool cables of her dress into my cotton shirt like she wanted to brand the pattern into my skin, barely letting me catch my breath.

I eased back. A smile pinched my cheeks, and laughter rumbled in my chest. I just felt so…so…happy.

"Wow," I said.

"Old people are so gross," the kid behind us muttered.

Eden giggled and buried her face in my neck. "Thank you for tonight," she whispered. "Even with the venue change and all the *messy*, I had a great time."

"Me too, Denny Dee."

And to prove it, I kissed her again.

19

She said, "You can talk to me."

Eden

APARTMENT 15C LOOMED AT the end of the corridor.

The carpet smothered the comforting clickety-click of my heels, so it was my heart pounding the beat as I dragged my feet to the door. I glanced at my phone to read Zach's message for the tenth time.

Zach

> How about a night in? I'll pamper you like a princess. We can get to know each other again. No pressure.

Except there *was* pressure.

Not from Zach. He was a gentleman. He only popped a kiss on my cheek after whispering to ask for my permission, and even though I didn't always say yes, he never grumbled, and it only made the next kiss all the sweeter. But tonight wasn't neutral territory. We weren't meeting at a bar or treading the familiar boards of the coffee shop. The door at the end of the corridor was Zach's apartment. His bed was inside, and I'd tumbled in his immaculately tucked Egyptian cotton sheets enough times to know it was worth diving back in.

My phone buzzed.

What was the point of checking? I knew it was Andie giving more of the 'helpful' advice she'd lumped on me at brunch about not rushing things.

I frowned at the screen.

Andie

> Keep your vulva out of the conversation tonight.

> Talking solves problems, not sexual intercourse.

I glared at my phone before stuffing it back in my bag and kept walking. Andie was trying to help. She was. And she wasn't...wrong. I made no secret about enjoying sex. A man hammering between my thighs as he yanked my hair and made me beg to come—heaven. But I'd bawled my way through enough therapy sessions to confront the fact there were times I used sex to avoid real intimacy.

Pound my pussy but stay the fuck out of my heart. Use me tonight because your use-by date is tomorrow. I decided. I held the power.

Not with Zach.

Sex with him had always been different. Our first weekend in bed together had been heaven, but not the kind fuelled by the short-lived lust of chasing my orgasm. My shy sweetheart was an unexpected surprise. He was intense. Insatiable. He had the naughtiest little potty mouth when he fully let go, but he would kiss me so very softly as the rest of him did unspeakable things.

When Zach was in control, sex was an intoxicating mix of rough but tender.

I was in trouble.

I gulped in a deep breath and raised my hand to knock, but the door swung open before my knuckles hit the wood.

There was no sign of Zach's thoughtful scowl. His warmth hit me in two waves—the hug sweeping me off my feet and the kiss on my forehead. I snuck my nose into the soft cotton of his T-shirt and sniffed the familiar soap and cologne. My heart fluttered. I'd missed his smell on my pillow.

"You're here." He murmured the words almost in disbelief.

"I believe you promised to pamper me like a princess," I teased.

"Oh, I'm going to pamper the pants right off you." The skin under Zach's glasses flushed a deep pink. "I—I didn't mean it like...*you know.*"

Laughing, I kicked off my shoes and watched with amusement when Zach neatly lined them up beside his. I followed him inside.

Speaking of pants coming off...

I snuck a peek at Zach. Jeans and a simple striped T-shirt. Eh. Nothing special. But hot damn, even if he were wearing a sack, he'd be a fine example of a man. He had a presence, a quiet but powerful masculinity. Those shoulders. I sighed. And that booty...

"Eden." A scowl turned over Zach's shoulder. "Stop looking at my butt." He had the nerve to wink.

"As if I was." The squeak in my voice betrayed me. "Stop being so obsessed with yourself."

My gaze drifted around the apartment. I'd never missed this place. The bitter memories of being on my own—wondering where Zach was—still stained the sterile white walls. A shudder skated over my skin, but I shook off the feeling. I closed my eyes, focusing on our fresh start and all the delicious smells floating in the kitchen.

"Bread...and herbs...and something sweet in the oven," I murmured. "Maybe a hint of coffee."

Zach laughed. "You've basically guessed my whole menu." When I popped my eyes open, he was leaning over the marble countertop, watching me with a smile as he tumbled a pile of tomatoes onto his chopping board. "I'm cooking Italian."

"That's my favourite!" I stowed my bag and wandered over, searching for an apron, hovering over his board, ready to help. "What can I do?"

"I'm supposed to be pampering you, remember?" He pointed at the uncorked bottle of white wine—the bougie kind I liked—and the empty glass waiting on the edge of the kitchen counter. "For you. Take a seat and talk to me about your day. I'll keep going with this."

I scooted my li'l booty onto the stool. Pouring the wine, I paused for a moment, letting a familiar feeling sink into my bones. This was nice. Cosy. Zach and I had shared a few dinners like this in our early days. I'd cooked. He'd cooked. We'd talked about nothing much important, and dinner had often gotten singed around the edges when we'd been distracted by an overheated kissing session. A flicker of warmth tinged my cheeks. Was that how tonight would end?

Ping.

I clunked down the wine bottle, my eyes shifting to where Zach had tossed his phone on the counter.

He wasn't interested in the slightest. He ignored it, focusing on the ingredients in front of him. "So, what did you get up to today?" His knife hit the board in smooth, steady strokes.

"Not much," I said. "Sometimes, you need a lazy Saturday. We opted for brunch and pedicures."

"Cute." His eyebrow lifted. "Even Andie?"

"*Especially* Andie. Don't let her tomboy aesthetic fool you. In some ways, she's as high-maintenance as the rest of us. What'd you get up to?"

Ping.

Zach ignored the new message and kept chopping. "Went into the office."

"Seriously?"

"I'm behind on a few files." The smile he attempted was strained. "My boss isn't exactly happy about it." He couldn't turn away quick enough to avoid the rest of that conversation. He fussed with the knobs on the oven instead.

Ping.

What the f—

Ping.

Paranoia clawed at my skin. I needed to trust Zach to make our relationship work, but my fingers itched to snatch the phone.

Zach skewered a toothpick into whatever he was baking in the oven. "Dee, can you please see who's ruining our night?" he asked absently.

"Oh, um..." A nervous laugh. "I respect your privacy." A total lie. I snuck another sideways look at his phone. I'd kill to know who kept messaging him.

He snorted. "The passcode is eight five three zero. I'm giving you full authority to tell whoever it is to buzz off."

I picked up the phone, the thump of adrenaline in my veins making my hand shake. I took a deep breath. Typed in the passcode. Opened the messages. Let my beady little eyes read all the terrible words. Except...

My smile stretched wider the more I read. The never-ending stream of messages was from Zach's mum.

Mum

> Is Eden there yet?

> Did you choose something nice to wear?

> Don't serve my future daughter-in-law an underbaked loaf of bread.

> Remember, no soggy bottoms!

"All good?" Zach's hands were stuffed in white oven mitts, and he held a bread pan. Before I could even get through a full nod, a new message popped up.

Mum

> Don't let that no-neck rugby goon get his baguette in her oven before you do!

My eyes bulged. Shock burst the laughter out of me. Zach's eyebrow rose.

"Your"—I swiped a tear from my lashes—"mum."

His face turned whiter than the oven mitts. "Oh, God." The pan clattered onto the stovetop, and he scrambled to strip off the mitts before racing to my side and grabbing the phone. His eyes darted over the screen. "No." His skin turned scarlet. "Oh *no*. Y-You read this?"

"Every last word."

"So, ah—" Embarrassed, he cleared his throat and forced a smile. "Yeah, that's Mum for you." He messed around with the buttons on his phone. "Okay, the phone's off. I vote we forget any of that ever happened."

"Sorry, no can do. I need to report back to Maree about the status of the soggy bottom. However"—I grinned—"I could be swayed to spare her the details of where your baguette does—or does not—end up by the end of this evening."

Zach grunted. "I appreciate your generosity. What are your terms?"

I nodded at the discarded bread pan. "What type of bread did you make?"

"Sourdough."

If he hadn't ducked his head so quickly, he would've seen the enormous smile overtaking my face.

"That's my favourite," I said.

He nodded. He knew. He wanted to prove things would be different this time. It was working. My heart was diving in loop-de-loops, giddy, ready to pack up my new apartment and move right back in with him. Too bad the cynical side of me wasn't convinced. It was easy enough for Zach to spoil me with a nice meal. The greater challenge for him—both of us, really—was how we handled when life smashed us with bigger issues than a few awkward messages or choosing what bread to bake.

I bumped his shoulder with mine. "Consider me swayed."

Zach beamed a smile. His cheeks still a dark pink, he directed his shyness into sliding the glass of wine along the countertop to me and returning to his salad prep. Off he went, chopping his tomatoes, dicing the onion, and moving on to a piece of celery. I tipped back a sip of wine and peeked at him over the rim of the glass. The sweet tingle did nothing compared to the zing shooting through me as I drooled over Zach's muscular forearm at work. I reached out and traced my fingertip along the corded muscle. It wasn't my fault. His sexy forearm *begged* me to do it.

Zach sucked in a sharp breath. The knife paused, and a cautious glance turned from the corner of his eye.

Gorgeous.

My tongue darted over my bottom lip as I let my hand wander a little higher to his bicep. "It's a crime you were born so sexy."

His laugh was nervous. "I wasn't born looking like this."

"No?"

He shook his head. "I shot up like a bean sprout. I don't think I had a pinch of fat on me until I was at least twenty...despite my mother's best efforts to fill me out."

"Where'd you get all these yummy muscles then?"

"The same way everyone else does." He tried to steady his breathing as my finger explored all the pretty veins that patterned his skin. "Working out."

Huh? "You go to the gym?" Since when? "Not just for herb deliveries?"

Zach laughed. "I go a couple of times a week on my lunch break. Well...*used* to. Work has been nuts lately, so I've skipped most of my sessions. I should try getting back in the habit. Maybe I will after the announcement."

"You lift weights?"

He snorted. That was a no. "Boxing, mostly. Punching something helps blow off some of the frustration when there's drama around the office." His smile pinched. "It's just a dumb thing the therapist recommended."

"You..." A rock lodged in my throat. *Therapist?* This was news. Big news. I'd shared so much with him, spilt my guts, and he hadn't said a word. "You see a therapist?"

The knife clattered to the chopping board. Zach's head bowed, his hand plunging into his hair.

"Hey. It's okay." I wrapped my arm around his waist and encouraged him to snuggle closer. "You can talk to me."

"I don't see the therapist anymore," he said. "It was a few years ago. I, um... I tried to..." His body slumped into me, his weight pressing me into the counter. "Chris made me see someone after Mum got sick."

I never thought much about my mother. Memories of her were misty. Maybe a smile or the faint smell of a freshly baked cake, but I could have imagined that because the one photo I'd seen had been the two of us on my second birthday. But I knew what it was like to lose my mother. I understood the gut punch that left you hollow. I knew why Zach took those big breaths to fill up the space gnawing inside him. I knew.

"Zach, I'm so sorry."

"It's hard to talk about. I can think about it." He tapped his temple. "But if I try to make the words come out, it—it doesn't always—"

"Shh." I feathered my fingers into his hair, gently stroking his head, my own pulse calming as some of the tension seeped from his muscles. "You don't need to say more. Your mum's okay now, right?"

He nodded. "She's in remission."

Cancer. Holy hell. "Are *you* okay?"

"You're here. I'm okay."

I was there, but what should I do to *show* him I was there in moments like this? The right words, the right actions—I had no idea what they were. No one had taught me. I did the only thing I knew. Falling back into old habits, I arched on my tiptoes to capture his lips. Short and sweet kisses melted into long and luxurious.

Zach knew the steps to our old dance, too.

Ragged, uneven breaths jumped in his chest. He pulled back. Dark eyes intense, mouth not quite smiling, he snagged the belt of my dress and tugged me across the room. Strong arms lifted me. Goosebumps prickled my skin when cold wood stuck to my thighs as I awkwardly bumped onto the dining table.

"Eden." A stubbly cheek pressed to mine. "Let me make you feel good." His big palm crept up my thigh. Stopped. Squeezed.

A promise, if I said yes.

I wanted to, but...

Should I?

20

She said, "You chose her."

Eden

I shouldn't have said yes.

I did anyway.

Conflicted, my heart twisting in my chest but the rest of my body needing—demanding—Zach to smother all my senses until there was nothing in the world except him, I captured his mouth in another kiss.

My hands slipped under his T-shirt. I was desperate to feel every bit of his skin that my greedy fingers could find—the warm, rugged ridges of his back, his chest, the patch of crinkly hair on his abdomen leading down... I sighed. Yeah, I knew where that led, and I wanted my hands there, too. I yanked at his belt.

"Eden, that's not—" He tore his lips off mine. "Slow down."

"Do you really want that?" I whispered the question as I rocked my hips, rough denim rubbing against delicate lace.

Zach groaned into my neck. Tension coiled tight in his muscles, his back rigid, but he didn't want to slow down. He jerked me closer, a possessive hand weaving into my hair, fingertips pressing into my neck. No, slowing down wasn't what he wanted at all. A shiver rippled down my spine, the world blurring with the graze of his teeth down sensitive skin and every insistent squeeze of his hand on my thigh. But the sensation muddled. Memories collided from all directions.

My hand went limp on his belt. I screwed my eyes closed. No, it wasn't just my eyes that shut. My entire body shut down. The words I'd always begged him to whisper when we'd replayed my favourite fantasy echoed in my head.

I don't fuck just anyone. I'm selective.

"Eden?"

Zach's voice was cautious, but my response stayed glued to my tongue. I couldn't speak. My heartbeat pounded in an erratic drumbeat, my fingers trembling on the cold belt buckle. There'd be no sweet relief of running away from my problems this time.

"You chose her," I whispered.

Zach's body went very still. The gentle pressure on my neck released. His hand disappeared from my thighs. "Michaela?"

My head bobbed. "You're selective, right? Isn't that what you always told me? You chose her."

"It wasn't like that."

I pushed away from him. "Stop lying to me!" Suddenly feeling too exposed, I shoved down my dress.

"Okay. Okay." Zach held up his palms and stepped back. "If you want the truth, we need to have a proper talk about what happened with Michaela."

Cold wood disappeared from under my thighs. Strong arms wrapped around me. A few steps, and I was sinking into cream suede. Zach dragged the throw off the arm of the sofa, bundled me up in it, and booped me on the nose with a sad smile.

"Michaela and I are—" He paused like he was searching for the right word. "I don't want to say we're friends because we're not." He hunched beside me, his chin in his hand.

"She was your girlfriend," I said flatly.

"No. I never thought of Michaela like that. We went to university together and had a few mutual friends, but we never dated. Our families are from totally different worlds. She comes from money and was driving around in a brand-new car, and I took the bus for years until I scrounged together enough money to buy an old beater my dad fixed up." He sighed. "She still gives me shit about that car."

"Can I interrupt to say one thing?"

"Please."

"What a bitch. Sorry, but what the hell? I'd tell her where she can shove those sorts of comments."

"I've called her out on it, although…maybe not quite as colourfully." He smirked.

'Colourful' was probably exactly what that viper needed. "Sometimes, you need to be blunt," I said. "It's the only way you get heard." I fought to keep the anger out of my voice. I hated he'd been treated that way, but I didn't want him to clamp his mouth shut and stop talking now. I needed to understand what happened if we were to have any hope of moving on. "Is that why you slept with her? You were searching for some kind of acceptance?"

"No." Zach took a deep breath but mainly spoke to the creamy tufts of the sofa he plucked at with his fingers. "When Mum was sick, I didn't handle it. Honestly, that's sugarcoating it. I was a mess. I was up for partnership and trying to slog through the same hours I do now, but somehow, I had to help my parents. Dad would be on his knees in the bathroom taking care of her while I tried to hold the rest of their life together. What the fuck do I know about hospitals and running a household? Turns out, fuck all."

I scooted closer to him and bundled him under the blanket with me. "I'm sure they appreciated your help," I said softly.

His chin dipped in a nod. "No matter what happened, I'm glad my work suffered and not my parents."

"Your boss didn't support you?"

"Hell no. Work got ugly. I..." He shook his head. Shame washed over him, his shoulders slumping even lower into the sofa. We were back to the roadblock I'd seen at my place and here in his kitchen. "I, um..." His hand was trembling when he pulled it through his hair.

"It's okay. Don't go there." I curled my arm around his waist and held him close. "Skip that bit. Tell me what happened after."

He nodded. "Chris put me on forced leave and told me to see a therapist to sort out my shit or to not bother coming back."

"Zach, that's—"

"Just the way it is at Worley. Personal lives stay personal."

I sat in stunned silence, but outrage burned a fiery trail through my veins. If one of my team was going through anything close to what Zach did, I'd be there helping, not telling them to fix it themselves. His boss sounded like an absolute bastard.

"The first night I was back, Chris took the team out for drinks to celebrate," Zach said. "Mum hadn't gotten the all-clear yet, though. What the hell was there to celebrate? I was so lost. I drank too much. Michaela sat with me, and she said we should get out of there...go back to her place..." His head bowed. "I said yes."

"You didn't want to?"

"I just wanted...*someone*. I felt so alone but had no one to talk to. Michaela said she didn't want anything serious, and honestly, I never wanted a relationship with her. I'm not even sure I respect her anymore. Sleeping with her was a mistake. I felt like garbage every time it was over, just so goddamn empty, and

I vowed I'd never do it again. Somehow, she'd always convince me back for one more night. After the fourth time...work got busy for a few weeks and gave me an excuse to avoid her...and then..." His shoulder bumped into mine.

"Then?"

"This incredible woman floated into Brew HaHa, and I was a goner. Wonder who that could be?"

I beamed. "Me!"

He nodded. "Michaela still wanted to meet up, but I always turned her down after I saw you. She didn't take it well. Got kinda aggressive about it and said some ugly shit in meetings. She tried rubbing my face in the fact she'd moved on to Chris, but I literally didn't care. I was glad to shut the door on that part of my life." A shy smile pushed at his cheeks. "The day I first talked to you at Clovelly, the reason I was out there was because Dad had called to let me know Mum was in remission. I hadn't been to the beach in months, but for the first time in ages, it felt like there was space to be—I dunno—okay? And then you were there. It was one of the best days of my life. Officially a fresh start. Michaela wasn't a part of my life then. She still isn't. Not in any way that matters."

I wanted to smile back, but flickers of anger swirled in my chest. If I hadn't hated the viper woman before, I certainly did now. "She took advantage of you," I said. "You were dealing with so much. She should've been supporting you and making you feel good in all ways, not playing stupid games and only being there when she wanted to bounce around on your, um..." I flashed a sheepish smile. "You know what I mean. And I say this as a master at avoiding problems with some bedroom action."

"Like what you were trying to do before?" Zach's tone was soothing, but the words arrowed right into my chest.

"I—I don't know what you mean."

"Adorable little liar. Why do you think I sometimes ask you to slow down?"

"You prefer long, torturous sex that lasts for hours?"

He laughed. "Yeah, sometimes, but also because I want you to think a bit longer about what you really want. If sex is really the answer. Tonight...is it?"

Dropping my gaze, I shook my head. "I don't think I'm as ready as I thought," I admitted.

"There's no rush. Let's take sex out of the equation until you're ready. *Really* ready."

I hated to admit it, but Zach was right. We needed to solve some of our issues—and keep my vulva out of the conversation, like Andie had said. I sighed. Everyone was so much better at grown-up relationships than me.

"If we wait..." I said. "What about hugs?"

Zach smiled. "Nah, sorry, I need hugs. We can't skip those."

"What about kisses?"

"You can have as many kisses as you want."

To prove his point, he bent over to peck a kiss on my cheek, but I whipped around to capture his lips instead. His eyes popped wide before fluttering closed, his hand finding my cheek and his mouth devouring mine.

Zach groaned and pulled back. "Okay, maybe not too many of those kisses. A man only has so much self-restraint."

I grinned wickedly.

A hint of laughter edged his next groan. "Please take *a little* pity on me. I am making you a nice dinner, after all."

"Pity is only for men who know how to make delicious desserts."

"Oh, there's *dessert,*" he drawled, then sat bolt upright. "And, ah...not in a dirty way. I'm actually making a dessert."

"What is it?" I bounced up and down, clapping my hands. "Tell me! Tell me!"

"Tiramisu."

"That's my favourite!"

Zach kissed my forehead. "I know."

21

He said, "A diamond's still a diamond."

Zach

"You're so wriggly," Eden huffed from behind me. "Hold still!"

Smothering a smile, I squared my shoulders, standing tall, but I couldn't help squirming when Eden's fingers lingered a little *too* long on my behind. She'd said she needed to smooth out the creases in my tuxedo. Adorable little liar. She was just trying to cop a feel.

Her hand slipped lower.

Lower.

I wriggled.

"Zach," my angry kitten growled.

"Keep your hands off my butt, and I'll stand as still as you want." A fair compromise. Announcing our arrival at this god-awful work function with a raging hard-on wasn't exactly on my bingo card.

Eden straightened up, lifted her chin, and planted a no-nonsense hand on her hip. "Tonight's important. We need to look our best for this art gala. I'm going to do my best to schmooze your boss, and I don't want us tagged on anyone's social media with 'should have taken the bus.'"

I arched a brow. I couldn't imagine Eden climbing into a bus in her slinky black frock. My eyes dipped lower. Or wearing those sky-high heels.

Her nose scrunched. She didn't appreciate my grin one bit. "It's a saying my favourite fashion critic uses when she notices all the wrinkles and creases in people's outfits. We need to look immaculate."

"Are you sure that's why you can't keep your hands off me?" I teased. "I've recently learned you happen to like my butt."

"As if." Eden made a scoffing sound, her eyes bouncing everywhere but on me. "I've never noticed your stupid booty."

She was too cute when she lied. "No?" I booped her on the tip of her nose. "I should probably tell you that the gossipy ladies at your salon spilled the tea."

"Spilled the tea? You don't say things like that!"

"Oh, yes, those ladies spilled *all* the tea, Denny Dee. It was suggested to me you might've been gushing about how hot I am for quite some time." Even the idea of it seemed ludicrous to say aloud, but I loved the way colour flushed to her cheeks.

She snorted. "As if I think you're hot."

"No?" I lowered my voice. "You didn't imagine digging your little fingers into me...when I'm on top of you...making you feel good?"

She swallowed. "N-No."

"You weren't imagining me repaying you for how pretty you moan for me?" I ran my fingertips over the silky fabric hugging her hip. "Fucking you even harder?"

"Um." She wriggled on the spot. "Def—definitely not."

"No. Of course not. We're waiting, aren't we?"

"Y-Yes." She cleared her throat. *"Yes."*

She tipped a smile up at me. She enjoyed playing this game, but I hadn't distracted her from her nerves. She stepped closer. Her eyes locked on my bow tie. Before her hands reached me, I captured them, warming her fingers on the spot over my heart.

"Eden, my bow tie is straight. My tux isn't wrinkled, and your dress, hair, and makeup are all perfect. You look crazy gorgeous. Everyone's going to love you."

But no one could ever love you as much as I do.

My smile strained, suddenly too tight for my face, and I lowered my gaze to the safety of my shoes. There was no clowning around when those words were so close to spilling out of my mouth. I pressed my lips together to stop myself from scaring Eden away again too soon.

"Zach?" A soft hand touched my cheek.

"Let's go inside."

I crooked my arm. The worry pinching between Eden's brows disappeared. Glowing with a supercharged smile, she took up my offer by hooking her arm through mine, and she marched through the doors into the crushing attention with her head held high.

"Zach!" she squealed, pointing across the room. "There's the quartet!"

Her nerves forgotten, Eden fluttered around the gallery. She nibbled canapés off white spoons. She dragged me from sculpture to sculpture and sipped martinis like a classy French maven. When someone wandered past, she was never afraid to introduce herself, bubbling effortlessly, striking up easy conversations, and charming the pants off everyone.

I was the awkward—but wrinkle-free—lump standing next to her. I didn't mind.

Eden was having the time of her life. She sparkled. She was in her element. Walking around with her on my arm made my chest puff out more than when I'd won the sixth-grade spelling bee. I-n-d-o-m-i-t-a-b-l-e. I grinned. Maybe the universe had tried to warn me about Eden.

She paused as we strolled along a row of ugly paintings. "What do you think the artist thought when they painted this?" she asked, nibbling the edge of the dainty quiche perched in her fingers.

I tilted my head. A plain white canvas splattered with blue dots and a red line. Did you need to think much to paint something like that?

"Ah, well..." I knew nothing about art, but I'd stood next to Chris at a couple of these functions and picked up a few keywords. It was time to unleash my inner wanker. "I feel this piece is a dialogue about consumerism in modern society. The single red line, in particular, highlights the battle line drawn between capitalism and the collective spirit of community."

Eden's mouth dropped open.

The older woman standing next to us turned. "Yes." She nodded with approval. "Yes! Such a thought-provoking critique of this piece."

Eden just stared.

I flashed the older woman a smile and scooted Eden the hell out of earshot. I stooped just a little, my lips grazing the shell of her ear, and whispered, "I made that up. That painting looks like an over-enthusiastic toddler slapped it together."

Eden giggled and butted her shoulder against mine. "You're just full of surprises, huh?"

We paused in front of another painting, not even glancing at the swirls of gold but enjoying the quiet space, just the two of us. Eden's cheek dropped against the sleeve of my jacket. I couldn't help tucking my chin into the molten waves of chocolate I knew she'd taken hours to perfect. She sighed and shimmied closer. Bliss.

"There you are, Zach."

Chris was all smiles, swaggering towards us, his arm draped around the slim waist of his fiancée. The doctor preferred watching her own careful footsteps rather than daring to glance up. I guess I wasn't the only person suffering in introvert hell.

"Glad you could make it," Chris said, leaving off the 'for once' dangling in the air between us. We shook hands before he gestured to the woman glued to his side. "I'm sure you remember my fiancée?"

"Of course. Lola." I offered my hand. A handshake seemed right, but what did I know about gala etiquette? "It's good to see you again."

Her glasses were turned down to her pointy heels, but when Chris nudged her, she lifted her chin to offer a wobbly smile. Tentatively, she reached out, but when her shawl slipped off her shoulder, Chris's head snapped to the side. Why was he glaring at her like that? She jerked her hand back without touching mine.

Awkward.

Brows furrowed, unsteady, I lowered my hand and turned a confused smile at Eden. She didn't smile back. Her attention narrowed on Chris. I knew that expression—the subtle scrunch of her nose and the grimacing smile. Eden hated his guts.

"Thank you for inviting us." I weaved my arm around Eden's waist to settle my hand on her hip. "Chris, Lola, this is my..." Girlfriend? Future wife? The reason I got up each morning? "Eden."

Lola chirped a soft hello.

Chris's brow lifted slightly. No movie star smile. "A pleasure to meet you." No handshake, either.

The smile he got back from Eden was nothing short of showstopping, but it was the same one I'd seen in her paparazzi pictures—one hundred percent fake.

"Yes, a *pleasure*," she said.

I winced. I knew that voice, too. It was the arctic tone she'd blasted at me after I'd screwed up by sending her those stupid roses. Did Eden and Chris know each other? If they did, they certainly didn't *like* each other.

Eden turned to the doctor with a real smile. "Lola, tell me where you found this gorgeous gown of yours!" Her gushing praise was genuine, too. "I haven't seen anything like this in the boutiques."

"I found it at, um..." Tiny blue eyes peeked out from behind enormous glasses. "The vintage store in Potts Point." Lola managed a timid smile. "They have some wonderful bargains."

"Frugally chic. I love it! See this?" Eden twirled to model the intricate lace on the back of her gown. "A rental. I adore fashion, but the designer price tags are outrageous for a one-off. The two of us prove women can look fabulous on a budget."

I snorted a soft laugh. Eden had absolutely no need to be on a budget. I was now well-informed that the mountain of shoes stacked in her closet probably cost more than my car.

Lola relaxed into a wide smile all the same.

Chris stood as rigid as a rock.

Self-conscious, the air crackling with too much tension, I tugged at my bow tie. Were parties always like this? The networking event at the stadium had been better than whatever was happening in front of me now—and Eden had figuratively chopped my balls off that night.

"So, um..." I gulped. What the hell did I know about small talk? What the bloody hell was I doing? "Lola, are you still working at the general practice in—"

"Why don't you ladies go get us some drinks?" Chris suggested.

Eden's eyes slitted. She didn't appreciate being snapped at to fetch a man his drink.

I jumped straight in and said, "There's no need to—"

Eden stopped me with a touch to my elbow.

"Yes." She pasted the fake smile back on her face. "Lola, why don't we get these *men* some drinks?"

Lola's gaze flickered to Chris, and he dipped his chin in a nod. Eden's eyes rolled to the ceiling. She thought she'd masked it by turning around, but I'd seen it. When the two women strolled off for the bar, I batted away my paranoia that my boss's eyes seemed to linger more on Eden than on his fiancée.

Chris raised one blond brow. "Eden Phillips?"

He knew her.

And I *hated* it.

Wary, I forced my voice to stay neutral when I asked, "You've met Eden before?"

"Very few rich men in this city haven't *met* Eden before."

"I beg your pardon?"

"I didn't take you for the type to chase after someone like her."

I didn't appreciate his condescending tone. "Eden's a talented businesswoman and one of the most sought-after stylists in the country." Every word was said with pride.

He snorted. "For more reasons than her skills with scissors."

"Sir, the way you're talking about Eden is entirely inappropriate—"

"Zach, you can do better. If she's the reason your billings have dropped..." He shook his head. "You're a top lawyer at one of the city's most exclusive firms. Value your real estate higher. Do you really want to be number one hundred in the line?" He flicked a strand of hair off his forehead with calm indifference, but his eyes were on the other side of the room.

On Eden.

I despised the words he was saying. I hated how he seemed to think he could say that trash and still look at her with envy boiling through his blood. *Personal lives stay personal?* Not tonight. He'd *made* this personal.

"I don't care if there were a thousand guys before me if she chooses me in the end," I said. "A diamond's *still* a diamond."

"Eden Phillips is one rough-cut fucking diamond. Zach, I understand you rose up the ranks from nothing. Chasing famous fluff is fine, but I shouldn't have to remind you what you're risking."

"Eden's worth—"

"We don't want a repeat of what happened two years ago, do we?"

I stuffed my hands in my pockets. I couldn't look at Chris, so I dropped my eyes to the floor. "It's not like two years ago."

"Partnership announcements are next month."

"I know."

"Do you?" He cocked his head. "What time did you leave work last night?"

My jaw clenched. Seven o'clock. Eden and I had enjoyed another re-date night trying out a new restaurant. Then, I'd worked from home until I fell asleep at the kitchen table around two in the morning. I was pulling my weight. I was pulling a lot of people's weight.

"My billings are lower, but they're still the best in the firm." I wasn't rattled. My voice stayed strong. Facts were facts. "It's not like two years ago."

Chris sighed. "Zach, I'm just looking out for you. Trust me. Don't risk your future on a piece of arse." Blue eyes roamed the gallery to where Eden laughed at the bar. He muttered, "No matter how luscious the arse may be."

The final straw snapped.

I clenched my fist but forced a deep breath to stop myself from punching him in the damn mouth. Blood pounded in my ears, fury burning so hot my vision turned red.

Who the hell *does he think he is?*

My mentor. The man who'd given me a career. The best in the business. But also, the man whose eyes wandered to almost everyone except the woman he'd promised his life to, lingering longest of all on the woman who I wanted to promise mine. Complicated feelings warred inside me, but the battle didn't last long.

"Sir," I said, the word an effort to bite out. "While I have the greatest respect for you, don't think for one second you won't find yourself on the other end of my fist if you ever talk about Eden like this again."

"Zach—"

"Not only does Eden deserve better, but so does your fiancée." I jerked a nod. "I hope you and Lola have a pleasant evening."

Chris Stone may have taught me everything about being a lawyer, but he knew shit all about acting like a decent human being.

Screw his networking event.

It was time to get my girl and go home.

22

She said, "I was too scared to ask you to stay."

Eden

I've never been so jealous of an ice cream cone.

The roar of the roller coaster spiralling overhead and the excited squeals erupting from Luna Park faded into the background. Nothing existed but Zach's mouth. He clutched a chocolate ice cream cone, and his tongue darted out for a lick, stalled, hovering midair as he turned a wary look sideways.

His brows lifted over the top of his glasses. "You sure you don't want to swap?" It was the third time he'd offered.

I stared helplessly at the melting orange mess in my own hand. "But you don't like mango."

"And obviously, neither do you. That thing is miserable. Come on." Zach hoisted the pink sequinned dolphin he'd won for me at the ring toss under his arm and offered his empty hand. "Swap."

No one was stupid enough to pass up a deal like that.

Excited, bouncing on the spot, I shoved my mango ice cream at him and greedily grabbed for his. Zach laughed—an easy kind of laugh that was getting rarer for him the closer we crept to his firm's big announcement.

Lowering my lashes, I curled my tongue around the melting chocolate. *"Mmm."*

Innocently, I glanced up. Zach stood there, frozen, mango ice cream dribbling down the cone to his hand. His gaze locked on the swirl of my tongue. What was going on behind his dark, dark eyes? Dirty thoughts? I certainly hoped so.

"You like licking the ice cream, sweetheart?" His voice was gruff.

Oh yes, he was thinking *very* naughty thoughts.

"Uh-huh," I said. My next lick was positively obscene.

Zach grunted. His eyes slowly lifted, pinning me to the spot, and then, ever so slowly, he raised his cone, flattening his tongue to lap up the melting ice cream.

"Wha—what are you doing?" My pulse fluttered. I remembered those long, luxurious licks.

"Enjoying...my..." Lick. "Ice cream..."

"That's—you're—" I gasped a little sound. My poor neglected pussy throbbed. It had been so long since his mouth had been on me.

Zach's lashes dipped, the picture of boyish innocence, and the evil smile tugging at the corners of his lips only disappeared when he took another taste. *"Mmm."*

I narrowed my eyes.

"So...good."

My mouth curled into an angry pout. I spun on my heel, casting furious looks at Zach over my shoulder as my legs pumped as fast as they could to the ferry terminal.

"Eden!" Laughing, he jogged after me, the dolphin's tail flapping with each effortless bounce. "I was just messing around!"

"Oh, *were* you just!"

"Yes." He planted himself in front of me, blocking each of the steps I tried to dodge around him. "I thought we were having a little fun with each other."

I huffed.

"No?" He scooped the dolphin from under his arm and bumped its sequinned beak into my nose. "Is the torment only meant to be one-sided?"

"No." I pouted.

"You're adorable when you lie." He booped me again with the dolphin. "Come on, the ferry will be here soon, and this li'l guy is up way past his bedtime."

We finished our ice creams with no more innuendo. A napkin appeared out of Zach's pocket when the ferry arrived, and he dabbed at my lips, wadded it up, and tossed it in the bin as he shuffled us both on board.

He bumped his shoulder against mine. "I had fun tonight."

"Me too. It's been a long time since I've been to Luna Park."

"Same." He rubbed the back of his neck. "I didn't think I was getting off the spinny ride without embarrassing myself, though."

"I happen to think you're cute when you turn green," I teased.

He wrapped his arm around my shoulders, and my head fell to his chest, listening to the thump of his heart. The wind whipped off the water and through my hair, and I snuggled closer, my fingers flexing on the hard lines of his chest.

"That feels nice," he murmured, kissing my head.

His shirt was still clutched in my fist. I didn't dare open my eyes. "Do you want to come over for…a coffee…or…" I nibbled on my lip.

Or stay the night with me.

Why was I suddenly acting like a bashful teenager? I wasn't shy. I'd begged Zach to fuck me more than once, and he'd always obliged enthusiastically. Even when my legs had been trembling from an orgasm, he'd happily dived in to help me chase another.

"I'd better not," he said.

Struggling under the crush of disappointment, I forced my eyes back up.

His gaze was lost over the harbour on the high rises looming over the city. Was he seriously thinking of heading back to the office? Forget the stupid ice cream. I've never been more jealous of a desk.

Zach kissed me and started to pull back. The fabric of his shirt slipped through my fingers.

I don't want to wait anymore. I'm ready.

But he was so close to his dream.

Please come home with me.

His work always came first, but maybe it wouldn't once he got promoted.

"Coffee tomorrow morning?" I asked.

"I'd love that."

When the ferry docked at Circular Quay, we kissed goodbye and walked through the city in opposite directions.

And nothing had ever felt so wrong.

· ♥ · ♥ · ♥ · ♥ · ♥ ·

Frustrated, I yanked open the closet door. One sneaker flew off my foot. The second bounced into the wall.

Whose dumb idea had it been to wait?

My dress was stripped over my head and tossed on the floor instead of in the hamper. I twisted to catch a glimpse of myself in the full-length mirror. Sexy black lace underwear. Decoration, zero comfort. Scorecard? Hotter than hell. Not that Zach saw my new lingerie. Not that he'd even tried to take a peek.

Sighing, I flopped into the mountain of pillows on my big, lonely bed beside the sequinned dolphin. A cute but poor substitute for the man I missed so much. Sure, sex for us had always been out of this world, but the thing I craved most was our connection—the laughing, the pillow talk, snuggling together, and sharing sleepy kisses.

I should've spoken up and told Zach I was ready. Why hadn't I?

I needed to fix this.

A scheme.

I snatched my phone off the bedside table. A satisfied smile spread across my face as I tapped out a quick message to Zach.

Eden

> Can you come over? We need to talk.

My wicked laugh filled the emptiness of the bedroom. If this plan worked, there would be very little *talking*.

I slipped a floral kimono over my underwear and spritzed some perfume in the air. *Oh, what the heck.* A spritz for me, too. I raced around the apartment, tidying the clutter to make sure Zach's neat freak eyes focused on nothing but me. Dishes flew out of the sink and into the dishwasher. A dirty towel finally made it into the hamper. Pillows on the sofa were fluffed and chopped—

Frantic knocking cracked through the silence.

Cinching the belt of my robe snugly around my waist, I let just enough satin slip off my shoulder to reveal the lacy black bra strap hiding underneath.

Let's see how long his pants stay on...

I opened the door, arching against it with my best seductive smile, but Zach's reaction was not what I expected. He barely gave my outfit—or me—a second glance before he burst through the door. His arms were overloaded with so much junk I didn't know where to look.

"Zach, what the fu—"

"Eden, I'm sorry. Was it the ice cream thing? Was it 'cause I nearly puked when we went upside down on the Moon Ranger?"

"What the hell are you talking—"

"Whatever I did, I'm sorry. More than sorry." My dining table disappeared under an avalanche of sunflowers, daisies, cookies, chocolates, and a bottle of wine. "Is this enough?" His hands clapped on his cheeks. "What else can I buy? What do I need to do? You know I'll do anything."

"Zach—"

"Was it because I asked you to go to Chris's birthday party?" Agitated, he paced the kitchen, pushing a hand through his hair. "I know you've got your doubts about him. Me too. I don't know how to separate the man I admire from the man at the gala. But we need to put on a brave face until the announcement."

"Zach—"

"Oh, God. Was it Mum? Did she say something to you? I begged her not to—"

"Stop!" I grabbed a pillow off the sofa and tossed it at him. It bumped into his chest and hit the floor, but thankfully, he stopped pacing. "What the hell is going on?"

"What's going on? You said we need to *talk!* That's code for—for—" Emotion choked his voice. Tortured eyes met mine. "Are you dumping me again?"

My chin dropped.

I was hopeless. Zach had been trying so hard for weeks, opening up and sharing more about himself, but talking still wasn't easy for me. I should've been honest with Zach and sent him a message with 'DTF' and an eggplant and peach emoji tacked on the end. Even he could decipher that, right? He would've already stripped me out of the stupid lace thong riding up my booty and been, you know, DTF.

Zach's chest still heaved when I cupped his face in my palm, and his gaze stayed locked on his feet.

"Hey." I urged him to relax with a kiss on his jaw. "Look at me." I waited for his eyes to lift to reassure him with a smile. "Zach, I'm not breaking up with you. I'm not. Okay?"

"O-Okay."

"I'm sorry. I was upset you didn't want to come over, but I was too scared to tell you."

His eyes widened. "You wanted me to...come...over?"

"Y-Yeah."

The line of his mouth was grim, dark lashes lowering when his eyes started to roam my body. His fingers skimmed the trim of the kimono to reveal another sliver of my skin. "Come...over?"

Teeth in my lip, I nodded.

He traced the ridge of my collarbone, pushing and bunching the satin. I shivered as cool air rippled over the black, lacy breast exposed to his greedy eyes. "Eden. I didn't realise you meant..." He groaned. "You want me to...stay?"

"Only if you want to." I hated the uncertain waver in my voice.

"Consider your invitation accepted."

My feet lifted off the ground. I let out a helpless squeal as he threw me over his shoulder.

"Zach!" I flailed my legs and whacked playful hands on his back. "Put me down!"

He smacked my backside with a loud crack. "Unfortunately, I'm unable to fulfil your request. Your waiting period has expired, and now, I must complete *all* my duties under our agreement." The bastard was laughing! "Point the way to your bedroom."

I kicked out a leg in the direction of the hallway. "That way."

Quick strides, one easy toss off Zach's shoulder, and I was sprawled on the bed. The room was dark, the only splinter of light from the kitchen, but I could see the grin on Zach's face. Two plonks on the wood. He'd kicked off his shoes. The mattress dipped. A big hand clutched my neck, pulling me closer, holding me in place for a toe-curling kiss.

"Are you sure you're ready?" His breathless question was whispered into the crook of my neck even as he frantically unknotted my robe.

I grabbed his hand and shoved it between my legs. His fingers blurred along the damp patch of lace, and a groan huffed against my skin. Dizzy on the cologne ghosted on his neck, I undid the buttons of his shirt, stripped the linen off his shoulders, balled it up, and tossed it on the floor where it belonged. His belt unbuckled. The button on his trousers popped off. I tugged down the metal zipper.

Zach tore his lips away. "Slow down."

"I don't want to." I tried to force his weight on top of me by pulling on the waistband of his trousers. I wanted to sink into the mattress underneath him. I wanted him to pin me down. Do his worst. "I want you."

"You know our rule."

"Forget the stupid rule," I said. "I want you. Inside me. Right now."

Zach chuckled, but he didn't hurry. In fact, he slowed down even more, pressing kisses on my shoulder and running his finger over the lace barely covering my skin. "This is so pretty." He fumbled trying to undo the clasp. "You always dress up so...so...*nice*." My bra disappeared. "What's our rule, Eden?"

"I always come first," I grumbled.

"Tell me how..."

"No." I pouted. "I want this." I cupped the bulge in his trousers.

My sigh was dreamy. God, he was *so* hard already. My aching pussy only throbbed more when he moaned from my touch. But he refused to give in. He tutted me softly and moved my hand from his cock to the safety of his bare chest. Little party pooper.

"Do you want me to use my mouth?" Zach's tongue flicked over my nipple in a luxurious lick that made me shudder. "My fingers?" A hint of friction glided along the damp lace between my legs. "What do you want?"

"I want it like after my birthday party."

He groaned—not in a sexy way. "Eden, you were *so* pissed off at me that night."

"I was," I said, shimmying his pants down his muscular thighs, yanking them over his ankles, and tossing them into the air, desperate to get to his underwear next. "But remember how many times I came riding you? I want that."

Zach's eyes softened, his hand trying to calm my frantic touch. "You want to be in control tonight?"

"I want you to do what you're told."

He chuckled. "So...yes?"

I glared at him. This wasn't the time for jokes. Didn't he know how long I'd waited? I might've been desperate, but I was in no mood for begging. "Give me your cock, Zach." I curled my fingers around the waistband of his underwear.

"Those aren't very pretty manners, Denny Dee."

"Give me your cock"—I smiled sweetly—*"please."*

"Oh, *well*... In *that* case..." Strained laughter echoed in his voice. "Be my guest."

His underwear—gone. Off and somewhere on the floor.

An easier laugh filled Zach's chest when I didn't bother hiding my delight to wrap my hand around his thick, veiny cock. I sighed. He'd been made *just* right. But he cursed me bitterly when I kissed the weeping tip to say hello. He threaded my hair around his fist and yanked me away. Bossy. I loved it.

"Don't you dare," he growled. "Not unless you intend to let me repay the favour."

I grinned. "Later, then?"

Pushing my lacy knickers to the side, I threw my leg over his waist, ready to reclaim the handsome man sprawled on my bed. A peaceful smile softened his face.

When Zach looked at me like that...

My chest squeezed, my heart pumping a frantic beat as I fought the swell of emotion bubbling inside me. I tried to breathe through the feelings, but my fingers still trembled when I took off his glasses and popped them on the nightstand. I kissed him. Long and slow. Explored his skin with less frantic energy, enjoying the feel of how different our bodies were, his hard muscles, and the crinkly chest hair tickling my nipples when I bent over to kiss his neck.

"Can I have you?" I whispered. "All of you?"

"I was yours forever the first day I saw you, Denny Dee."

It was the final invitation I needed to lift my hips and guide him inside me. And it was good. So good. Better than good. I was stretched and full and just...floating.

Zach's eyes screwed shut tighter and tighter the lower I sank on his cock. Dark hair crushed into my mountain of white pillows. The sequinned dolphin squished under the desperate arch of his neck as he strangled out a moan. "Shit, I—" He gasped. The grip he'd clamped on my thighs became a brutal squeeze. "W-Wait."

I froze. "Wait?"

"Fuck... *Fuck*. It's been—" He grunted, almost like he was in pain, tiny beads of sweat glistening on his brow. "I didn't prepare enough for this."

Oh, this was getting *sexy*. "Prepare?" I traced my fingers down the rugged ridges of his chest, smiling as he squirmed. "How do you *prepare*, handsome man?"

His mouth pressed down into a flat line. Cute. But his stubbornness wasn't going to stop me. I rolled my hips to slip up and down his hot length. A bit of torture might coax the truth out of him.

"O-Okay." His fingers dug even deeper to try to stop me from tormenting him. "J-Jerking off."

"And when's the last time you jerked off your big cock?"

Zach strained against me, shaking his head, not willing to tell me. What was there to be ashamed of? Everyone did it. The thought of his big hand fisting his cock had my pussy clenching. A string of filthy curses left his mouth, and I grinned down at him. Maybe now he'd give up his sexy secret.

"This...morning," he panted.

"Where?"

"S-Shower."

"And what did you think about?" I pinned his shoulders under my hands. "Tell me."

"Y-You."

"Yeah?" I let the roll of my hips press into his hot, hard skin. "Doing what?" Another roll.

Zach grunted with appreciation. "My tongue. On you. In you. Eden, you taste so good. Let me."

"Later."

"We've got a long list for later." His chuckle was strained.

"Is that a problem?"

"Only for the little schemer who likes torturing me." He smiled. "It's payback time."

"Wha—"

Zach bucked his hips.

I answered him with a moan, loving the way his hand latched onto my rear, urging me up, brutal thrusts starting to pound deeper and deeper inside me. He'd found his rhythm and—God—did that man know how to fuck.

Was I in control... Or was he?

My head fell back as thick fingers slid over my clit and circled. Barely any air reached my lungs. Every breath was saved to moan a thank you. I was in heaven. With every rough stroke of his cock, I soared closer to where I wanted to be. I was drugged on the way his face contorted in ecstasy and agony. I did that. He suffered with each groan rumbling from his chest. He was waiting for me. Putting me first. Like this, he always had, but now I knew he would in other ways, too.

"That's it," Zach urged me on. *"That's* fucking *it."*

Finally—but still too soon—I tipped over the edge, exploding into a hundred happy pieces, blissfully complete when I coaxed out Zach's deep, long moan of relief next.

I folded over on top of him. His grip loosened on my backside, but he still held me in place, steady and sure. His other hand reached up to tuck my hair behind my ear. He wanted to see my face. His brows furrowed, eyes swimming with an emotion I'd seen before but never quite understood. What was he searching for when he looked at me like that? His mouth opened, but he snapped it shut before saying a word and left me only with a smile.

I wanted to ask him, "Why?" But what if I didn't like the answer?

I kissed him instead.

When would we both be able to say all the words we needed to say?

23

He said, "I want it all, Denny Dee."

Zach

Opening the car door was a breeze. Getting *out* of the car? A whole different story.

I groaned when my feet hit the driveway. Exhaustion gnawed up my calves, my muscles protesting in a scream, everything aching.

I'd survived another Saturday helping at the salon. Barely.

The two hours I'd spent at the office before heading uptown had been as easy as falling off a log. Six hours at the salon was the equivalent of being smacked with a log across the shins...a hundred times...and if the log was actually a freight train.

How did those three women do their jobs day in and day out?

Eden had promoted me to Chief Executive of Towels, Hanging Robes, and Restocking. When I'd served the champagne and coffee quickly enough, I'd earned her slap of appreciation on the backside. The overheated make-out session in the colour mixing room had been my bonus payment.

Andie had thrust open the door and glared daggers at us.

"This is a goddamn workplace," she'd barked.

Eden had fallen against me, giggling, not bothered at all. "Mighty words from the woman who's been sneaking into the laundry room with Yvette."

Cheeks red, attempts at a retort spluttering to nothing, Andie had slammed the door and stormed off.

But otherwise, a perfect day.

I rounded the car to pop the boot. Eden had insisted that meeting my parents for the first time had certain gift requirements. No amount of reassurance had convinced her otherwise. I leant over and stuffed my arms with the oversized fruit basket, two beautifully wrapped presents complete with frilly bows, and a bouquet of tulips. Eden had noticed they were Mum's favourite after scoping out her social media page...right after she'd hit the 'request friend' button. Mum had sent me three messages gushing about it.

I lumbered up the driveway.

Eden hadn't even unbuckled her seatbelt.

She was still sitting in the passenger seat, staring out the windscreen, her eyes locked on the orange bricks of my parents' house. Carefully, I set down the gifts, risking Eden's wrath by tucking the tulips into the fruit basket, and headed to the passenger door. Opened it. Held out my hand. Flashed an encouraging smile.

She didn't budge.

"Coming in?" I asked.

"Um." She fumbled to unclip the seatbelt. "Y-Yeah."

She tripped as she got out of the car, but I stuck my arm out, catching her before she toppled to her knees on the driveway. I frowned. I'd never seen her this unsteady on her feet. She charged around in six-inch heels more comfortably than I walked around in my old Chucks—the pair of shoes I would've worn to my parents' place if she hadn't recoiled in horror.

"You okay?" It wasn't the first time I'd asked her that.

"Yeah," she lied, not for the first time, either. Except now, she was sucking down breaths like she'd run across town. She bent over, scrambling to get a hand on the car bonnet to steady herself.

I touched her shoulder. "Denny Dee?"

Eden's head shook from side to side. "I can't go in there." Wide eyes barely skimmed the modest house over my shoulder. "I can't."

Was she worried about...the...house?

Although the style was dated and had little street appeal, people passing always commented on Dad's perfect lawn and Mum's messy cottage garden. It was the only house I'd ever known. It wasn't on the 'right' street or in the 'right' suburb for the people I worked with, but this was Eden. She wasn't like them. She'd spent her last weekend off working at a barbecue fundraiser to raise extra money for the youth centre. She was there two nights a week. She didn't care where people came from, only wanting to lift them up so they got where they wanted to go.

No, the house wasn't the problem.

"Come on," I said, making sure the low tone of my voice was reassuring. "Let's go inside."

"I *can't*. It's a *home*, Zach. A proper *home*. A *family* lives there."

My heart twisted in my chest. There it was. The real reason she was nervous. "Yeah, a family does live there. *Your* family."

Eden jolted up straight. "M-My..." A blink.

"Hate to break it to you," I said casually, trying—probably failing—to keep the mood light, "but I'm pretty sure Mum has adopted you whether or not we stay together."

"But—"

"No buts."

"What about all my, you know...*issues?*"

I shrugged. "If I can deal with your leftover toast crumbs, so can my parents."

Eden's eyes narrowed. "That's not what I meant." She took a deep breath, trying to be brave, but spoke to the hands twisting her dress into a crinkled mess. "My *daddy* issues."

I stomped down the anger exploding behind my carefully guarded expression. I hated her labelling herself because of her father's abuse. She was strong. She'd achieved so much. But it wasn't going to be an easy road to prove to her that not all men were like him. And that was okay. I was all in no matter how long it took.

"You know what?" I said. "Girls wouldn't have any issues if their dads were good men who did the hard work. So, you've got some stuff you need help with, hey, guess what, so do the rest of us. Did you run away screaming when I told you how I coped—didn't cope—when Mum got sick?"

She scoffed. "Of course not. You did the best you could."

"And you are, too. The woman you are today is because of all your experiences, good and not so good." I touched her cheek. Dropped a kiss there. "And I want it all, Denny Dee."

She bit back a cautious smile. "All the drama?"

"Until the curtain's called."

"All my schemes?"

"I'll hit play on your villain theme song."

She covered her mouth with her hand, but the grin was there. The crinkles around her eyes were a dead giveaway. She'd hated the card I'd sent her all those months ago, but I honestly loved her smile. I wished I could see it. Not just in that moment. Always.

"I..." Emotion gripped my throat. My breath was gone, stuck somewhere in lungs that didn't work anymore, but the words were back, ready to burst out of me.

I love you.

Something achingly hopeful danced in Eden's dark eyes, but if I finally said the words, there was no guarantee she'd whisper them back. Did that matter? Hadn't I always wished I'd said the words sooner? What was I waiting for?

I took a deep breath. No stammering. All courage.

"I love you, Eden."

"Y-Yeah?"

I nodded, and she...burst into tears.

"Shit!" I scrambled to my feet. "Shit!"

I bounced on the spot in a strange sort of dance to nowhere. Adrenaline pumped through my limbs. Run for help? Fight off...nothing? My brain was going haywire. Eden's eyes lifted, helpless, tears dribbling down her cheeks, her hands flapping in a panic.

I dropped to my knees. "Your makeup." I stuck my hands in my pocket and fumbled for a tissue. *Nada*. I bunched up the sleeve of my sweater and dabbed under her eyes. I tried to smile, but it probably wasn't reassuring. It was twitchy, wobbly, all over the place. "This isn't exactly the reaction a man hopes for when he says I love you." I pressed the cotton against the wet spots on her cheeks.

"It's the only one I can give at the moment," she admitted in a quiet voice.

I hid my disappointment by kissing her temple. "I'll take it." It would've been great if she'd said it back, but I didn't regret telling her how I felt. The words weren't stuck inside me anymore. The tightness was gone from my chest. I could breathe again.

I picked up the gifts, stuck the fruit basket under my arm, and lobbed my free arm around Eden's waist.

"I can walk," she huffed.

"Yeah, but you're a flight risk." I chuckled. "And I like it when you're beside me."

Eden stuck close to me up the driveway and angled even closer when I rang the doorbell. I'd never pressed that doorbell in my entire life.

A shadow moved behind the door.

Mum was already there but desperately trying to hide her excitement. Another beat passed before the door flew open. My mother stood there, her smile almost a rictus grin, her entire body stiff. She'd promised not to overwhelm Eden, but I had a feeling everything we'd talked about on our phone call that morning was about to be forgotten.

"Zach and—" She pressed a hand to her heart. Oh no. She was already crying. All restraint evaporated. "Eden! It's so wonderful to meet you!" She flung herself across the threshold and crushed my shocked girl in a hug. "You're even more darling in person! So tall! No wonder you always look so lovely in all your photos."

"So much for playing it cool, Ma," I muttered.

Mum swatted me. "Shush."

"It's nice to meet you, Maree." Eden shuffled from foot to foot. "We, um—" She waved a hand at the gifts tucked under my arm.

"What's all this?" Mum readjusted her glasses. "Honey, that's so thoughtful of you! I just love presents. Zach's dad, John—you'll meet him—he's absolutely *dreadful* at giving presents. Last Christmas—"

"Ma."

"—you wouldn't even believe it if you saw it with your own eyes! He bought me fertiliser—"

"Ma," I said through gritted teeth. "He chose it because you like gardening."

"*Fertiliser!* For *Christmas!*" Mum scoffed. "If Eden's going to be part of the family, she needs to be prepared for whatever terrible—"

"Ma!"

Eden laughed. "I'm looking forward to our first Christmas." She squeezed my hand.

"Me too." Our first Christmas. Together. My heart skipped. "And have no fear—as you know, I happen to be excellent at choosing gifts." I wiggled my eyebrows.

"You're...improving."

I grinned. "I'll take it."

Mum waved for us to follow her inside. "I hope you haven't eaten! We're having lamb with all the trimmings."

"Ma." I groaned. "You didn't need to go to all the trouble of making a roast."

She ushered us into the living room. "You don't fill tummies with salads, Zachary," she hissed as she shoved me towards the sofa.

"God help me," I mumbled.

I was arranging the gifts on the coffee table under Eden's watchful eye when Dad wandered into the living room.

"Hey, mate." He patted a quick hello on my shoulder and then fussed with the collar on his shirt, looking at me, Mum, and finally Eden. After staring at her with an uncertain tilt of his head, he eventually stuck out his hand. "Nice to meet you."

Mum glared at him.

Self-conscious, Dad glanced at his hand. "I washed up." He rubbed it down the front of his jeans just to make sure and stuck it back out.

"John, really." Mum sighed. "A handshake?"

"Yeah, what's wrong with that?"

"She's Zach's, erm...well..." Mum twittered a laugh and fluffed her hair.

Sensing the awkwardness, Eden stuck out her hand, catching Dad by surprise when her fingers closed around his to pump his hand up and down in an efficient shake. "It's nice to meet you, Mr. Rawles."

"John." He broke out with a rare smile. "Strong handshake. Better than the little punk who runs the mower shop."

Mum let out a mortified groan. "John, really!" She quickly recovered to flash Eden a warm smile. "Ignore that big lug of a man. You two sit down. We'll bring in some drinks and a few nibblies so we can chat before dinner."

Dad tugged at the collar of his shirt again. "You never said anything about chat—"

Mum yanked him away. "We'll be right back."

Once they'd left the room, I turned to Eden with an apologetic smile. "Sorry," I said. "That's, ah—yeah, so that's my parents."

"Zach, they're amazing! And look at this place!" Her head swivelled to take in the walls jammed with knickknacks and photos. "I love it. It's a real home." She was grinning when she headed straight for the row of pictures in the china hutch. "Oh my gosh! Are these you?"

"Ah, yeah." I started flipping down all the frames. "We don't need to see those." *Ever.*

Eden squealed. "Stop that!" She swatted my hand. "Teenage Zach is adorable."

My brows rose. I'd shot up to six feet by the time I was thirteen and would've been lucky if I was fifty kilos sopping wet. Gangly arms and legs. Glasses. Braces. The whole bingo card for an awkward youth.

"You need glasses, too, Denny Dee?"

Eden poked her tongue out at me and shuffled around the living room, lifting the frames to peek at all my embarrassing photos, her fingers almost reverent on all the dusty knickknacks and along the back of Mum's prized suede sofa.

My phone pinged.

I sighed. If Mum was texting me instructions from the kitchen... I slipped my phone out of my pocket.

"Huh."

Chris

> I'm sorry if I said something to upset you on Friday night. I'm only looking out for you. If I overstepped, I apologise.

> Let's get a coffee tomorrow morning.

"Everything all good?" Eden asked.

"It's Chris."

Her chin dropped. "But it's Sunday night," she whispered.

She was worried I was going to abandon her and head to work. I had before. Not tonight. I didn't even bother responding to Chris's apology. Something about his message left me cold. I turned off my phone and put my hand to much better use clutching Eden's waist. I dipped my head. Kissed her shoulder.

"He apologised for what happened at the gala," I said.

"Which was...?"

"Like I told you, he overstepped his mark."

Eden huffed. She was still pissed off at me for not telling her why I'd grabbed her hand and dragged her away from the bar. What good would come of telling her? Chris's comments had been cruel and entirely uncalled for. I wasn't letting one word of that filth come out of my mouth.

"He made some bullshit comment about me, didn't he?" she guessed.

"Dee—"

"I know you admire him—he's been a big help to your career—so I'm being *very* selective with my words."

"But?"

"I don't like him. Not one bit. Even if I somehow manage to put aside the way he treated you when your mum was sick—which I don't think I can—I don't like the way he glares at his fiancée, and I *loathe* the way he talks to her. He barks orders at her like she's his damn servant." Eden's nose went in the air. "No thanks."

"He gave me a chance when no one else would."

"And you've paid him back a thousand times over by being fantastic at what you do. The way he treated you, Zach. I just—I—*ugh*. It makes me furious! You don't owe him anything!" Eden breathed out, slow and steady. "Sorry." She touched a hand to her cheek. "I'm sorry."

"You have nothing to be sorry for." I slung an arm around her to pull her close and kiss her forehead. "Thanks for looking out for me."

A flash of grey hair disappeared from the doorway.

Without turning, I said, "We see you, Ma."

A long laugh trilled from the hall. "Sorry. I didn't realise you two were, um—" Another nervous laugh. "I've bought a few little things to nibble on." Mum breezed into the living room with an overstuffed charcuterie board. "Your father's bringing some wine." She bent closer to whisper as she passed, "From the *fancy* section."

"Geez, Ma, no one's going to need dinner after all this."

She glared at me and slid her wooden board neatly into place on the coffee table. She perched on the sofa and patted the spot beside her when Dad lumbered in with an open bottle of red and a handful of glasses.

Once the drinks were poured and shared, Mum asked, "Shall we toast? John?"

Eden grinned and held her glass the highest.

"May we be loved by those we love," Dad said.

The glass trembled in Eden's hand, but she was the first to lean over and clink with everyone.

"Oh!" she cried. "We can't forget the gifts!"

She set down her wine, panicking when a drop sloshed on the glass coffee table, frantically scrubbing the spot clean before snatching a present to pass to Mum.

"Such pretty wrapping." Mum positively beamed as she tugged off the ribbon and carefully nipped open the paper. "Oh." She pressed a hand over her mouth. "Oh, honey, this is too much." Loving fingertips hovered over the designer purse inside.

"Every woman needs her signature accessory." Words Eden lived by, but her voice wavered, nervous. "Zach said your favourite colour's purple."

"Oh. It's—I just—oh, honey, I love it!" Eyes brimming with tears, Mum launched from the sofa to capture Eden in a fierce hug. "John." She flapped a hand at Dad as she shimmied in next to Eden. "Open yours."

Dad dropped a suspicious look at the present resting in his lap.

Eden laughed. "I *promise* it's not a purse."

One of Dad's lopsided smiles flashed, and he tore off the paper and flipped the lid to the box. His thick brows shot up. "Tickets to the final?" He rubbed the back of his neck. "Oh, um..."

Eden didn't know his subtle signs yet, and the longer he tried to process receiving such a nice gift, the more she chewed on her lip. "Front row seats!" She hyped it up even though she had no idea why it was so special. "My friend Sam arranged everything."

Mum sniffed. "Friend."

"Ma," I warned.

"Zachary, do I need to remind you about the *baguette?*" She skewered me with a glare.

Eden burst out laughing.

Mum's eyes darted between us.

"Eden saw the message," I explained. "She knows what you mean when you refer to the *baguette.*"

Eden patted Mum's knee. "Sam's *definitely* just a friend," she reassured her. "I'm also happy to report there was never any, um...*baking.*"

Frowning, Dad glanced at all of us, uneasy. "What on earth are you lot talking about?"

It had been a long time since so much laughter filled my parents' living room.

24

He said, "Since you asked so sweetly."

Zach

I WAS ALREADY AWAKE when the rest of the city stirred in a torrent of rain. Only a sliver of daylight sliced through the storm clouds and the open curtains into the bedroom. Perfect weather for sleeping in.

I blinked at the nightstand. The clock was fuzzy without my glasses, but when I squinted, I could just make out the numbers.

6:00 a.m.

I groaned. Sleep-in over. A mountain of work waited for me at the office. I needed to drag my backside out of bed—my very naked and very *cold* backside, courtesy of the sheet thief beside me.

"Quit wriggling," a muffled voice grumbled. "I'm being cuddled here."

The pillow lifted. I was greeted by a tumble of dark hair and chocolate eyes crinkled by a sleepy grin. My smile back was automatic. A pleasure. How was Eden always so lovely? Palming her hip, I urged her soft skin to press closer and bent down for a kiss—

Eden slapped a hand over her mouth. Wide eyes stared up at me.

"Move your hand," I said. She refused with a shake of her head. Impatient, I grazed my nose along her cheek. "I want to kiss you."

Her fingers inched apart. "I haven't brushed my teeth yet!"

"I don't care about your morning breath." It was all in her imagination, anyway. I nibbled her neck, loving the way she squirmed. "I want to make you messy again before I head to work."

Eden's eyes shifted to the clock on the nightstand. Her brows drooped.

I could read her like a book. She was thinking, "This early?"

Could she read my face as easily to see I was thinking, "This late?"

Frustrated, I rolled away and flopped onto the pillow, a sullen glare pointed at the ceiling. Priorities were blurring. I'd been spending more and more time with Eden and even more time distracted from work. My billable hours were plummeting. The money I was bringing in was still well beyond the minimum, but for me, low.

The lowest it had been in two years.

Eden propped herself on her elbow. The tangled ends of her dark hair tickled my cheek before her lips did. "Zach?"

"Mmm?"

"When you become a partner at your firm, will it make you happy?"

I stared at the ceiling. Would it make me happy? Waking up next to Eden, sneaking my palm over her belly, and letting it linger while I listened to her adorable snores melted my anxiety. She made me happy. I dreaded walking into work, and my stomach roiled at the thought of turning on my computer or opening another email. I'd been on this hamster wheel for a long time. Twelve years. I was exhausted, but...

"I've been working towards becoming a partner since I graduated from university," I said. "It's all I've ever wanted." I reached up to touch her cheek. "Well, it used to be."

Eden smiled. "What changes when you become a partner? Will you get to work less?" She kissed my neck with enough of a lick to drag a sigh out of me. "Maybe sneak in a few mornings so we can snuggle in late?"

"Yeah, I think so. I'll have more say in how the firm's run and how we treat people." The first thing I planned to do was give Sue a raise. "I'll finally get proper recognition in my field. I'll actually be someone worthwhile—"

The gentle press of Eden's index finger stopped my words.

"Hey, none of that." She frowned. "You're worthwhile. You're more than your job."

"I know it won't make sense to someone like you."

"It makes perfect sense. We've walked the same road; I just climbed to the top of my ladder a little earlier than you did. But that's cool because I can give you a hand up the last few rungs."

"Behind every great man is a great woman?"

She smirked. "You seriously think I plan on standing behind you?"

"Charging out in front?"

"Nah, let's go one better. Side by side. We're going to be the ultimate power couple."

"No, Denny Dee."

Her face fell.

"We're going to be a family," I said.

Eden's lashes fluttered in rapid blinks. I understood that look now. Emotions. Tears. She kept both locked behind the veneer of a smile. When would she feel safe enough with me to let go?

Her arms latched around me.

Oh—*now?*

Suddenly, she didn't care about morning breath. Her lips burst against me in feverish kisses, urgent fingers clawing at my skin to roll me on top of her. I chuckled against her collarbone. I wouldn't be heading to the office as early as I'd thought. Warm hands sailed over my skin. Scorching kisses stole the breath out of my lungs. I barely had enough air to grunt when her fingers curled around my cock.

"We should spend a little longer on foreplay, don't you think?" I ground out.

"No. I do not." Her hand worked me up and down in a gentle pull. "God—just—" Her head fell back on the pillow.

"Mmm?"

I asked the question, but I already knew what she wanted. She'd wriggled underneath me and sweetly spread her legs. One of her hands clung to my hip, urging me to give her what she wanted. The hand she'd used on me was now stuffed between her legs, furiously working her clit.

"Zach! Just—" More squirming.

This was so, so fun. "Mmm?"

"Just hurry up and put your big dick in me, would you!"

A laugh rumbled in my chest. "Since you asked so sweetly."

I slipped the tip of my cock along the wetness slicked between Eden's thighs and slowly slid into the spot she begged to be filled. Pleasure shuddered through me before sinking deep in my bones, urging me to plunge deeper, possess even more of her. She didn't mind. Oh no. She loved it. Her eyes squeezed shut. Her mouth went slack with a long sigh.

I kissed her jaw. "That's what my girl wanted, isn't it?"

"Yeah." She licked her lips and tilted her hips to force me even deeper. "Fuck, yeah."

I groaned with her. "Yeah."

For once, Eden didn't try to rush me. She lay back, letting my hips control the pace, rolling with each thrust, her breath panting against my neck until my skin prickled. Her fingernails grazed over the stubble on my cheek.

"Why is it always so good with you?" she whispered.

I planted my palm beside her head and arched up on shaking muscles. My first kiss brushed one of her closed eyelids. "Because"—my second kiss landed on the other side—"I love you."

"Yeah—*oh*—you do, don't you?" Eden's eyes snapped open, searching my face. "When did you know?"

"Hmm?" I didn't want to talk. I wanted my lips on her when I was inside her. I wanted to kiss her again. So, I did. And then I licked her neck. Nipped it.

"When did you know you loved me?" she insisted.

"I was—fuck, Eden—I was falling for you forever." I tried resisting the urge to buck my hips. No. That wouldn't do. We could still fuck slow and steady and share sweet words. "I knew for certain the day you moved in. When I—*oh*—when I saw your—your toothbrush next to mine."

"Why did you wait so long to tell me?"

"I was scared."

"Of what?"

"That I wasn't good enough for you. But I will be soon—"

Eden's index finger pressed against my lips. "Don't say that again, okay? You're good enough. You're incredible. Not your job. *You*. Hear me?"

I nodded.

"Now, come here," she said. "I want you to show me how incredible you are."

·♥·♥·♥·♥·♥·

Eden's eyes darted around the coffee shop.

"Stop that," she whispered.

"Sorry." I peppered a trail of kisses up her neck. "What did you say? I couldn't hear you over all of the kissing noises."

She fought the giggle, but a bubble of laughter escaped before she flattened her lips in a frown. She lifted her chin. Oh, yes. The little liar just hated all the attention. I laughed into the crook of her neck.

"People will see you," she said, sounding slightly thrilled about it.

"No one's looking."

I peeked over the top of her hair. Hazel eyes stared back, frozen wide open.

I was wrong.

Michaela was watching.

♥ • ♥ • ♥ • ♥ • ♥

PEOPLE PLODDED INTO THE boardroom.

I dumped my files at the head of the table and sank into the leather seat next to Chris. Absently, I drummed my fingers and glanced around the room. These meetings were a waste of time and another one of Human Resources' attempts to build a 'culture of positivity' when none of us had the time to think, let alone care. Hopefully, Chris would make this one quick. I had a thousand messages to catch up on.

Michaela slunk into the room and sat four seats down. She forced her lips to curve whenever someone said hello or asked about her weekend, but no one could call her pinched look a smile. She had no time for them. All her attention was on me. Daggers shot down the boardroom table.

Chris's eyebrow rose as he shifted a glance between us, but he said nothing. He shuffled his papers and started working through his agenda with his usual ruthless efficiency.

"Zach, I've heard word we've been recommended to the buyer of the shopping centre complex out in Campbelltown," he said. "I'll book drinks and feel them out, but I'd like you to lead the team if we can get the deal across the line. Can you be ready?"

I nodded even though my stomach plummeted to the floor. "Sure."

The sale was massive—months of work. The current projects we had on the books were already stretching everyone to breaking point. My promotion couldn't come quickly enough. Right after I gave Sue a raise, I'd hire more people. We'd all been drowning for too long.

Michaela snorted with annoyance. "It's great Zach has the opportunity to get back to his childhood." She leant over the boardroom table to make sure I saw her smirk. "Does your mummy shop out there?"

I turned away and let the snide comment slide into silence. I hadn't grown up that far west. Why would it matter even if I had? Or did Michaela want it to matter because of the scene at the coffee shop? She was floundering. Nothing between us—including the few times we'd been in bed together—had been close to matching the pleasure I felt doing something as simple as holding Eden's hand. Michaela had seen the difference with her own eyes now. She couldn't deny it.

She also didn't appreciate being ignored. "Maybe you could take the sl—I mean your *girlfriend*—along to survey the site?" She batted her eyelashes. "Show her your home soil?"

Chris bristled beside me. I didn't have to look at him to know he was about to blow a gasket because his meeting was being derailed with insults about my girlfriend—especially after what had happened at the gala.

"I don't think this is an appropriate time for you to raise my relationship," I said to Michaela in a measured tone.

"Ashamed of her, are you?"

"Absolutely not—"

"You *should* be," Michaela sneered. "This firm is revered for excellence. Integrity. Our names shouldn't be dragged through the mud because of the inane celebrity antics attached to your girlfriend. She's exactly what's wrong with this world."

The fingers I'd been drumming on my files stopped. My eyes narrowed. I'd warned Michaela. She couldn't keep speaking to me like this, and she absolutely couldn't say trash about my Denny Dee.

"Truly? She's what's wrong?" I tilted my head with the question. "How does she compare to a person who knowingly sleeps with someone in a committed relationship every second Tuesday? Surely my girlfriend has more *integrity* than a person like that."

Michaela's mouth dropped open.

She'd told me in confidence, but I didn't care. I'd never been okay with the idea of her and Chris, and I was even less comfortable with their reality. I'd heard the rhythmic thumps through the wall of my office late at night. I'd seen Chris and Michaela leave together—more than once and more often than every second Tuesday—and hadn't uttered a word.

Personal lives stay personal.

What a fucking joke.

Chris leant back in his chair. I hadn't mentioned any names, but I could feel his eyes on me, calculating what to say next. Nobody else at the table knew he was still involved with her. But if they were even half as smart as they pretended to be, they'd know I was referring to Michaela. I frowned. I should've been more careful. Not let her bait me. I'd dumped her right in it.

"How *dare* you?" she spat. "You think *you* have the right to say that to *me?*"

And that was the moment I gave up caring.

"Sometimes, people need to even the playing field," I said. "They need to take the opportunities they're given in life and make the most of them. You try to belittle me, but that's what I did. That's what my girlfriend did. Then, there's using people, deliberately hurting them to get what you want, and acting like a cruel, petty bitch. That's what *you* do."

A murmur rippled around the room. Chris cleared his throat to stop the whispering, but it didn't work. Chairs squeaked as people restlessly tried to get comfortable in the tension closing the walls in around us, waiting to see what happened next.

If I'd read the room, maybe I would've snapped my mouth shut, but I was too angry, so sick of Michaela's games.

I shifted my gaze from her stunned face to Chris. "I won't work with her anymore," I said. "I want Michaela off every single one of my files, or I walk."

Chris cocked his head, trying to figure me out. I'd never stood up for myself. I was loyal. I'd always done my best never to create a scene and follow his rules—and it had almost cost me the woman I love.

Michaela leapt from the chair. "Chris! You can't! He's a liability. You—you *can't*—"

Her words choked away when my boss pushed back his chair and rose to his feet. Not blinking, his face far too calm, he pointed at her to sit down. He didn't have to say a word before she sank back into the overstuffed black leather. His hands braced the boardroom table. Blue eyes fixed on me.

"Done," he said.

"This is fucking bullshit!" Michaela was already back on her feet and marching to the door. "If you think I'm just going to let you effectively fucking *demote* me—"

Chris barked a laugh. "Walk out, and you don't come back."

Michaela's hand froze on the door handle.

Void of any emotion, he sat down. "Have a bitch session with your little girlfriends in Human Resources if you need to." His voice was glacier cold. "But if you want to keep your job after bringing your personal life into my boardroom, you'll sit your little arse back in that chair and finish the meeting." He rearranged his papers without sparing her another look. "Do you understand?"

Silently, she slunk back.

Chris picked up his pen and started working through his agenda as if nothing had happened.

The only sound in the boardroom was his voice.

No one said a word.

No one moved.

We were a bunch of adults cowering in our seats, no better than children who'd been scolded by their teacher.

And I stared at the boardroom table, questioning for only the second time in twelve years if this career—working for this firm—was *truly* what I wanted.

25

She said, "I'm Eden fucking Phillips."

Eden

"When can we leave?" I whispered to Zach.

I gulped another sip of champagne, hoping the fizz would numb my boredom. The yacht club was so exclusive someone had forgotten to invite the fun. The splattered red flowers on my dress were the most interesting thing to look at in the sea of greige.

I glanced over Zach's shoulder. Even the birthday boy wasn't having fun. Chris kept his poor fiancée leashed to his side like he was worried she'd flitter away on the ocean breeze. I scoffed into my champagne glass. Lola should flitter away. *Run.* I'd known too many men like Chris. That guy was one hundred percent bad news.

"I thought you liked parties?" Zach teased.

"I *love* parties," I said. "This is no party."

"There's food and booze and way too many people. It's a party."

"That's also the perfect description for a wake, which, by the way, would still have more life in it than this shitshow."

"The venue's good, though, right?" Zach didn't sound convinced.

I rolled my eyes, lowering my voice to imitate one of his greige colleagues. "Oh, look at me," I crooned. "I'm a rich, fancy lawyer in a fancy yacht club. Listen to me talk about boring paperwork and my new sports car because I'm overcompensating for having no personality."

"The truth's out, huh?" Zach smirked. "That's what you think about me?"

"Nah." I kissed his stubbly jaw. "You don't drive a sports car."

He laughed. "I promise we don't have to stay much longer."

"Just here for appearances?"

Zach dipped his chin in a solemn nod. "The partners are meeting tomorrow."

"Almost there."

"Almost." His nose found its favourite spot under my ear, and the warm, minty press of his lips landed there next. He responded to my shiver with a sigh. "I can think of a thousand things I'd rather be doing right now."

"Are we naked in any of them?"

"Behave, Eden."

I pouted. "Make me."

Zach's cheeks turned pink, his expression shy as his finger drifted along the lacy seam hidden under my dress. A spark zipped up my spine, and I squeezed my thighs together. This naughty game was more fun than the party. Was Zach remembering, too? Before the party, when he'd bent me over his sofa, slipped down my knickers, and fucked me so rough and so good I'd sobbed into the cushions? After that, when he'd gently dabbed me clean and glided my knickers back up my legs as if nothing had happened?

"Later," he said.

"Tease," I huffed. "If we're not playing our naughty game, I'm going to dash to the ladies and freshen up." I smoothed my hair. "I don't want to be all messy when the cameras come out for the cake cutting."

"I prefer you messy." Zach bent down and guided me into a long kiss too intimate for his boss's birthday party.

"That wasn't fair," I whispered against his lips.

He eased back, drooping eyes barely there behind fogged glasses. "All's fair in love and...*schemes*..."

I laughed, and he sent me on my way with a party-appropriate squeeze of my booty.

He should've sent me with a packed lunchbox and a map.

The elusive sign for the bathroom led into a rabbit warren of confusing corridors and dead ends. I turned. Stopped. Turned again. Annoyed, I marched along the hardwood floors, clicking up a frenzy, finding nothing but blank white walls.

The hiss of a man's voice stopped me. Old fears clawed around my lungs.

"—Don't you dare embarrass me again—"

The unmistakable sound of a slap on skin. A gasp.

My hand flew over my mouth to cover the cry begging to escape. I crept along the corridor to where struggling shadows spilt around a corner.

"Do you hear me?"

A whimper.

"Do you?"

I'd heard him loud and clear.

My father had made his demands in the same menacing voice with the belt wrapped around his hand. It didn't matter whether you answered yes, no, or said nothing at all; the outcome was always the same. I'd wished a million times for someone to save me from him.

My heart slammed in my chest, cold sweat sticking my satin dress to my spine, but I wasn't about to turn my back on someone who needed help.

I edged around the corner.

Lola cowered against the wall, the telltale mark of a slap hidden behind the slender fingers fanned on her cheek. Chris towered over her. His hand jerked away from her arm when he heard my footsteps on the hardwood behind him, but the reminders of his grip still dented her pale skin.

That evil bastard.

Not that he seemed at all bothered to see me. He casually buttoned his jacket and flicked back the strands of blond hair that had fallen across his forehead.

"A pleasure to see you again, Eden." His lips twisted in a smile as if nothing had happened.

All the fancy canapés I'd scoffed sloshed around in my stomach. My mind screamed at me to walk away. Their relationship was none of my business. Chris held Zach's future in his hands—but those were the same hands he'd used on the woman cowering in the corner.

Maybe I should've walked away.

But how could I?

How *could* I?

Out came my dazzling smile. "Lola! There you are!" I sang in my best performance yet. "I've been looking absolutely everywhere for you! You won't believe the gossip I just heard on the deck."

Chris scoffed. He'd bought the act. Not surprising—that jerk had pegged me as a bimbo since day dot. Towering over her, he murmured, "Run along," and pecked a frosty kiss on her cheek.

I clenched my fist until my fingernails bit into my skin.

Lola peeled herself off the wall, shrugging the delicate gauze shawl into place over her shoulders and knotting it tight so the bruises on her arms disappeared. Before her head could turn to seek his approval again, I'd already huddled her to my side.

"Come on," I urged her away from him. "Let me fill you in on all the details." *About how to leave that man.*

I hurried her down the corridor, constantly checking over my shoulder, my hip bumping into the wall because I was moving too fast and not paying enough attention. Another dead end. Another turn. The restroom. I nudged open the door with my shoulder, ushering Lola through a small crowd of women to get to the basins.

"W-Where's y-your"—I took a deep breath—"makeup bag?"

She bit her lip. She didn't have one.

"Ladies!" I called to the women milling around the basins. "Makeup emergency!"

Women rushed over, tipping out their foundations and powders for us to test until we found the perfect match. The hot red handprint scorching her pale cheek blurred behind the tears in my eyes. I tried to distract myself by tucking wisps of blonde hair behind her ears only to see the bruises dotted on her neck. My heart squeezed so tight I couldn't breathe.

"Thank you," Lola whispered.

Frantically, I dabbed at her skin to cover the marks. "We need to get you out of here." Hoarse words rushed out of my mouth. "A taxi—or—"

"But i-it's Chris's b-birthday."

"So bloody what! He *hurt* you!"

"He didn't mean to. I'm sure Zach's told you. They work so many long hours. It was my fault for—"

"It wasn't your fault!"

"He's been under so much pressure."

I forced down gulps of air, trying to stop my hand from shaking as I dusted a coat of powder on her face. "Take it from someone who grew up around a man like him. Chris *won't* change. He'll get worse. It's not the hours. Or the pressure. It's *him.* Lola, please, I know people. I can help you find somewhere—"

"N-No. Thank you. I appreciate you helping me with this." Her fingers hovered above her cheek. "But I don't want to cause any more trouble."

"Please," I begged. "Let me help."

Lola's head bowed. She wasn't ready for this conversation yet—not from me, anyway. I wasn't a superhero. I was a stranger. As much as I wanted to swoop in and save her, that wasn't how life worked.

"No matter what that bastard says, you *don't* deserve it," I whispered. "I know you'll find your strength one day. And if I can do anything to help you get there, just ask. Everyone knows where to find me."

Lola nodded. She rose to her feet and carefully checked her shawl in the mirror. She was going to walk out that door. Not to escape, but to stand beside the same man whose handprint was hidden under the makeup I'd applied to her pale skin. *Me.* I'd hidden it.

My heart cracked down the middle.

I couldn't stay.

I couldn't stand there knowing what would happen to her tonight...or tomorrow...or every day until she left him.

With a sad smile, I edged away and... I ran.

I flew out of the door, stumbling down the suffocating corridors until I burst back into the function room. My eyes desperately searched the crowd. I needed to find Zach. The partnership announcement was so close. He needed to know the truth about the man he idolised. Even if Lola wouldn't listen, *he* would. I needed his arms around me so I could crumble into a fit of tears. He was safe. *Home.* The opposite of the monsters who walked around in the world undetected until you stumbled on them in a corridor.

Where *was* Zach?

I rushed onto the deck, the salt breeze a relief on my burning skin. I leant over the railing, sucking down breaths, trying to dull my anger—and the fear it masked—by watching the swell of the ocean bobbing to the horizon.

I'm...done.

Done with small talk. Done pretending Chris wasn't the boss from hell. Done seeing another broken woman who hadn't found her wings. I growled. I'd left her in the bathroom! I should've dragged her into a taxi! I should've—

A hand palmed my backside. I swallowed down my emotions, plastered on my bravest face, and, shimmying a little, turned around to sass Zach.

"So," I drawled. "We're back to playing this ga—"

My smile vanished. Chris stood eye-to-eye with me. I considered Zach's promotion for less than a nanosecond before my fight instinct flew out with a vengeance, and I smacked that smug bastard's hand away. Hard.

He laughed.

Laughed.

"Keep your fucking hands off me," I hissed at him.

Chris was too close to my ear and stinking like the expensive alcohol boring bastards like him preferred drinking. "Is that the best you've got? I'm disappointed."

"Step away, old man," I warned him. "This ain't happening."

"Rugby players more your thing? I remember you had quite a thing for musicians back in the day." A blond eyebrow arched. "You certainly get around, Eden."

I lifted my chin. *Please*. Slut-shaming? Nothing emasculated a man like him more than a woman who enjoyed sex on her own terms.

I restrained my anger under the fakest of smiles. "Don't believe everything you hear."

"Oh, I've heard plenty." Chris's eyes locked on my chest as his fingers reached for a feel, but I was even quicker. A harsh crack rang out as my hand connected with his cheek. Chris's eyes flashed. Not with anger. He was laughing again.

"You're fucking *perfect*, Eden."

"You're fucking *disgusting*, Chris," I seethed. "Take your drunk arse back inside and find your fiancée. *If* you can find her. One day soon, she'll realise she can do a lot better than your abusive arse."

Saying those words was a mistake.

The mask slipped. Chris's face twisted to reveal the monster he was, and his fingers clawed around my arm. He yanked me closer. The pressure digging into my skin was so punishing the blue ocean blurred to black, and I fought with every ounce of strength inside me to hide just how much it hurt. The bruises all over his fiancée told me he was capable of worse. It was the same story of every girlfriend my father had ever had. *Of me.*

Defiant, I hiked my chin and stood even taller. "Is this how you convince the pretty doctor to stay with you? What a *man* you are."

Sneering, he shoved me. My back bounced off the railing, and I yelped as the pain snapped up my spine. His hands were off me, but he stalked closer and crowded me into the corner until there was no escape.

"Who the fuck do you think you are?" he spat.

"I'm Eden fucking Phillips."

He smirked. "White trash who jumped on every eligible dick in this city to make some money."

"Oh, honey, is that what you need to tell yourself to feel better? Can't handle a woman who sees opportunity and takes it?" I fluttered my eyelashes. "Or are you disappointed that even after taking *all that dick*, I still wouldn't be caught dead on yours?"

His lips pressed into a straight line.

"I can't wait to tell Zach all about the piece of shit you are," I said. "He will end you."

"Is that what you think?" Chris barked a laugh. "Zach's career ends with a snap of my fingers. It wouldn't take much to convince the other partners to hold him back for another few years while he sorts out all his...*problems*."

My bottom lip caught in my teeth.

Chris smirked. "How do you think Zach will handle that?" His head cocked. "After everything he's been through... We both know it'd destroy him. But... I'm sure we could come up with some kind of...arrangement." My bones chilled when his fingers ran down my arm. "You're a savvy businesswoman, aren't you? You know how to negotiate terms. Make...deals..." He slurred over the last two words because he was too busy leering at my boobs. "You keep your mouth shut about me, and I'll make Zach's dreams come true."

"That's blackmail."

"No, honey, that's business." Chris's mocking voice chilled even more. "Do you really think he'd believe a bit of trash like you over me?"

I shoved him off me.

"You may think you matter," Chris said, "but you're not more important than the future Zach's been working for his entire career. He owes me everything. He chose *me* over his *own mother*. I suggest you choose your next move *very* fucking carefully."

His smug smile was the last thing I saw as he left.

My hand trembled as I fumbled to steady myself on the railing. My breaths were shallow and shaky, and every emotion I'd been holding back threatened to flood out of me. Fear. Anger. Humiliation. Devastation.

But I forced everything behind the walls I'd built in childhood. Barely. I held myself together. Somehow.

What the hell was I going to do?

26

He said, "I need to go back to work."

Zach

Something was wrong.

The mattress bobbed. Cotton sheets rustled. Eden rolled over to face me, her hair tangled on the pillow. I'd convinced her to switch off the lights, but she hadn't tugged the drapes closed, and enough of the urban glow wedged through the gap to show the worry creased between her eyebrows.

"Denny Dee, is everything okay? You haven't said much since we left the party."

An understatement. Eden hadn't spoken a word in the taxi back to her place. No brutal commentary about the dull outfits. No scorecards for the food. She was an anxious cloud suspended in murky silence.

"I want you to be happy," she whispered.

"I am." The truth. "Talk to me about this." I gently pressed my finger into the line knitted between her brows. "What can I do?"

"Will you hold me?"

Grinning, I rolled on my back. "I've got just the spot for you." I thumped my chest. "Right here."

Eden scooted along the sheets, quiet as a mouse, tucking against me with her head on my heart and an arm slung over my waist. Her hair tickled my nose. She smelled like tropical cocktails, coconut and lime—a reminder for me to book a romantic vacation once the partnership announcement was behind us.

"Feel better?" I kissed the top of her head.

Eden answered with a light touch to my jaw and a kiss on my chin. "Can I show you how I feel?" she whispered.

I nodded, but the logical side of my brain tracked each movement, none of the puzzle pieces clicking neatly into place yet.

She was trying to distract me...but...from what?

Eden's kisses started on my neck, and she propped herself up, her hair hanging in a dark curtain, shielding the truth on her face. A soft kiss dropped on my mouth. Another. Harder. Longer. I only dared to cup her cheek to keep her sweet mouth on me. I'd always loved kissing Eden. Time slowed down. Worries—work—disappeared. The world revolved around her, the only noises my accelerating heartbeat and the needy rumbles in my chest that made her hum happily in reply.

Her fingers curled around my hand and dragged it down...down...until my palm swallowed her breast.

Again?

"Denny Dee?" I searched through the dark for her gaze, but I didn't understand the eyes that blinked back at me. "Please, talk to me. What do you need?"

She bit her lip, silent as she continued to explore my chest, my abdomen, following the trail of hair from my belly button with the tip of her index finger until she wrapped a firm grip around my cock. I choked back a grunt of surprise.

"Yeah." She moaned long and low as she stroked the hard length from base to tip. *"That's* what I need."

Eden was an expert at distracting me.

Logic switched off. My questions went unasked, unanswered, when she straddled me, her fingernails sharp in my chest, her dark eyes drilling into mine, some hidden message behind the intensity as she rode me hard, unrelenting, demanding pleasure to erase whatever was bothering her. When I was still catching my breath from the first orgasm, she nudged my hand between her thighs to sweetly ask for her second.

I knew Eden. Sex was a Band-Aid. She was craving validation. Feeling vulnerable. But... Why? Dread swirled in my gut. I'd screwed up again. I must have. But every path my mind wandered down led nowhere. Nothing made sense.

And sleep never won over.

When the birds chirped their morning greeting outside, I was exhausted but awake, boneless from all the sex, but my muscles taut with nerves. Groaning, I rolled over and tried to untangle myself from Eden's death grip. Cold air hit my backside as I edged out of the sheets.

Eden's eyes snapped open.

"Where are you going?" she demanded, her arms latching around my waist.

"Sorry, Denny Dee. I have to head back to my apartment to get ready for work."

"No." She pouted.

"Eden." My best grouchy dad's voice was a lost cause. Her grip only tightened. I chuckled as I pried her arms from my waist. "I'll make it up to you."

She dipped her gaze, smiling sweetly. "Now?" Her fingertips danced along my bare chest.

"Later." I kissed her. "Promise."

And my promises meant something these days. Eden knew. Still, her gaze locked on me as I stumbled blind through the clutter to pick up my discarded clothes. I threw them on, found my glasses on the nightstand, and sat on the edge of the bed.

Seemingly defeated, her head bowed.

"Eden, is something wrong? I know I haven't always listened as much as I should, but I'm listening now." I brushed the strands of her ruffled bed hair behind her ear. Coaxed her chin up with gentle fingers. "You can talk to me."

"It's your big day," she whispered. "Is the promotion still what you want?"

"More than anything."

Her smile seemed forced. "Almost there."

"Almost."

My body left Eden's apartment, but my mind stayed stuck there all morning. She occupied every thought. I thought about her when I drove back to my apartment. When I showered and dressed for work. When I stopped for a coffee, and she wasn't with me.

Zach

Love you. Can't wait to see you tonight. xo

Little dots flashed. Eden typed a message...that never arrived.

Something was very wrong.

Robotic, I plodded through every mouse click, every signature, every email.

I'd screwed up again. I knew it. What did I do wrong? Was she leaving me? Like last time?

When another text message went unanswered, I dialled the salon.

"Sweetie, Eden's not here," Yvette said. "She called in sick this morning. I'm literally trying to reschedule all her—"

Panic shot me out of the chair. Away from my desk. Out of my office.

Sue's heels clicked after me down the corridor, and her shout for me to come back echoed as the elevator doors closed.

· ♥ · ♥ · ♥ · ♥ · ♥ ·

Eden's front door cracked open.

Rumpled chocolate hair poked through the gap. Pink blotches coloured her cheeks, matching the tip of her nose. My heart cracked. She'd been crying long before my frenzied knocks scared the wits out of her.

"Let me in, Denny Dee."

And not just through the door. I needed her to unlock the spot where she kept all her secrets from me.

The door inched open enough for me to squeeze inside.

"Why didn't you tell me you weren't feeling well?" I hugged Eden's stiff body against my chest. "I would've stayed if I knew you were sick. I can take care of you. Can I get you something? Should I call a doctor?"

She waved off the concern and shuffled through the living room, heading for the kitchen. "Do you want a drink?" she asked, her voice empty without her usual sparkle. "I can make you a coffee. I have some of those fancy pods you like."

I frowned. I didn't want a bloody coffee. "I want to talk about what's going on."

Eden kept her distance on the other side of the kitchen, an arm hugged tight around her middle, her tank top riding up to show her fingers pinching into the skin of her belly. Her wary glance pinned me as she fussed with a jar on the kitchen counter. I pressed my palm over the lid. I didn't care about the stupid coffee pods.

"Stop." My command was soft. I wanted her attention on me, not avoiding me.

She froze.

"We're getting better at talking." My throat bobbed painfully on a dry swallow. "But, Eden, please don't make me jump through the hoops of some bonus round trying to figure out what I did wrong. Just tell me."

"You didn't do anything wrong."

"So, you're sick?" I touched her forehead with the back of my hand. She wasn't hot. "Really sick?" I tipped up her chin with my finger. She closed her eyes to avoid my gaze. "Eden?"

Nothing.

Locking a sigh of frustration behind flattened lips, I dropped my hand from her chin, running a soothing touch down her shoulder to her arm. Her face screwed up. A wince. She fought to shutter her expression, but I'd seen it. My heart plunged to my feet when I saw the bruises—deep crimson spots tinged with indigo—dotted on her arm.

I ghosted a hand over the violent marks. Perfectly spaced...just like my fingers. "What happened to your arm, Eden?"

"N-Nothing."

"Why are you lying?"

"It's nothing to worry about."

Like *hell* it was nothing. "Tell me the truth!"

"Zach—"

"Who did that?"

Her lower lip wobbled. "I ruined everything, didn't I?" A fat tear trickled down her cheek.

Shit. *Shit!* "No... No... I'm sorry." I took a deep breath and buried the fear deep in my chest. It wasn't helping. "I'm sorry I raised my voice. I'm just freaking the hell out because—" Helplessly, I pointed at her arm, my own resolve crumbling. "Please, tell me what happened."

Eden shook her head. "I—I can't. Not yet. Not until after..." She hugged herself into a tighter shell.

"No. There's nothing more important than this. Tell me right now."

"You'll hate me. I should've walked away, but I couldn't." She hiccupped through every strained breath, and wet lines trickled down her cheeks. *"I couldn't."*

"Tell me," I insisted.

Eden didn't speak. For the longest time, I thought this was another secret she'd lock away and toss the key. "I saw...Chris...at the party." She refused to meet my eyes. "He hits her, Zach. I saw him."

A freight train barrelled into my chest and forced me a step back. "What? I don't—Lola—but—" My fingers speared into my hair, tugging at the roots, my eyes frantic on all the clutter. Nowhere was safe to look. I had too many questions and no answers. *Wait.* My fingers hovered over Eden's arm. Those bruises were an answer. "Not just Lola."

"Zach—I—"

"Chris touched you?"

Eden still refused to meet my gaze, but her chin jerked down in a nod.

"Grabbed you?"

Another nod.

"Hurt you?"

Another nod.

"Did he threaten you?"

She didn't speak, but the way her big eyes lifted and stared at me, not blinking, I knew the answer was yes.

Rage boiled inside me until it scorched so hot, so deep, it ate away every other emotion. Nothing was left but a dark void in the hollow of my chest. Chris had hurt Eden, and where the hell had I been? Protecting her? No. I'd been sipping a drink while some moron from marketing yammered on about the stock market.

Eden didn't protest when I scooped her in my arms and carried her to the bedroom. She was a mess of tears and snot and hiccups. I slipped her safely in bed, folding the floral sheets snugly around her chest, and blotting her tears with a tissue I snagged from the nightstand.

This time, when I rang the salon, Andie's gruff voice answered. Only a few words passed between us before she declared she was coming.

Eden turned her head into the pillow, clutching it tighter to her chest. "Do you still...love...?"

I smoothed back her hair and tucked the loose strands behind her ear, but I couldn't reassure her. My mind had flipped an off switch. Time passed. Maybe a minute. Maybe an hour. I wasn't sure of anything except the circles I patted on Eden's back to coax her to sleep. It was like I'd shut down.

Just like two years ago...

The front door creaked open.

"Andie's here," I whispered, pressing a kiss to Eden's forehead. "She's a good friend. Watches out for you. Everything's going to be okay." A rusty smile creaked onto my face. Eden really was worth burning the entire world to ashes.

Her sleepy hand slipped off my knee when I stood up.

Andie stalled in the doorway. "How's Ed?" she asked, her voice low and eyes glassy with worry.

"Not good."

I edged past. Andie's angry scoff stopped me. I turned. Her nostrils flared, and she clenched her fist by her side. She was debating whether to take a shot at me.

"Where the fuck are you going?" she spat.

"I need to go back to work."

"You son of a bitch. Are you abandoning her *again?* She *needs* you!"

I ignored Andie and headed for the door.

I needed to go back to work.

27

He said, "It's always the quiet ones."

Zach

"Chris is on the bloody warpath," Sue said, her short legs struggling to totter behind me as I charged past reception and down the corridor to my office.

"Is he," I said.

"You—Jesus, boss, will you slow down? You missed the mediation for the boundary dispute."

"Did I."

"Michaela went instead," she reassured me. "Chris got pulled out of the partners' meeting to sort it out. He wasn't happy."

"Heaven forbid."

I kicked the chair out from under my desk and sat down. Sue's cautious steps stopped at the door, her hands squeezing an old tissue as her gaze skittered around the office, unable to find a safe place to pause. She was anxious. Was I scaring her?

"Boss, i-is everything...okay?"

Guess so.

"Everything's great." I forced my lips to twist into a smile.

Sue reared back, her eyes wide.

Just like two years ago.

My smile hadn't help. Sue's brows stayed pinched tight, but it was all I could offer when a silent rage twitched through every nerve, my self-control stretched into a thin line, the ends already unravelling, ready to snap.

Chris touched Eden. He hurt her. It's his turn to suffer.

Another smile crept on my face.

"Zach...hon—"

"Give me a minute, okay, Sue?"

"Y-Yeah." She inched backwards. "O-Okay." The glass door snicked shut behind her.

My gaze drifted around my office. My reward. I scoffed a hollow laugh. A white-walled prison with a harbour view. Once upon a time, that had meant something. The claps, the green eyes, and forced smiles when I'd moved into the office next to Chris's had been a prize. Achieving partnership was supposed to be my happily ever after. The moment I'd worked for my entire career. The time I'd finally risen from the ashes of poverty to become a success instead of the skinny loser with the beat-up Corolla.

I glanced at the photo of Eden on my desk and touched my fingertips to my lips before pressing them to the glass. My beautiful girl. She was my *real* happily ever after.

Tension short-circuiting my stiff fingers, I focused on the computer and clicked open a new email. The cursor blinked in the white box. How should I word the message to implode my career? If I'd planned better, I would've forwarded a photo of the card Eden had sent me all those months ago—the one with the cat that said, "Giving zero fucks." The final middle finger.

I started typing.

I can no longer work for this firm.

It has been my pleasure to work with some of you, but continuing to turn a blind eye to the toxic practices of a partnership who prioritise money and ego over its people only lowers me to the bottom of the barrel with them.

We all deserve better than to work for a man like Chris Stone.

I'm sorry.

I clicked send.

Twelve years of my life ended with a few sentences, but I'd promised Eden action, not only words.

I slipped off my glasses, arranged them neatly beside the laptop, and rose on steady feet. I shrugged off my suit jacket and tossed it on the desk. Diamond cufflinks dropped on the wool. Off went the carefully knotted tie. Finally, I folded my shirt sleeves to my elbows.

Action, not only words.

How long would it take someone to call the cops? Would I be arrested? I'd never been arrested before. I'd barely been in a fight. Dad had taught me it was better to walk away. I'd been a good kid and kept my fists to myself even when the other boys had teased me and knocked me down just because I'd worn glasses and preferred reading to sport. I was tired of being knocked down. The bullies didn't always have to win.

The door to my office burst open. Michaela stumbled inside, her chest heaving, cheeks red.

"Zach, your email—" She gulped in a breath.

I headed for the door, but she smacked it shut and barricaded the handle and every possible escape route with a windmill of arms. It would've been laughable if there was a drop of emotion left inside me.

"Move," I said.

"Think about what you're doing!" The words scratched out of her in a desperate shriek. "Sit down at your desk and retract that fucking email! Zach, I know you—"

"You know *nothing* about me."

"I know you've worked your arse off for twelve years. You're the best lawyer in this firm. That woman you're with is poison, Zach. If she told you to quit—God—whatever lies she's told you—"

"Bruises don't lie."

"Bruises?"

"Chris."

Michaela's face turned white, but somehow, she didn't look shocked.

"Move."

"Okay." She nodded. "I'm moving." Her hand shook when she pulled down the door handle.

I shouldered past her without another word.

People stared at me, and heads popped out of offices as I charged down the corridor. Two colleagues tried to stop me. So many questions.

What happened? Where are you going? Are you okay?

What would everyone say when this was all over? Would it be like when the news anchors interviewed people in the neighbourhood after someone snapped?

It's always the quiet ones.

The glass-panelled walls morphed into rich, dark wood on the other side of the floor. Those walls hid the partners, but I knew they were in there, crowded around the boardroom table, planning everyone's future—*mine*—with the devil himself sitting at the head.

I'd faced those same eight people two years ago. Chris had stood over me, spitting hatred into me like bullets for letting down the firm, and no one had said a word. Billings too low. Mistakes being made. Couldn't have a weak link leading a team. Not his fucking problem my mother had cancer. Those partners had twitched uncomfortably in their seats, but every last one of them had kept their heads down.

No one had even asked about Mum.

No one had said a word to me until two days later. The woman from Human Resources had waltzed into the hospital in her burgundy suit and parked her arse next to my bed, even though Dad had demanded for her—and everyone else—to fuck off and leave me alone.

She'd asked a lot of questions, too.

Did you really mean to walk in front of that car? Are you sure you weren't just tired? Maybe you should talk to someone?

That night had been the second time I'd seen my father cry. He'd folded over on the plastic chair in the emergency room and tried to hide the tears behind his hands, and I'd never felt so damn low.

But this wasn't like two years ago.

I yanked open the boardroom door. Ignored the shocked faces. My eyes zeroed in on Chris. His chair flew back, and he scurried backwards like the coward he was.

"Zach, you need to calm down."

"I'm calm." *So* calm.

He tried to dive past me, but he was too slow. My hand snatched the collar of his overpriced shirt, dragging him back. A panicked shout yelped from someone behind me. Chairs crashed and toppled around the room, and a stampede hurtled at me, but they were stuck in quicksand compared to the speed of my anger.

Chris wrestled an arm free to shield his face, but my fist connected with his cheek, pain searing up my arm, and the sickening crack of bone-on-bone scorching a wave of vomit up my throat that I forced back down.

"I warned you." I ploughed my palm into his chest to force him against the wall. "Hurt Eden, and I'll hurt you."

Air whooshed out of Chris in a strangled grunt when my other fist slammed into his stomach. He bent over, gasping for breath, until he turned to me, his lips curled in a taunting sneer. I lunged for him, but a mix of hands gripped my shoulders, my arms, my side—too many people to fight off. They hauled me back.

"All this over some hairdressing slut?" Chris laughed. "You're really going to throw away your career over her?"

"Why not? Didn't you?" I spat back. "I saw the bruises on Eden's arm. I know what you did. The same abuse you inflict on your fiancée, you evil piece of shit!"

The hands clutched around my shoulders disappeared as one of the partners stepped back...as if they were shocked by what I'd said...as if we hadn't all been pretending not to see exactly who Chris was for years.

Smirking, Chris touched a hand to his cheek. He squared his shoulders. He wasn't fazed. He *loved* this. "I hope joining the queue to fuck that whore was worth it."

The boardroom turned scarlet.

My fist smashed into Chris's jaw so hard he reeled backwards, crashing past a chair that rolled away under his grip. He hit the floor with a thud.

"You'd be *nothing* if it wasn't for me." His voice was a broken wheeze as he struggled to stand. "How many times have you failed everyone in this room?"

"I never failed you."

"You walked in front of a fucking car!"

"Because *you* failed *me!*"

His laugh was manic. "You're soft. A fucking loser from the gutter. Take your pathetic pound of flesh, Zach. This changes *nothing* about where you came from or the fact that I'm sending your sorry arse back there."

The insults shouldn't have meant anything. He'd said them all before. But hatred and disgust fuelled a rage inside me I didn't understand. I launched for him.

Eden. My parents. Even Andie. My people.

Every punch I landed on Chris was for them. Blood soaked my hand, and thick red smears whipped and splattered over Chris's face and crisp white shirt. Swollen patches of his skin were already purple.

What...am I...doing?

Strength dissolved from my legs, and without the rage to keep me upright, I crumpled to my knees. My fists were cut and broken, and every muscle ached. I couldn't move. I watched with a horrified fascination as the man I'd once admired crawled like a shattered crab across the boardroom floor, his breath shallow rasps, the movie star smile missing under the blood and swelling my fists had put there instead.

In the end, I'd been no better than Chris.

What did that make me?

What?

A monster.

"You're"—Chris gasped a breath—"finished."

There was nothing left inside me to care.

28

She said, "I love you."

Eden

"Don't hang up!" The frantic shriek of Michaela's voice was the only reason I didn't instantly end the call.

"You've got less than a second," I warned her.

"It's Zach. He—oh fuck—he just—" Shaky breaths echoed down the line.

I hurdled over the back of the sofa and raced to the front door. "He *what?* Is he okay?" My heart pounded as panic shot my feet into my sneakers. I covered my phone and called out to Andie.

"He lost it! Like. Fucking *lost it!*" Michaela said. "I tried to stop him. He sent this fucking email saying he was quitting, and then he goes into the boardroom and beats the absolute shit out of Chris!"

The hallway spun. I blinked rapidly, trying to focus on Andie standing at the kitchen doorway, a tea towel over her shoulder and a wet bowl in her hand. Her eyebrow went up. I waved her closer.

"Where's Zach?" The watch house, probably. Did I know any lawyers? Yvette did. She knew everyone.

"I don't know where he is."

"What do you mean you don't know? You aren't *with* him?"

"I tried to get in the elevator with him when security escorted him out," Michaela said. "He yelled at me to fuck off. I wasn't arguing with him. He looked—he looked—" She sucked in a breath. "Crazy."

My mouth pinched. *This woman.* Did she know Zach at all? He'd been edging closer to his breaking point for months, and now he'd shattered into a thousand pieces. I should've realised how much pressure was on him. My stomach dived. I shouldn't have told him what happened with Chris. I *never* should've let him walk out the door.

"Did you go to his place to check on him?" I asked Michaela, grabbing my handbag off the hook and slinging it over my shoulder.

"I don't know where he lives! Sue, his EA, yeah, she told me to fuck off, too. You're the last person I wanted to call."

I would've rolled my eyes if the situation weren't so serious. "Why *did* you call me then?"

"You're listed as his emergency contact."

I clutched the phone tighter to stop the tremor in my hand. My gaze shot to the front window. The sky was already turning dark. Zach hadn't called. He hadn't responded to any of my messages. I'd assumed...

I'd assumed he wasn't coming back. That he'd chosen his path, and it wasn't the one we'd walk together.

I'd misjudged him.

And now he was alone.

"Michaela, I'm giving you a one-time-only thank you," I said. "I needed to know this. But you're not part of our lives. Zach made his choice over and over again, and it was *never* you. It's over. Never call either of us again. I won't be polite the next time I see you, do you understand?"

"I—okay." The defeat sank her voice lower. "And it's possibly worth nothing...but...tell Zach I'm sorry?"

"You had the chance to tell him yourself."

I hung up.

Andie tossed me a pained look. "Zach snapped?"

"Sounds like it." I sighed. "This is all my fault. God, he was *so* close to achieving his dreams. If I'd just shut my stupid mouth and he'd made it through one more day—"

"He would've hated himself even more for signing his life away to those people," Andie said. "This was a long time coming. We need to find him."

"You don't need to come."

"You're right. I *want* to come." Her hand twisted the knob, pushing the front door open. "When have I ever let you run off into the night alone?"

"What about the party after I caught that dude screwing someone else?"

"It's sweet you think I wasn't behind you the whole way 'til you got home." Andie smiled. "Come on."

Zach's apartment was dark.

Swallowing my fear, I fumbled for the light switch. Even when the warm glow flooded the narrow hallway, I couldn't shake the dread turning my blood to ice. I toed off my sneakers and kicked them next to the door.

"Zach?" I called out.

Silence.

I raced to the kitchen. Flipped another switch. Empty. Panic jolted me from room to room. No one. My chest caved in, and

I sagged in a heap on the edge of his bed, almost bursting into tears because I'd messed up his neatly tucked sheets.

What now?

I should call Zach's mum, but what if he wasn't there? She'd be so worried. His dad, too. They'd already been through so much. I needed to be strong. Figure this out. *Help.*

But where else could he be?

Another helpless look scanned around his bedroom.

Wait.

I edged off the bed.

Was that...?

My heart split. Tears squeezed out of my eyes even though I fought to hold them back.

Barricaded in the walk-in closet, Zach huddled in the corner, scrunched into a ball with his arms wrapped around his knees and his head pressed against the wall. How long had he been there? Hours? Even a minute on his own was too long.

I shuffled into the closet, dropping to my knees, crawling closer. My hand landed on his back. He flinched.

"Zach?" I hiccupped through the tears. "You...okay?"

He buried his head deeper into his knees and pushed up his shoulder to shield his face from me.

"I'm here," I said.

I blanketed myself around him, my cheek resting against his back. I was going to sit in the terrifying darkness and protect him like a warm mama bear whether he liked it or not.

It was as if the comfort of someone being there let him snip through the last frayed knot. His shoulders started to quake, and my insides shattered with each of his quiet sobs. I'd never seen a man cry before. I didn't know what else to do but hold him.

"I was so worried about you." I kissed his shoulder even though he probably wouldn't feel it through the cotton damp from tears. "You never came back."

A dark chuckle echoed in his chest. "Why would you want me to come back? I'm a failure. *No one.* Not a partner. Not even a fucking lawyer anymore. Why would you want me?"

I could've listed a hundred reasons, but I settled for whispering the one I hoped would mean the most of all.

"I love you."

Tear-stained cheeks turned. Dark eyes—no glasses—dipped in a tormented blink. "Denny Dee?" A desperate hand reached out, pulling me closer. "Do you really?"

"I do. I really do. I have for the longest time."

"When?"

"Before the toothbrushes." I bit my lip. "If I'm honest, I think it was the first night I stayed over. The way you looked at me…"

The first time he'd pushed inside me, his hand had cupped my cheek, and his dark eyes had fluttered closed only for a moment as he'd kissed my forehead and whispered, "Are you really here?" My true favourite fantasy. The one I'd never dared to tell him. Not just because he'd chosen me, but because he treasured me. He treated me like no one else ever had—like I was the most precious gift in the world. He made me feel safe. *Whole.*

"Things are different now," he said.

"They're better now."

"I lost my job."

"And that's going to be a huge adjustment for you, but it doesn't change the fact I love you. And, spoiler alert, but your job never even cracked the top ten things I like about you."

His head turned, a small smile tugging at his lips. "What's number ten on your list?"

"You've got a hot li'l booty."

His smile spread wider. "Nine?"

"This list will be mostly X-rated until we reach the top five. You're a wonderful man, Zach, and I'm so lucky to be with you. You're sensitive and kind. You listen to me—really listen—and you share all the same hopes I have for our life. It also doesn't hurt you're so handsome and have a nice"—I wiggled my eyebrows—*"smile."*

A chuckle rumbled under his ribs. "A nice *smile*, huh?"

"Uh-huh." I tightened my arms around him and kissed his cheek. "No matter what happens with your old work or your new work, we're in this together. I love you."

He sucked in a breath.

"What?" I asked.

"I'm getting used to hearing you say those words." He smiled against my temple. "I like it."

"Good, because now that I've said it, I'm never going to shut up about it."

"Promise?"

Giggling, I kissed him on the chin. "I love you."

"I love you, too." His sigh was deep...*content*. "I liked saying the 'too' for the first time."

My brows drooped. I'd waited a long time to say the words back to him. Stubbornness. If I was truly honest—fear. "Zach, I know I haven't always been good at showing you how much you mean to me. I understand now that I was scared, but when I think back about how I treated you sometimes, I'm not proud. I did so many stupid things I regret."

"I deserved it."

"No, not always. You've worked hard to change, but I haven't always kept up. I'm trying. I really am. And I'm going to try even harder."

Sadness flickered through Zach's eyes, and his bruised hand clutched mine, pressing it close to his heart. He pecked a kiss on my fingertips. "Eden, if you're really trying, I want you to consider talking to the police about what happened with Chris."

"It was nothing—"

"A man touched you without your permission. He left bruises on you. That's *something*. Bad men shouldn't always win."

"Will you go with me?"

"Of course," he said without hesitation. "I'll be with you every step of the way. No matter what. We're a team, right?"

"Always."

Zach gusted a sigh when I stroked my hand through his hair to pull him closer, capturing his perfect mouth. The kiss tasted like salty tears—his or mine, I wasn't sure—but the urgent press of his lips was almost enough for me to forget.

Almost.

"Let me take care of you," I whispered.

His big hand slid up my waist, a question in his eyes. I shook my head. For once, I wouldn't try to solve our problems with sex. I tugged him to his feet and led him to the bathroom. When I flicked on the tap to fill the tub, fussing with the water, making sure it wasn't too hot, he perched on the side. Sad eyes watched me as I tended to all the broken skin and tender bruising swelling his usually beautiful hands.

"You shouldn't know how to do that so well," Zach murmured, his voice barely rising above the roar of the water.

"We both got here walking a rocky path."

"You know I'd never use my hands on you, right?"

I nodded.

Slowly, gently, I reached for him, unbuttoning his shirt, peeling the blood-stained clothes off his skin, stripping off my own, and coaxing him into the warm water. A bath bomb plopped in. The fizz of jasmine cleared the air. I slid into the tub behind him, soaped him up, and massaged the clenched muscles in his shoulders, the broad muscles pulled tight in his back, his arms, until he melted against me. My arms wrapped around his chest.

It was intimate, but not sexual. Half-blind from tears, I let myself sink into the uncomfortable feeling. Actual, real, unconditional love. No trade-offs. No orgasms required. Zach in my arms was all I needed. He was safe there. I was happy.

We bobbed about in the bath, not saying anything, until the water turned cold. Then, armed with a fluffy towel, I patted him dry, combed his hair, and still as naked as the day we were born, I pulled back his crisp cotton sheets and encouraged him into bed so I could tuck him up tight.

Zach's eyes drooped. "Denny Dee." He reached for me. "I don't want it to be o…" He never finished what he was going to say. All the worry creasing his brow finally disappeared when he drifted to sleep.

I sat on the edge of the bed, soothing soft swirls over his back, but I stared out the balcony doors at the moonless harbour.

No stars tonight.

No way to wish away his worries. This part of loving someone was so hard. To see him suffering but be unable to do anything but simply *be there*… It tugged at my heart. Made me feel helpless. Useless. Yet, my feet stayed stuck. I didn't run.

When Zach stirred, his hand searching for me on the pillow, I curled my body around his and listened to the steady thump of his heart under my cheek. My own heart thunked along with it. I only untangled myself when I ducked into the living room to call his parents—they needed to know he was okay—and to pop to the front door to collect the food Andie and Yvette left outside.

I shuffled back to the bedroom and slipped under the sheets, my breath catching when Zach rolled over. A rough palm curved over my hip.

"Come closer, Denny Dee," his sleepy voice commanded.

I scooted along the cool cotton.

"Closer," he whispered.

I wriggled a little more. Soft skin fused with hard.

He sighed. "Better."

His lips found my neck, the bristles on his jaw grazing against the tender skin before he nipped a bite. "Yeah." A hand drifted from my hip to cover my breast. "This is what I need." He kneaded my nipple between his fingers. Bent down. Kissed it next. He moaned when he followed that with a torturous lick that made me gasp.

"You play by my rules tonight," he murmured. "Which are actually your rules." A laugh rumbled over my skin. "Usually."

"We can't solve our problems with sex." I pressed closer to him just the same.

"I'd like to give it a damn good try." Without even a sliver of moonlight, I couldn't see the expression in his dark eyes, but the squeeze of his hand on my waist was only questioning, not demanding. "Am I still yours?"

I nodded. "And I'm yours."

His fingers traced a lazy trail from my belly button until he reached my pussy. Biting back a moan, I shivered, my hips tilting on their own, begging for the thick fingers exploring smooth lips to find just the right spot.

"You first, tonight," he said. "Please?"

I grinned. "Oh, I suppose if I *must*."

A smile ghosted his lips as he edged down the bed until his handsome face disappeared between my thighs. Warm fingertips traced all the intimate lines first, his mouth only dusting kisses on the dips of my thighs until my perfect spot was plump and aching for his tongue.

I rocked my hips. "I want," I whined.

And he was only too happy to give me everything I wanted.

His wet mouth was like fire against my skin, igniting all the lonely places inside me to burn with an urgent need for him. Just him. The room didn't feel so dark when it lit up with my breathless pants and his muffled groans. He loved how I responded to him. He loved *me*.

"Stop." My neck arched off the pillow. "I-I'm supposed t-to take care of you."

The tangle of his dark hair didn't lift, and his words whispered in a cool gust on my heated skin. "You did."

Had I? It didn't feel like I'd done enough. I tried to wriggle from Zach's grip and pull him up, but he pinned my legs to the bed. Despite my protests, he kept me locked there, gasping, *begging,* until an explosion of pleasure shot up my spine, sparkles dancing from my toes, and his hair nothing but a matted mess from my desperate fingers.

"I love you," I choked out.

His smile pressed into my skin as he kissed his way up my thighs, my stomach, my ribs. "I love you, too," he said.

"I loved you first."

Zach lifted his chin so I could see his smile this time. That was his favourite secret about me. "We made it."

My heart floated. Zach was right. We weren't almost there anymore. We'd arrived. Not to the future we thought, but in the end, a better one than we'd ever imagined when we'd first started smiling at each other in the coffee shop. We'd wasted so much time assuming things about each other, never saying the words we needed to, but every painful, lost minute had been worth it.

We were so much stronger now.

Bruised fingers laced through mine, anchoring my hand against the soft sheets, Zach's big body crushing my hips into the mattress. I wasn't going anywhere. My heartbeat raced, skin tingling with anticipation...not just for the pleasure but for the *possession*. And just like our first time, when he moaned low, so very satisfied to finally slide his cock inside me, his long lashes fluttered against his cheek for a moment as his lips pressed on my forehead in a kiss too tender when he was buried so deep inside me.

"Say it again." His demand was strained.

"I love you."

His mouth flattened into a grim frown.

Oh, hell yeah.

This was another side of Zach that I loved. The confident version of him. Each controlled thrust was brutal, powerful, and unrelenting, even when I writhed beneath him, begging for relief. He was so rough with me, but he never hurt me. Dark eyes locked on mine. I finally understood that intense gaze—the careful way he watched my face as he took what he wanted from my body.

He wanted to mould us even closer together.

He needed to show me how much he cared about me because sometimes he struggled to find the words.

That look mirrored our first night together. Other nights since. Zach had said he first knew he loved me after I'd moved in, but maybe it was before then. Maybe he'd fallen first, after all.

But, in the end, it didn't matter.

All that mattered was us.

29

He said, "Be brave with me."

Zach

"John, talk some sense into him," Mum said, shoving a tray of raw meat at Dad. Her gaze narrowed on me.

"Mmm?" Dad didn't look up from fiddling on the knobs of the barbecue. "What's he done this time?"

"He hasn't *asked* her yet."

"Ma," I warned, hiding a smile behind the top of my beer.

"Don't you 'Ma' me, Zachary." Mum swatted me on the shoulder with a purple and white chequered tea towel. "A girl like Eden is one in a million. If you don't snap her up and propose, someone else will!"

My gaze drifted across the deck. Laughter bubbled from the group crowding the oversized table crammed with too many chairs. Eden, Andie, and Yvette gossiped away, sipping champagne—well, not Andie. A beer sat in front of her. Some of Mum and Dad's friends were there, and a neighbour or two. I wasn't paying attention to the satellites orbiting the edges of my universe. My eyes always gravitated to the sun in the middle.

Eden.

She noticed me and blew a kiss across the deck. I pretended to catch it and smack it on my cheek. Even brighter laughter fluttered in the air.

What the hell did I do to deserve her?

"I think I'm okay, Ma." Better than okay. Better than ever.

"Oh, do you just?" Mum snipped. "Should I remind you about a certain rugby player...hmm?"

Dad chuckled. It did him no favours. Mum's glare shifted to him.

"Well?" she huffed.

One of Dad's brows went up, but he smiled it away and went back to the barbecue. "Zach, have you showed Eden the new kayaks we bought for our trip next weekend?"

Mum snorted. "No one wants to see your stupid kayaks! Especially not a classy girl like Eden. Did you notice the new heels she has on?" Mum leant over and whispered, "Designer."

"Those kayaks are designer," Dad said. "Real showstoppers—"

"Stop distracting him!" Mum cried. "Zach needs to plan his proposal. Something special. *Memorable.*"

"Memorable, eh?" A smirk played on Dad's lips. "Zach, maybe you should propose to Eden the way I asked your mother."

Mum's face burned redder than a fire truck. "Absolutely not."

"Yeah, that's right. Not like the second time." Dad's voice was low as he grabbed Mum around the waist, pecking her cheek. "The *first* proposal."

"John!" Mum hissed.

"This is news to me." I shot a confused look at the two of them. "You proposed twice? I thought you asked Mum after driving down to Mollymook. You asked her on the beach at sunset, right?"

"That was the *second* proposal." Dad grinned. "Or was it technically the fifth?"

"John," Mum warned.

I took another sip of beer, interest piqued. "What is this highly secretive first proposal?" I was happy for any inspiration at this point. "Dad?"

Mum's glare stayed on Dad. "Don't you dare!"

He smirked. "I asked her during *cuddles*—"

"John!" Mum shrieked.

Dad ignored her protests and winked at me as he tossed a steak on the barbecue. "I asked her four times during those...*cuddles*."

The swig of beer I'd gulped turned into concrete in my throat. I couldn't swallow. I couldn't breathe. My chest heaved in a fit of embarrassed coughs. Mum was frantic, trying to pat my back, but I shook her off.

"I'm—f-fine—" I wheezed. I was just shocked. The idea of my parents having 'cuddles' was—

Nope.

Not going there.

Never *ever* going there.

"John! Honestly! You've scarred the boy for life." Mum whacked him on the backside with her tea towel and hissed, "None of those *cuddles* for you tonight."

She stormed across the deck, disappearing into the kitchen, but not before shooting another death glare back at him. He didn't seem bothered, chuckling away as he flipped the steaks.

"That'll keep your mother's agenda in check for a couple of hours," Dad said. "And don't listen to her talk about needing something over the top. You don't. Tell your girl some words from your heart and ask. You still got your grandmother's ring?"

I patted my pocket with a slow smile. "I've always got the ring."

"So, what's holding you back from asking, then?" Dad asked. "You've been thinking about this for a while."

"What do you think about talking to Andie first? She's the closest person Eden has to family. Is it stupid to want her approval?"

Dad shook his head. "I like Andie. She doesn't pull any punches, and she has decent taste in beer. Show her the Ford F100 I'm restoring in the garage. She'll get a kick out of it. And once you've had your talk, you need to find your girl."

I dropped my head.

"What's going on, mate?"

"What if Eden says no? I've had plenty of job offers since I left Worley, but I haven't settled on anything yet. I've just been sitting around on my backside for two months, wasting time reading books and trying to sort my shit out with the therapist."

"Healing takes time. Don't worry about the job for now. You've needed to slow down for a long time, mate, and you've been sensible putting away for a rainy day—not that Eden's with you for your money."

"He's right." Eden's sweet voice melted me to goo. Her arms wrapped around my waist. "I don't need your lousy money."

I smiled into her hair, the bouncy waves and soft coconut smell tickling my nose. "What do you need?" I kissed her temple.

"More of these kisses. Lay one on me, big fella." She tapped her cheek, and I obliged.

Dad's expression turned solemn. That was a look I hadn't seen since making the cut for the Under 14's cricket team. Was it relief? Pride? Maybe he was hoping for all the same things as Mum—a new member of the family, grandkids, and buying a ridiculous minivan—but never said so. I hoped I wouldn't let him down. I sure as hell had on that cricket team.

"Hey, Andie!" Dad called out. "Zach's gonna show you the Ford F100."

Andie's eyebrows shot up with interest. "Seriously?" She launched off the lounge and smoothed down her jeans in record time. "The one you mentioned before? What year?"

"1966," Dad called back like it meant something.

It must have. Andie was already barrelling down the back stairs. The impatient look thrown over her shoulder screamed at me to hurry.

After I flipped on the lights for the garage, I made my way over to the rust bucket taking pride of place in the centre. I knew less than nothing about cars. I wished Dad had suggested an awkward conversation about the lawn mower or the vegetable garden. That was more in my wheelhouse than the stupid car.

I pointed at the rusty old truck. "The car," I said with a shrug.

"This is so fucking cool." Andie's voice was awestruck as she wandered around, inspecting everything under the open hood in close detail. "Your dad said he's replaced the crow cams, all the pistons and valves, and he's just re-cored the radiator."

Whatever that meant. "Ah...yeah."

I fidgeted. Standing like a dolt in the garage reminded me of too many school holidays. Sweltering heat, sweating through my shirt, bored out of my mind and dreaming of my books upstairs, Dad had forced me to sit there with him while he'd rebuilt some engine or another. Torture then, even worse now.

Andie skimmed a loving touch along the dented metal before she propped her hip against the car. "What's a cylinder head?" She folded her arms. Waited.

I shrugged. "Stuffed if I know."

"Okay, so clearly, this is a setup. You know fuck all about cars."

I stuffed my hands in my pockets. "I, um..." My eyes searched for a safe place to look.

"Are you going to look at your shoes all day, or tell me what you want?"

I took a deep breath. Looked up. Spat the words out. "I want to ask Eden to marry me," I said.

Andie snorted. One of the most important conversations of my life was off to a fabulous start.

"You're the person closest to her in the world," I continued. "I'm not asking for your permission because Eden's her own person, but it would mean a lot to me if you, um..." I shrugged.

"You want my approval before you propose?"

I nodded.

Andie stood there. Silent. Head cocked. Watching me. She didn't hate me like she used to—at least, I didn't think she did—and it helped Yvette sang my praises. Andie was easily swayed by the bubbly blonde. But I suspected I hadn't fully earned her trust yet.

She sighed. "I always had my doubts about you... but..." Out puffed a breath. "Ed's more settled than I've ever seen her. I'm worried about what'll happen when you go back to work—"

"I swear it'll never be like it was. I walked away, and I won't be going back. Hell, I don't even have to do legal work. I could help around the salon and continue my role as Chief Executive of Towels, Hanging Robes, and Restocking."

Andie smirked. "You know that's a bullshit title Eden gave you to get in your pants, right?"

I laughed. "Yeah, I figured that out when she dragged me into the colour mixing room."

"Please. No reminders. Gross." Andie laughed. It was rare for her to laugh around me, so I took it as a small win. "Look, you know Ed's family. She stood by me when no one else did, and I'd do the same for her. I'm never going to stop looking out for her, but..." She shook her head with a smile. "For whatever fucked-up reason, she loves you, and you make her happy. So, if you want to propose, I won't stand in your way."

Andie would never understand how much her words meant to me. Based on the wariness in her eyes, I didn't think she'd appreciate the hug I wanted to give her, so I nodded slowly with a relieved smile instead.

"Alright, fuck off," Andie said. "Leave me to drool over this beautiful machine, and you go make my best friend's dreams come true."

I didn't need to be told twice.

As I rushed back up the stairs, my mind raced, running through options. Grandma's ring had been burning a hole in my pocket for weeks, waiting for just the right moment, but the proposal had to be amazing, didn't it? It had to be social media worthy with balloons and fanfare and... *Shit*. I just didn't *know*. Maybe I should wait another day or two? A few weeks? I could surprise Eden with a vacation somewhere romantic, like Fiji, or even the snow. Neither of us had seen the snow before. A candlelit dinner at her favourite restaurant might be better. I could hide the ring in a piece of cake...or...something.

I paused at the screen door.

Eden and Mum huddled around the wooden counter, slicing oranges—probably for Mum's signature punch that was boozy enough to knock anyone's socks off. Yvette was sitting on a stool. The three of them chatted, but Eden's arm around Mum's shoulder punched me in the heart. She was the daughter Mum never had. They were always video chatting, and Eden ended every call by singing, "Love ya, Maree!"

She was the missing piece for my family. For me. She slotted perfectly into place. She was the stormy skies soaring above my calm sea. She was my biggest cheerleader. I was hers.

I'd wasted so much time.

I stuffed my hand in my pocket and slipped the cool platinum of Grandma's ring over my pinkie. *Still there.* I smiled.

Yvette noticed me first. Her hands clapped on her cheeks. Did she know?

Nervous steps landed me in the kitchen.

Yvette was in a panic. "Maree! Ah—" She hopped off the stool and raced to Mum's side. "Why don't you, um…show me the lovely new throw rug you were telling me about?" She tugged at Mum's sleeve. "In the living room?"

Mum flapped a hand, distracted as she grabbed more oranges. "Not yet, hon, we need to finish—"

"No. Now." Yvette cackled a nervous laugh. "Just, um—" She looked helplessly in my direction.

Mum's gaze snapped up, finding me standing there like a dumb fool. Her eyes rounded. "Oh, yes!" She yanked off her apron. "Yes! The, ah—the *throw rug*."

The two of them bolted out of the kitchen, heads together to share excited whispers, and a lot of winking back at me.

They knew.

Eden had no clue.

She watched the scene with her brows knitted together and the knife hovering above an orange. "What the hell got into that pair?" She shook it off with a laugh and went back to slicing. "Want to help?"

I shook my head. Every word I wanted to say was stuck in my throat like glue. I shuffled closer by her side.

"There are heaps of people here today," she said, touching my arm. "You doing okay?"

I nodded, stuffing my hand back into my pocket and fumbling to check the ring. *Still there.* Blood pounded in my ears. My mouth was dry enough to drink boatloads of the punch Eden was making. What was I meant to do? My mind looped in blanks, and every plan was out the window.

"I love you," I whispered.

Eden looked up at me with a soft smile. "Yeah?" She didn't always say it back, but I didn't mind.

"You mean everything to me. You always have, you know?"

She wedged herself closer. "What's got you so talkative?" She kissed my cheek. "Was it the guy perving on me at the supermarket? I wouldn't have noticed him if you hadn't gone all caveman." Her grin was sly.

She liked it when the jealous caveman glared at all the other men…and even more when I tossed her on the bed afterwards to prove to her exactly who her man was.

"I got something for you." I nudged my shoulder against hers. "In my pocket."

"Oh!" She waggled her eyebrows. "You know I love this game." Grinning, she stuffed her hand down deep. I was hoping she wouldn't try to cop a feel—an erection accompanying a proposal might lead to some awkward looks from the people outside.

Eden's smile wobbled. "Z-Zach?" Her hand was still in my pocket. Had she found the ring? "Is this…" She pulled out the antique platinum band with its one diamond. She blinked. A tear blotted down her cheek. "I-It's, um…"

"It's my grandma's ring."

She bit her lip. "Why?"

"Oh, I got this all wrong, didn't I? We always mess up the order, don't we?"

I dropped to one knee. My heart jumped like a jackhammer in my chest, and the speed only ramped up when I looked at Eden. She held the ring in trembling fingers, eyes swimming in tears. I'd ruined the proposal. I should've practiced more. I should've—

"Ask me," she whispered.

I hesitated.

I could feel too many critical eyes on us. Mum and Yvette peeked around the corner. Dad and Andie pretended not to be interested from their spot outside by the barbecue. I hadn't planned on an audience, just like I hadn't rehearsed what to say. Eden deserved better than a nervous proposal in my parents' kitchen. She deserved better than me too, but here we were.

I'd waited long enough.

"I saw you a month before you saw me," I said. "I used to hang out on the back wall of the coffee shop, and then you came in one day...and the next. I wanted to talk to you so bad. You were just...*everything*. Clever and gorgeous, a big ball of sunshine who lit up my whole day with only a smile. It took me a month to get brave enough to step away from the wall. I pushed past two idiots in baseball caps to get a spot up the front, but you finally saw me."

"I remember that day. You were so sweet with your shy smile."

I couldn't help giving her another one of those smiles. "I want to be brave again, Denny Dee. I'm stepping from the wall, but I want you to be brave with me this time. Will you...?"

A huge smile threatened to burst across her face, but she bit down on her lower lip to stop it. "Even with all my drama?"

"This ring locks us in until the last curtain call."

"And all my schemes?"

"I know I promised to hit play on your villain theme song, but I'll make you a whole damn playlist if you agree to marry me."

Eden fell to her knees and threw her arms around my neck. Her lips landed on mine for one delirious kiss before she nuzzled in the crook of my neck. "I want you to hear my answer before any of those cheeky busybodies get in on my moment," she whispered, waiting a breathless pause, before simply saying... "Yes."

Our adventure started when I walked up to a girl crying on a step in Clovelly, and I said, "Hey."

Our next chapter would start with just one other word: "Yes."

And that word was so much better.

It was the best damn word I'd ever heard.

Epilogue

Zach

Three years later

A CHUBBY HAND WRAPPED around my finger. Not the one where I wore my wedding band, the one next to that.

I glanced down at the tiny girl hovering beside me. The wispy chocolate pigtails on her head bobbed as she peered around my parents' backyard, and she clutched her threadbare pink bunny under her chin, her thumb in her mouth.

My little girl. Josie.

I squatted, steadying myself with a hand on the grass. Closer to forty than thirty, my knees creaked, not quite what they used to be. Josie shuffled her tiny high-tops along the grass, the soft pad of her diaper butt in pink overalls parking on my knee.

"What do you think, JoJo?" I asked. "Excited?"

Her enormous brown eyes tore away from the corner of the yard where Dad and Andie scrambled to finish building her new jungle gym. She blinked up at me. Her thumb dropped out of her mouth with a slurpy pop.

"Yeth!" A toothy smile flashed but quickly disappeared. She'd inherited her mother's scowl...and impatience. "All done?"

"Soon."

Not a word she enjoyed hearing. "No" was high on the list too. Josie's thumb popped back in her mouth—precisely where she liked it—and she sucked furiously, surveying her domain with serious eyes.

"We might be here a while," I muttered.

The whole jungle gym debacle had taken longer than the motley crew had estimated over breakfast. A *lot* longer.

"Three hours," Andie had promised Eden.

"Two." Dad had upped the ante. "Tops. Our girl will be in her tux, ready to leave for the awards on time."

"Promise." Andie had crossed her heart.

And now it was—I glanced at my watch—yep, six hours and counting.

Dad and Andie were usually a good team. They'd constructed the sandpit in record time. A few trips to the nursery had finished the landscaping for the new pool.

But I'd learned never to trust Dad and Andie to finish anything except a lot of beers when the cricket was on. They'd been distracted by the TV. I'd covered Josie's ears to avoid her hearing most of the ranting when a guy in baggy whites was "out" for something called a "duck."

Those shenanigans also gave me a clue Andie was probably the bad influence behind Josie declaring, "Fut that," with her hands on her tiny hips when I'd told her tea party time was over.

I huddled Josie closer. She giggled when Dad hollered out to Andie. He'd gotten himself tangled in the metal ropes trying to hang the swing.

"Pop, I told you to wait!" Andie dropped the yellow slide she was lugging over. "You'll put your fuc—I mean, *fudging*—back out again." She flashed a sheepish grin in my direction.

"Smooth save," I called out.

She bowed.

The slide was fastened in record time. The two of them surveyed the bolts, tugged on the ropes, and rattled the frame to make sure everything was secure. A couple of slaps on the back for a job well done, and the jungle gym was finally complete.

Josie's hopeful eyes turned to me. "Me go?"

"Yep!" I nodded with a big smile. "Pop and Andie all done." Finally.

Josie grinned and threw her tiny arms around my neck. Bunny came for a cuddle, too.

"Lub oo, Dada."

Her chunky tooshie toddled across the yard to the new swing she'd been dying to ride for hours. I hopped back up, watching Dad lift my little girl onto the yellow seat. His hair was threaded with so much more silver, but somehow, he looked younger, lighter. With her Bunny stuck safely under her arm, Josie glared straight ahead as Dad pushed the swing. She was wary at first, sizing up the new situation, but she was soon giggling and demanding to go "Hi-wa, Pop!"

Andie jogged over. "Dude! Did we do good or what? That play set is a work of art." She grinned. "I didn't think we'd get it built in time. So, ah"—she rubbed the back of her neck—"how pissed off is Ed?"

Smirking, I cocked my head. "What do you reckon?"

"Tsunami?"

"I'd scale her mood somewhere around Summer Storm Surge." I puffed out a sigh. "She's freaking out about the awards."

"Dunno why. This is her year."

"I've told her. You've told her. Until the Hairstylist of the Year trophy is in Eden's hand, it's a lost cause. She thinks she didn't send enough gift baskets or word her 'Thank You' social media posts properly."

Andie winced. "I still have nightmares about those baskets. At least you knew how to arrange the fruit correctly." She rolled her eyes. "I'm so bloody glad we're going rock climbing next weekend. I love our girls, but fuck, I need a few hours to decompress. This world has way too many extroverts."

"Hearing you loud and clear. I seriously underestimated the importance of award season."

I spared Andie the details of just how much I'd used my powers of distraction in the last month. Sex hadn't been this off the charts since Eden and I had eloped to Falls Creek—the first and, thankfully, *last* time either of us had seen snow. Sex the last two weeks had even eclipsed when we'd started trying for a baby. Two or three times a day sounded great in theory—fun in practice, too—but I still worried Eden used it as a tool to avoid her anxiety.

Then again, I always worried about her in some small way.

Love was like that. Life was less about me and more about my family, and I wouldn't change it for all the promotions in the world.

I'd thought less and less about the old days at Worley and Stone as time went on. Chris had battled his own demons, disappearing into the wilds of Tasmania instead of answering for the day he'd laid his hands on Eden. Michaela had been nothing to me. She stayed that way. The past was in the past. The future was so much brighter without those people darkening it.

I dipped a nod at the house. "Heading upstairs to put your penguin suit on?" I asked Andie.

"Yeah, I'll help Pop tidy up otherwise he'll overdo it like always. Otherwise, I'm right behind you."

I took a final look over the backyard. Josie shoved Bunny at Dad for safekeeping, jumped off the swing, and barrelled up the climbing frame, ready to test the slide. I smiled. The best sight in the world.

I raced up the back stairs two at a time until I landed at the top.

Mum shuffled around the deck, drizzling water over her potted herbs. "Eden's getting ready in the guest room," she said. Before I could escape, she caught my arm, dragging me down to her. Fierce eyes glared up at me. "When are you putting another baby in my daughter's belly, Zachary?"

"Ma..."

"We're not getting any younger here. Always so many excuses! First, it was getting married."

I smirked. "I feel like getting married is a pretty standard step for a lot of people before having kids."

Mum huffed. She often chose to conveniently forget she'd blubbered her eyes out to be one of only six people invited to our wedding. "Then, it was all that time looking for a house," she said. "What a waste! You already had such a lovely apartment."

"Eden didn't want to raise kids in my apartment." Or any apartment, for that matter. "She had her heart set on a house."

A big house. The perfect house. And she'd driven everyone—including herself—absolutely bonkers finding it. After eight months of searching and attending open homes, we'd gotten a tip-off about a house coming on the market in South Coogee—of all bloody places. Eden had fallen head over heels the second we'd pulled up out front. The white weatherboard overlooking the coast was everything she'd dreamed about. The commute uptown in rush hour was awful, but she'd never complained. Not once. She loved that house.

"I could help more during the week," Mum said. "Now Josie's older, she could stay for more sleepovers. And two littlies are basically the same as one, really."

"We'd love more kids, Ma. It's just not the right time. I'm about to take on some new lawyers—"

"About time." She spritzed me a little with her hose. "Less days in the office means more time for babies."

I rolled my eyes. I only worked three days a week. I was hardly chained to my desk. I'd been sceptical when Eden had first encouraged me to start my own firm, but every afternoon when I pulled into the driveway, I was grateful she'd supported me to take the leap. I chose how many clients I took on. How many hours I worked. More time for family.

"I'm only running a small firm, Ma. All my staff only work part-time—even Sue. I need to step up for a few months and settle everyone in, but once they're happy, I'll talk to Eden about more babies."

Mum stuck her nose in the air and returned to watering her herbs. "Some son you are," she grumbled.

I bent down and pecked a kiss on the top of her head even though she huffed at me. "Eden said she wants three," I whispered.

Mum grinned, misty-eyed, and shooed me into the house. The screen door snapped closed. I peeked out. She wandered around the deck, humming as she watered her plants. Another tick off the agenda. No need for a minivan—*yet*.

I walked through the house, down the hallway, to the guest room, and leant my shoulder against the doorframe.

Eden sat primly on a stool in her silk robe. Her designer dress—rented, of course—was hidden in a garment bag on the bed. She wanted her outfit to be a surprise. Her makeup was done, but Yvette still fussed behind her, rolling a fat hairbrush and blitzing the hairdryer on Eden's dark hair so it hung in long, glossy waves over her shoulders.

I sighed. Eden was beautiful. Crazy beautiful.

Yvette's eyes met mine in the mirror. "We're not quite done," she said over the whirr of the hairdryer. "Is my woman still outside building that"—she waved the brush about—"contraption?"

Eden hummed her disapproval through pursed lips.

"They're packing up," I said.

"She won't have enough time," Eden snipped.

"It takes Andie literally two seconds to get ready," I reassured her.

Yvette nodded. "Shower, clothes, gel, out the door to grab the coffees. I see it every morning." She stepped back and started to wind up the cord for the hairdryer.

I ducked in the gap. My arms hugged around Eden's middle. I smacked a kiss in the crook of her neck, and she squealed, swatting at my thigh. With a quick spin of the stool, practiced in a hundred situations just like this, she faced me so I could finally kiss her properly—deep and long until she was breathless.

"Missed you," I said.

"Love you," she whispered back.

"This is all very touching, darling lovebirds," Yvette said, "but this updo won't get done if you hog our future award winner." She flapped a handful of bobby pins at me. "Outta the way, Mr. Lawyer Man!"

Eden grabbed my hand and kissed it. A faint lipstick imprint was left behind. "Go put on your tuxedo. You can help zip me up"—she wiggled her eyebrows—"once I'm ready to put on my dress."

"Mmm." I captured her lips in a lingering kiss. "Deal."

Eden spun around to face the mirror. "Vettie," she said, lifting her chin, looking every bit a queen. "I need my pep talk."

"Let's do this." Yvette started to pin Eden's hair. "Whose night is it tonight?"

"Mine."

"Who's the best damn colourist in the business?"

"I am."

"And who are you?"

Eden's eyes met mine in the mirror. "I'm Eden fucking Rawles." She grinned.

Her salon, earning her place at the award gala, and the fact she was about to be—*officially*—the best hairstylist in the country were her achievements. She'd done the hard work—mostly on her own.

But she'd whispered to me one morning that I'd given her the things she'd wanted most in the world. A name no longer attached to her father. A daughter. A family. A home, not just a house. She didn't need to flip all the lights on anymore. She didn't keep secrets about her fears or worries. She shared them with me. We worked through them together.

And what had Eden given me?

Simply...everything.

The End

About Aubrey

Aubrey Whitten writes contemporary romances with an Australian twist. She has a soft spot for flawed characters who are down on their luck and loves to weave happy endings by mixing heartfelt moments, humour, and a dash of romantic steam.

Aubrey lives in the sunniest part of Australia and juggles time for writing around a busy day job and her small but mighty family.

Connect with Aubrey
www.aubreywhitten.com
www.facebook.com/AubreyWhitten

Made in the USA
Middletown, DE
25 March 2025